Cybele:
An Extraordinary Voyage
Into the Future

Adolphe Alhaiza

Cybele:
An Extraordinary Voyage
Into the Future

translated, annotated and introduced by
Brian Stableford

A Black Coat Press Book

Visit our website at www.blackcoatpress.com

Introduction

Cybèle, Voyage extraordinaire dans l'avenir, by-lined Jean Chambon, here translated as *Cybele: An Extraordinary Voyage into the Future*, was originally published in Paris by Georges Carré in 1891.

Jean Chambon was the pseudonym of Jean-Adolphe Alhaiza (1839-1922), about whose early life little is known, although he achieved a celebrity of sorts late in life when he became the editor of *La Rénovation*, the periodical of an organization established to carry forward and popularize the sociological theories of the utopian socialist philosopher Charles Fourier (1772-1837). Fourier remained famous long after his death, particularly for his design of hypothetical "Phalansteries" as the focal institution of communal residence, and he probably inspired the foundation of more experimental communities, especially in the U.S.A., than any other social theorist.

The biography of Alhaiza that appears on the Fourierist organization's current website at charlesfourier.fr relates that he was born in Tarbes in the Pyrenees, the son of Paul Alhaiza, an upholsterer, and Thérèse Chambon, and that he went to Paris at an early age in search of work. The story is then picked up in 1889, when Alhaiza published the first of the two books he wrote as Jean Chambon, *Catéchisme naturaliste: Essai de synthèse physique, vitale et religieuse*, [A Naturalist Catechism: An Essay in the Synthesis of Physics, Biology and Religion], at which time he was apparently employed as a commercial traveler. Although it is inevitably risky to take any biographical inference from a work of fiction, the evidence of *Cybèle* suggests that he might well have been to school in Marseilles, and that he probably spent some time later in life, perhaps in his days as a commercial traveler, in Algiers.

Either the catechism or the novel—which might have been stated earlier as a pure adventure story, and only adapted belatedly into a vehicle the ideas contained in Alhaiza's "new synthesis" of science and religion—came to the attention of Hippolyte Destrem (1816-1894; not to be confused with his later namesake, a banker and journalist), who was then the director of the Fourierist Society and the editor of *La Rénovation*. Destrem contacted the author and invited him to join the society; it is not entirely clear why, as neither of the Chambon texts has any evident affiliation to Fourierist ideas—the only mention of Fourier in *Cybèle* is distinctly equivocal—and Alhaiza's thesis is more appropriately interpreted as an attempt to graft an idiosyncratic version of deism on to the positivist ideas of Auguste Comte.

Indeed, Alhaiza does not appear to have taken an active part in the Fourierist movement until Destrem died in June 1894, when Alhaiza promptly took over his position. That appointment does not seem to have been welcomed by all the members of the movement, and seems to have caused something of a schism between the fraction that was devoted to practical utopian experimentation, and wanted the movement's primary aim to be the establishment of experimental colonies putting Fourier's Phalansterian ideas into practice, and the members who were primarily interested in active political propaganda.

Alhaiza belonged to the latter camp, and did succeed in making *La Rénovation* into a more active and more combative instrument of political criticism—albeit criticism that appears to have given far more prominence to his own idiosyncrasies than the ideas of the movement's founding father. In particular, Alhaiza was vociferously anti-Jewish, severely critical of several of the other socialist movements that were current at the turn of the century, especially the one spearheaded by Jean Jaurès, and nurtured a particular hatred for his rival Naturalist Émile Zola—although the utopian ideas developed in the futuristic sections of Zola's later works bear a much greater similarity to Fourier's than his own.

Thus, although Alhaiza undoubtedly raised the profile of the movement slightly during his tenure as its leader—he only resigned his position in January 1922, shortly before his death—some of its members might well have thought that he did not do their ideals and prospects any favors. The website of the rejuvenated movement suggests, delicately, that by the time of the Great War it had virtually ceased to exist, except insofar as the continued appearance of *La Rénovation* preserved an illusion of life. In the meantime, however, Alhaiza maintained a steady stream of publications alongside the periodical, issuing numerous books and pamphlets, all of them signed "Adolphe Alhaiza." He had earlier issued a revised version of his catechism under that signature, retitled as a *Catéchisme dualiste*, presumably to liberate it from any suggestion of Zolaesque naturalism. Had he ever reprinted *Cybèle*—in fact, he did not—he would presumably have signed it in the same fashion, thus licensing my substitution of his more usual signature on this translation.

At the time when *Cybèle* was published, there was something of a boom in Utopian futuristic fiction, partly stimulated by the success in the U.S.A. of Edward Bellamy's best-selling *Looking Backward, 2000-1887* (1888), which awakened a great deal of controversy and called forth numerous replies in kind in America and England. France, of course had a much older tradition of Utopian futuristic fiction, extending back to Louis-Sébastien Mercier's unlicensed pre-Revolutionary bestseller *Mémoires de l'an deux mille quatre cent quarante* (1771; tr. as *Memoirs of the Year Two Thousand Five Hundred*), and French writers did not generally dignify Bellamy with any specific response, although they were probably glad of a potential opportunity to capitalize on a new wave of international interest in such endeavors.

Indeed, French readers and writers might well have thought, with some justification, that Bellamy was stealing thunder from a revivification of interest in futuristic utopianism that had already taken place in France in advance of the

7

American writer's effort. In particular, they would have been aware of Émile Calvet's *Dans mille ans* (tr. as *In a Thousand Years*)[1], which had been serialized in the popular *Musée des familles* in 1883 before appearing as an illustrated book the following year. That work probably played some part in stimulating "Alain le Drimeur" to produce *La Cité future* (1890: tr. as *The Future City*)[2] as well as lending encouragement to Alhaiza. Alhaiza undoubtedly knew, however, that such works belonged to a long and reasonably sturdy tradition, which had long had a particular fascination with the future of Paris—and, in particular, the ruins that the city in question might leave behind when the forefront of civilization moved on, as described in Joseph Méry's "Les Ruines de Paris" (1844; tr. as "The Ruins of Paris")[3] and Alfred Bonnardot's "Archéopolis" (1857; tr. as "Archeopolis")[4]. Both of those much-imitated stories propose, as Alhaiza also does, that the future of civilization and of "France" might involve a decisive shift into northern Africa.

Alhaiza's familiarity with at least some of the works in this rich tradition is evident in *Cybèle*, in the manner in which he echoes them while consistently trying to add his own particular twists to them. The most interesting features of the novel are, in fact, the narrative moves by means of which he tries to solve the intrinsic problems of the subgenre, and the manner in which he deliberately introduces themes and images that exceed or contradict the devices employed by his predecessors.

The most remarkable of the moves in question is the notion of Cybèle itself. Alhaiza was clearly aware of the dilemma generated by the fact that the only plausible way of gaining narrative access to the future in 1891 was by means of some

---

[1] Black Coat Press, ISBN 978-1-61227-192-7.

[2] Black Coat Press, ISBN 978-1-61227-114-9

[3] In *The Tower of Destiny*, Black Coat Press, ISBN 978-12-61227-101-9.

[4] In *Nemoville*, Black Coat Press, ISBN 978-1-61227-070-8.

kind of prophetic dream, and the corollary circumstance that the device was bound to seem both hackneyed and unconvincing if it could not be given a particular twist that would make it seem both novel and somehow more solid. He knew, of course, that some previous writers, including Bellamy, had used the device of suspended animation to transport their protagonists into the future, and was also aware of the implicit penalty of that stratagem, in that it left its users with no way to report back to the present, let alone transport themselves back to their starting-point. He does deploy the notion of suspended animation in *Cybèle*—and, indeed, considers its implications much more enterprisingly than any author before him—but evidently rejected the possibility of employing as a fundamental means of transportation, in favor of a much more adventurous stratagem.

The device used by Alhaiza is not unique; variants of it were subsequently to be employed by the American grain-merchant Elmer Dwiggins, who wrote *Pharaoh's Broker* (1899) under the pseudonym Ellsworth Douglass, and by the popular French writer Henri Duvernois, in *L'Homme qui s'est retrouvé* (1936; tr. as *The Man Who Found Himself*)[5], but both those novels employ it as a means of "time travel" into the past rather than the future, thus producing novels of a markedly different kind. Nor was Alhaiza, strictly speaking, the originator of the idea, although he does seem to have been the first to make use of it in fiction. Although no source is credited in the text, Alhaiza had almost certainly come across it in a remarkable essay by the French socialist Louis Blanqui. *L'Éternité par les astres* [Eternity via the Stars] (1872), which argues that, if the universe is truly infinite in space and time, then among the infinite number of planets it contains, there must be an infinite number that are exact duplicates of the Earth in all but contemporaneity, so that, even though every human individual dies, he or she will also be replicated indefinitely, thus granting all of them a curious kind of immortality.

---

[5] Black Coat Press, ISBN 978-1-935558-04-0.

Taking advantage of this logic (which we, unlike Blanqui and Alhaiza, now know to be based on a false assumption), Alhaiza draws the inference that there must exist, elsewhere in the universe, worlds that are identical to Earth but historically displaced, so that our present is, for the moment, their past or future. All that a "time traveler" has to do, therefore, is find a means of instantaneous translation to one of these sister Earths. Strictly speaking, of course, this does not get around the problem of the temporal displacement functioning in exactly the same fashion as a dream, at least in narrative terms, but it does at least lend a certain eccentric muscle to the dreaming process, which is illustrated by the elaborate and highly unusual account given in the story of the journey through space that delivers Alhaiza's hero to his exotic destination—whose inhabitants, perhaps wisely, have long since got out of the habit of calling their word "the Earth" and have given it a more dignified title.

Although more recent writers have tended to prefer the Greek Gaia as a personification of the natural world in its entirety, Alhaiza's preference for Cybele—originally an Anatolian goddess assimilated by the Hellenes as one of the attributes of Gaia—was quite natural at the time, given that Cybele became a much more popular object of veneration in Rome, where she became the *Magna Mater* [Great Mother] and was reinvented as a mythical ancestor of the Roman people via the Trojan Aeneas. In the same way, it would have been natural for him to use the Latin Gemma as the name of the star that modern astronomers call Alpha Coronae Borealis, rather than alternatives such as the Greek Gnosia and the Arabic Alphecca, although the function the star serves in the plot might have been even better served by its Hebrew name Asteroth (rendered Astarte by Decadent writers like Jean Lorrain, for whom the goddess of that name became a baleful imperious influence).

Most literary time-travelers tend to either to aim for a future year bearing the label of a conveniently round number—

2000 A.D. used to be the favorite, although it has inevitably lost its currency now—or displaced from the present by a round number of years, a hundred being the most popular choice, although more daring writers opt for one or several thousand and Mercier had plumped for the alternative symbolism of 666. Alhaiza is among the boldest in his attempted reach of six thousand years, but his numbers are somewhat distorted, in consequence of his employment of a new dating system based on a highly idiosyncratic theory of cyclic history, which does not quite fit into a conveniently decimal scheme, being based on a cycle of approximately 21,000 years, derived from the astronomical precession of the equinoxes.

Specifically, Alhaiza borrows a thesis set out in a book entitled *Révolutions de la mer, déluges périodiques*, published in 1860 by Joseph-Alphonse Adhémar, which attempted to combine recent discoveries about the "ice ages" that had afflicted the northern hemisphere in times past with various other kinds of data, including the Biblical account of the Deluge, to produce a catastrophist geological theory, whose implications included a calculation of the date when the next such catastrophe would either put an end to the progress of human civilization or pose a very stern challenge to it.

We now know that Adhémar's thesis is completely false, because we—unlike him and Alhaiza—now have reliable methods of geological and archeological dating that reduce his hypothetical chronology to absurdity, and it did not attract many adherents in its own day, although it has a certain appealing ingenuity if one is prepared to overlook its woeful incompetence in deploying the notion of a drastic shift in the Earth's center of gravity. In spite of its lack of rational plausibility, however, development of Adhémar's hypothesis does allow Alhaiza to pose and address an interesting question, with regard to a future that has benefited from thousands of years of scientific and technological progress in addition to that already made in the 19th century, but which is uncomfortably aware of the fact that it is facing an imminent and potentially-apocalyptic catastrophe. The manner in which the author sketches out that situation in *Cybèle*, and then handles its narrative development, is interesting, even though he was obviously overstretching his competence in both imaginative and literary terms.

It is undeniable that *Cybèle* has some glaring faults. There is a long section in the middle of the book where the narrative voice appears to forget the characters entirely and to begins speaking directly to the reader in a quasi-historical manner, and not in a particularly coherent fashion. Indeed, it looks suspiciously as if various segments of prose that originally belonged to other works—including some satirical comedies as well as earnest essays—have simply been dumped into the text, with little or no attempt being made to make them consistent, either with one another or the narrative frame.

Even when the characters are securely positioned on the narrative stage, they mostly serve to deliver commentaries, rather vaguely as well as haphazardly—save for the protagonist's attempts to cope internally with his particular psychological predicament—but there is frequent, if slightly incoherent compensation for that narrative awkwardness in the profusion, and the occasional originality of the ideas introduced. It is certainly possible that a reader might wish that Alhaiza, having eventually built up his stock of ideas, had then gone back to square one, and started building them much more intricately and coherently into a sturdier and better-planned plot, but there were very few writers around in 1891 who would have been willing or able to do something of that sort.

In addition, the story suffers, as the Fourierist movement was later to do, from the particular bees buzzing in Alhaiza's bonnet, which occasionally deliver nasty stings, either in the shape of singular gratuitous insults or substantial rants, the most unpleasant and irrational of which are those directed against Jews, although he is also unfair and unnecessarily rude in his treatment of Americans and the English. I was strongly tempted simply to omit the crude abuse directed against "Judah," as its relevance to the story-line is distinctly marginal, but eventually decided that it was probably best to leave the passages in question in place, partly in order to maintain fidelity to the original text, but partly also to illustrate the fact that, although Alhaiza was virulently and appallingly prejudiced, even by the poor standards of his uncouth times, his notion of what might count as a "final solution" to the "Jewish problem" is very different in kind and temper from subsequent aspirants to that title.

In the final analysis, however, what makes Alhaiza interesting as a thinker and writer is not the things that he was against, which cannot and do not lead to any productive speculation, but the things of which he was in favor, which can and do—in particular, his deism and his "naturalism."

Given his presumable ancestry, it is perhaps not surprising that Alhaiza wanted to move beyond the dogmatics of both Islam and Christianity, condemning them both to future extinction, while nevertheless resisting atheism and wanting, like Auguste Comte before him, to design a new kind of religion shorn of unnecessary superstition but still possessed of lofty ideals. What is slightly more unusual, for its time, is his commitment to a holistic view of nature in which humans are by no means the only participants in an ongoing evolutionary process potentially and actually capable of bringing various other animal species to sentience and cultural development, and also capable of producing a further stage in human evolution: a superhuman species destined to carry biological progress even further.

Alhaiza only addresses those latter topics sketchily, but he does approach them in a resolute manner that was exceptional in his era. In spite of being something of a hotchpotch, therefore, *Cybèle* does have authentic claims to be a significant contribution to the development of French futuristic fiction, and it contains a good deal of material that is still capable of stimulating the thought and imagination of the modern reader.

This translation was made from the copy of the 1891 Carré edition of *Cybèle* reproduced on the Bibliothèque Nationale's *gallica* website. I have made one significant modification to its substance, omitting the long headnotes that summarize in advance what each chapter contains, which serve no function except the unhelpful one of serving as "spoilers."

Brian Stableford

CYBELE

I

"It's really him! It's Numa!"

"Ah! The dear child!"

"The worthy friend!"

"My dear brother!"

"Oh, what an excellent surprise!"

It was by these affectionate exclamations that a young naval officer was welcomed on the threshold of a beautiful house, shortly after arriving at Martigues on the five p.m. train.

Numa Honorat, almost constantly at sea, sometimes in the Far East, where he had valiantly taken his place among Admiral Courbet's brave mariners, and sometimes in some distant station in our establishments in the Antilles or Madagascar, no longer made any but rare and too brief appearances in his family. This time, however, granted a longer leave than usual, he had returned to France aboard the *Revanche*, after having exchanged, at eighteen years of age, the rank of ensign for the triple stripes of a lieutenant.

Among those who hastened to greet him in that manner was, first of all, the young officer's mother, the respectable Madame Honorat, who leaned on his shoulder, testifying to her joy at seeing her son again, as mother do, with moist eyes: soft tears, soon followed by bitter ones, at the memory of her husband—a memory often suddenly reanimated by the presence of the living portrait of the late Commandant Honorat, killed in 1871 at the fort of Vanves by a Prussian shell.

Next came a charming young woman, Numa's sister, who attached herself, radiant with pleasure, to the officer's other arm. Sustaining the two women thus, he responded, smiling broadly, to the questions put to him by his childhood friend, Marius Foulane, a tall, handsome fellow, all heartiness and frankness, whose mobile southern features were presently exhibiting the most expansive joy. The two friends had not seen one another since a vacation they had spent taking a pleasant Mediterranean voyage together, and Marius had often been disappointed to find that his friend, always far away, was not there at the times when he would most have liked to have him beside him. Now, when he was no longer expecting it, his wish was being realized.

"He's arrived just in time for the wedding—and without any warning, the sly dog."

"When on campaign, my friend, can one ever be sure of tomorrow? Then again, in truth, when I left the ship, Toulon is too close to Martigues to refuse myself the pleasure of giving you a little surprise."

Also there were Monsieur Foulane, Marius' father, whose habitually serious face had lighted up joyfully at the others' reunion, and his maidservant Martine, practically a member of the family—for it she was the one who had raised Marius, whose mother had died in his infancy, and she had seen him grow up with his friend Numa.

They all celebrated the arrival of the young mariner wholeheartedly, in the excess of joy that his presence brought—for there was already a full complement of joy in the house, where one of those unions was about to be celebrated that combines two kinds of happiness: the profound affection of young fiancés commenced at the most tender age and increased with the years, and the fusion of two families already brought together by long intimacy, a respectable social position and an honest fortune. What more could one wish? They had desired, without daring to hope for, the return of the brother, the absent friend—and the absentee had return just as the marriage contract was about to be signed.

Maître Démosthène Foulane's house was a rather impos-ing dwelling. Among all the neighboring houses, it attracted the gaze by virtue of its elevated summit and its elegant pro-portions; it was immediately recognizable as the house of a notable individual. In fact, above the arched portal whose two battens opened on to the pretty Rue d'Aiguevives, the badge of the notariat could be seen, which is only usually found on handsome buildings. At the precise moment that this story begins, the oblique rays of the setting Provençal sun, striking the polished copper, put a kind of brilliant meteor on the front of the dwelling. One might almost have thought it a second sun, descended from the firmament to honor with its visit the abode of a predestined mortal, as in the distant times when celestial signs came to announce some extraordinary destiny.

Here, however, nothing was in preparation but the mod-est destiny of a new head of the Foulane office, who would, in fact, be the third in line, for Maître Démosthène Foulane, who had inherited it from his own father, Aristide, was ceding it in his turn to his son Marius. Everything being thus arranged, with a happy marriage on the point of consummation, it there-fore seemed that the future of the young notary, set on such excellent foundations, was absolutely secure and utterly un-shakable.

For the moment, there was no room in Marius' thoughts for anything not attached to the charming individual who was about to become his wife; and certainly, anyone who had ever caught a glimpse of Mademoiselle Jeanne would have under-stood that, and envied the fate of the joyful Marius. One would have searched all of Provence in vain to find eyes of a more celestially profound blue beneath a forehead as pure, where abundant black hair was graciously parted.

If Marius loved Jeanne madly, Jeanne loved Marius with all her soul, and the two hearts that had understood one anoth-er for a long time had given themselves to one another so nat-urally that the fiancés would not have been able to say exactly when it had happened. There had been no futile sighs, no co-quetries, and no jealousy either. There had, however, been young Monsieur Camoin, the justice of the peace, who had also been madly smitten with Jeanne and whose passion had led to insistent actions that were a trifle humiliating for a magistrate—but Jeanne's heart could only feel sorry for him, for that heart belonged irrevocably to Marius, and the latter was so well aware of it that he had ended up feeling sorry for his unfortunate rival himself.

The solemn moment was approaching. Truly, Numa had arrived in the nick of time, for the marriage was to be celebrated the next day. The church and the Mairie had been forewarned, the invitations had been sent out, the details of the banquet expertly worked out, and all the old furniture in the restored apartments carefully rearranged—everything, in fact, had been reviewed and put in perfect order under the vigilant eye of the valiant Martine, who had been working herself to death for a week.

A short distance away, on the first floor of another habitation, whose windows overlooked a garden adjacent to that of the Foulane house, which formed a rather large space covered with verdure and tall trees, was the bedroom of a young girl about whom Marius had often thought.

An abundant branch of a pomegranate tree climbed along the wall and surrounded a certain little window that opened, delightfully framing the laughing face of the girl when the voice of Marius, escaping between drafting two documents, had become audible in the garden. Sometimes, the girl, leaning out, had extended her arm to pick one of the beautiful red flowers, which fell from her hand as a gesture of farewell when Marius went away. The young man caught it in mid-air and returned at a run to resume his work.

There was, at the present moment, something unusual in that bedroom: an opulent wedding-basket had been brought in, with jewels glittering in open caskets, and a vaporous whiteness brightened the shade of the peaceful retreat, in the form of a magnificent wedding-dress carefully laid out on the blue velvet of the chairs backed up against the wall.

We already know the people of the little town of Martigues to whom we were introduced at the beginning of this story, and who will reappear in due course when the time is ripe. We would, however be guilty of a regrettable omission if we did not also mention, in his modest place, another faithful friend of our hero: an excellent animal that answered to the name of Houzard, a brave spaniel full of affection, and who, by instinct, had already attached himself to his future mistress, to the extent that when one did not see him at Marius' side, one was almost certain to find him at the heels of Madame and Mademoiselle Honorat

Numa being unable to divide himself between the two families equally desirous of possessing him in those first hours of effusion, the notary's table brought everyone together again that evening. They had the pleasure of hearing the young mariner recount the incidents of his great voyages and describe the mores of the black populations of Senegal or the Congo, and became terrified in witnessing with him, at second hand, the duels of the paltry French torpedo-boats with the Chinese fleet of Fou-Tchéou.[6]

Numa had chosen his career by vocation. Enthusiastic by temperament, with an inquisitive mind, and an indefatigable worker, his shipboard duties only took up a part of his activity. His narrow mariner's cabin had become, for him, a study, and one would not have believed how many books, instruments and specimens of natural history that small space could contain. He had already learned enough, and cultivated sufficient understanding, to glimpse an immensity beyond received knowledge. He sometimes astonished his colleagues in the officers' ward-room with the audacity of his hypotheses or the unexpectedness of his conclusions.

---

[6] This implies a slightly earlier date for the beginning of the story's composition than the date of 1890 that is subsequently cited; the Battle of Fuzhou, between the French Far East fleet and the Qing dynasty's Fujian Fleet was fought on 23 August 1884.

Once, in the days of their early studies at the lycée in Marseilles, and later in the course of conversations in their all-too-brief meetings, one commencing his nautical career at Toulon while the other studied law in Paris, Marius had been able to appreciate all the bizarre aspects of his friend's habitual ideas. With him it was not the same as with so many others, whose depths are soon plumbed and fathomed; with Numa one quit the ordinary banalities of current life and departed for far horizons, always new, filled with surprises and the unexpected. When he got astride the charger of his imagination, there was nothing to do but let him go and allow oneself to be drawn along—and that was what Marius did; his own mind, more disciplined by professional tradition, could only share feebly in his friend's enthusiasms, but he always took a keen pleasure in allowing himself to follow in his wake.

Perhaps Numa had acquired that vagabond mental orientation during his early years at school, under the influence of the fantastic digressions gladly indulged, within and without his courses, by Monsieur Coral, the teacher with whom, doubtless by virtue of a conformity of natural tendencies between the master and the pupil, he had had the greatest sympathy. At that age, which receives indelible impressions, the young Numa had, as it were, hung from the lips of the worthy professor while the latter, going back to the Deluge, attempted to render in broad hyperbolic strokes the philosophy of the entire history of humankind, and then, departing from points already acquired, continued into the future, prophetically tracing the grandiose trajectory of human destiny. The first great chagrin the young man had known was the dismissal of Monsieur Coral, the beloved teacher, accused and easily convicted of deviance in academic philosophy.

It required several joys to come together at the same time to set all the springs of a lively and generous nature like Marius' quivering. Under the influence of an overexcitement that he had not previously known, his mind lit up at that moment with spontaneous internal gleams that rendered present the slightest aspects of his past live, in which Numa occupied such an important place. It was thus that, after many other memories of their youth, he came to remind his friend of Monsieur Coral's exciting lessons and the adventurous hypotheses in which the ultra-classical philosophy of the excellent man delighted—as when, for example, he placed a Pythagoras or an Archimedes in the middle of the present epoch and had them react, in accordance with the knowledge of their time, to our modern sciences, our electricity, our telescopes, our steam engines, our formidable weapons and discoveries of all kinds: aerostats, photography, telephones, etc.

"The men of the remote past certainly had no suspicion of the marvels that their descendants would realize," Numa observed, "but are we not plunged in our turn into a darkness comparable with theirs? Is not our time the nebulous past, the distant antiquity of the people who will live in the fortieth century? How will the science that is just beginning, and the discoveries of which we are so proud, appear to the eyes of future generations that will scarcely distinguish our memory from that of the Greeks and Romans?

"Do we know what is potentially contained in the ultimate development, the effective and practical application, of the great universal laws and the conquest of natural forces that we have scarcely begun to utilize? Do we know what those still-confused things that we call magnetism, hypnotism—words that we employ without understanding their hidden means—promise in terms of immaterial liberation for humankind to come?

"And what material and mental advancement, what development of all the human faculties, what truly superior civilization that future, magnified by all that the irresistible march of progress, will bring? How will that future humankind, which will be in full possession of its planet, and will have set its hand on the most secret springs of nature, be able to speak of our time, except as an epoch of profound barbarism?"

"In the meantime, let's be content with our own time," the notary put in, visibly desirous of changing the slightly untimely slant that the conversation was taking. "Barbaric as it may be, it still offers a few pleasures, doesn't it, my dear children?"

The smiles exchanged by the fiancés responded eloquently to that favorable interpretation of the present, and the ladies, who had other things on their minds, took the conversation in a different direction. But it was fated that the occupants of notary's house would hear a veritable lecture that evening, akin to those that fashion had recently introduced in many places. A further comment resumed the thread of the interrupted dissertation.

"Will you be with for long, my dear Numa?" Marius asked. "Will this expedition to the North Pole in which you're due to take part claim you soon? I haven't forgotten the enthusiasm with which you spoke about it to me during our great Mediterranean excursion. It was in Algiers, if you remember; we were strolling around the government square, taking in the cool evening air. I tried to dissuade you, but none of my reasons carried any weight before your ardent faith in its success."

"The North Pole? No one is going to the North Pole. Back then, I believed, as others did, than an open sea might exist beyond a circle of ice during the polar summer, which a single day of six months during which the sun never quits the horizon—but in view of what I know now, I've given up on that utopia."

"Oh! Now you're intriguing me again. It isn't, I suppose, the failure of the English mariners of the *Alert* and the *Discovery*, whose ran into insurmountable barriers of ice, or the misfortunes of the brave Americans of the *Jeannette* that have discouraged someone as intrepid as you. You must have more powerful reasons."[7]

---

[7] *H.M.S. Alert* and *H.M.S. Discovery* were two of the ships engaged in the British Arctic Expedition of 1875, commanded by George Nares, which set out to search for the hypothetical Open Polar Sea. The Jeannette expedition, led by the Ameri-

Very gravely, Numa collected himself momentarily, and seemed to be hesitating over his response, but before the interrogative gaze of Madame Honorat, who had always trembled at the thought of the project that her son had now renounced, he came to a decision and continued:

"Since you want to know the reason why the North Pole is inaccessible, and will become increasingly so, you need to know that there's an astronomical question, quite simple, that you'll grasp immediately. You know that our globe, in addition to its movements of axial and orbital rotation, which determine the day and the year, also has a retrograde conical movement of 50.1 seconds of arc per year, which results in the precession of the equinoxes, and then a fourth movement, that of the line of the apsides, which determines the slow horizontal movement of the major axis of the orbit in the same retrograde direction, at a rate of 11.8 seconds per year. That total of 61.9 seconds, relative to the 360 degrees of the entire circle, means that our globe resumes the same position after a period of 20,937 years.

"Now, by virtue of that incessant displacement of the elliptical curve of the terrestrial orbit, the inequality that exists in the duration of the seasons is necessarily subject to a kind of cycle that gradually transmits that inequality of one season to the following one, similarly passing through the solsticial and equinoctial points to return to the same order in 20,937 years, or, to round out the number, about twenty-one thousand years.

"One notable point, seemingly unimportant at first glance, but which has considerable consequences for our planet, struck the clear-sighted mind of a man who remains almost unknown to the public, and who published an essay on the subject a long time ago, which hazard recently put into my hands: Adhémar's *Les révolutions de la mer*. It is that our

---

can George Washington DeLong, set out on the same quest in 1879, but it came to grief in 1881.

spring and summer combined, which between the spring and autumnal equinoxes correspond to the broadest arc of the elliptical path of the planet, are about a week longer than the autumn and winter, while the opposite is true in the southern hemisphere, where the seasons are inversely related to ours. It results from that inequality that the northern pole has 4,464 hours of daylight in a year, compared with 4,296 hours of night—a difference of 168 hours of night, of which the other pole has more than ours.

"Now, although 168 hours of nocturnal cold in a year is not very much, it is a different matter when the figure is multiplied by several thousand years. The chilling of the less favored pole, which is, at present the southern pole, increases to colossal proportions, and we can then understand the enormous accumulation of Antarctic ice, which extends to the sixty-fifth degree of latitude, while the permanent ice of the Arctic pole scarcely extends beyond the eightieth parallel. When the movement of the apsides has accomplished half of its evolution, of course, the inverse will be the case relative to the comparative duration of the seasons in the two hemispheres.

"It is therefore established that in the course of a complete cycle of that slow displacement of the seasons, which lasts 21,000 years, each of the Earth's poles will experience in its turn the maximum cooling and the accumulation of ice, at intervals of 10,500 years., and that the alternation of the principal ice-cap will continue for as long as the astronomical conditions of our planet endure."

"I can't help finding all that logical and comprehensible, and adding my own adherence to Adhémar's theory," Marius interjected, "but from the fact that it's the southern pole that now has the principal glacial cap, doesn't it follow that the northern pole is at its minimum invasion of ice, and that now or never is the time to attempt the enterprise?"

"Wait a little, my dear Marius, and you'll see that not only are we no longer at the minimum of northern ice, but that the same theoretical reasoning about the formation of the polar ice destroys forever any hope of finding an open sea in the location where, on the contrary, the ice will pile up increasingly toward the center of the pole.

"The epochs of maximum and minimum arrive, of course, once in every 10,500 years, when the winter of one hemisphere and the summer of the opposite hemisphere coincide exactly with the passage of the Earth through the extremities of the major axis of its orbit. Thus, it was in the year 1248 A.D. that the first day of our winter fell at the moment when the Earth was at perihelion, and the figures we calculated just now are thus exact for the epoch that we are now in. Since the year 1248, the north pole has been getting gradually colder, and while the southern hemisphere has seen its summers, which coincide with out winters, getting longer and its ice diminishing, the ice has been increasingly piling up on our pole, which, far from being free of ice in any season, in spite of the estival melting at the perimeter, also possesses a permanent glacial cap, which will only increase as the years go by, and become, inconsequence, increasingly inaccessible.

"Adhémar has calculated that the mass of ice that accumulates specifically on one of the poles, and which, by the weight added to it by the incessant snowfall, sinks down to rest on the solid crust of the globe, exceeding considerably in weight and extent the ice of the opposite pole, can attain twenty leagues of thickness is the center of the cap, with a surface area of 78,500 square leagues, which represents sufficient weight to alter the equilibrium of the globe and displace the center of gravity of the whole liquid mass by nearly 400 leagues. Hence, necessarily, a flow of water toward the pole that has become heavier, and the submersion of all the land situated in the same hemisphere, up to a certain altitude.

"No more is necessary to understand that this is the reason for the immense extent and depth of the ocean in the southern hemisphere, which distinguishes that half of the world, where the principal glacial ice-cap is presently located, and where it is observed that the mean temperature is about ten degrees lower than that of our hemisphere.

"When the slow displacement of the duration of the seasons has transported that considerable surplus of polar ice into our hemisphere, it will be the north, in its turn, that will receive the influx resulting from the new displacement of the equilibrium of the oceans, and will see its continents buried beneath liquid masses—which, for France, will be more than a thousand meters deep. Those geographical and climactic modifications accompanying the movement of ice are very slow to occur, since the movement extends over a period of 10,500 years. It is, however, easy to recognize to present the significant signs of change since the year 1248, notably in the lowering of temperature that is gradually overtaking the land we inhabit.

"Already, the half-dozen centuries that have elapsed since the epoch that one can call the maximum Austral Sea and the minimum Boreal Sea, or rather, the maximum chill of the southern hemisphere and the maximum warmth of the northern hemisphere, has been sufficient to render the northern lands less habitable, and the proofs of that are abundant.

"Thus, the now-desolate land of Greenland still retains the roots of vanished forests, which testify to a relatively recent vegetation that has become impossible in the present temperature of that frozen country. Iceland, with its fifty thousand inhabitants, has scarcely a third of the population that the island nourished a few centuries ago, when cereals were harvested there that can no longer be cultivated today. Closer to home, did not vines prosper in England until the precious shrub was finally obliged to retreat from a climate that had become inadequate? Even in France, was it not still the case that, in the time of Louis XII and François I, certain vintages in the vicinity of Paris considered among the best in the realm? Nowadays, I believe, the wines of Suresnes and Argenteuil that Parisian strollers now drink on Sundays no longer have such high pretentions.

"These changes are, moreover, merely the repetition of similar changes accompanying the glacial cycle that repeats every 21,000 years for each hemisphere. Thus, the similar period anterior to the present period has left traces in the fossil forest of Ankerdluk in Greenland[8] and the numerous coal-bearing strata of different ages encountered at various depths in the five continents of the world. On the other hand, if we consider the mineral realm, does not the subsoil of Paris, with its successive strata of Neptunian terrains, corresponding to as many invasions of the sea that alternate with epochs of emergence, offer visible and material proof of these periodic revolutions? That past predicts for us with certainty the sad future that awaits the capital of the civilized world.

"It is, therefore, clearly demonstrated that the annual sum of solar heat that we receive in this hemisphere of the globe will diminish from century to century. Well, that cooling will continue to increase until France is in the same glacial period familiar to geologists, and which, notably in the Pyrenees, has left traces signifying a depth of four hundred meters, when our Provençal winters attached Mediterranean ice-sheets to ours shores, like another Baltic."

"Oh, my God! What am I hearing?" cried Jeanne, consternated.

The young woman, whom a devoted governess, an exceptional woman who had remained her intimate friend, had educated more seriously than is usual for young Frenchwomen, had been able to understand the things that her brother had just explained, but her vivid imagination and sensitive nature had been struck as if it were a matter of an imminent disaster.

"Don't worry, little sister; there's nothing alarming in it for us. The olive groves will continue to prosper for centuries to come in our beautiful Provence—but woe betide the men who will live in the eightieth century of our era, when the era of the great Arctic tide has come! In six thousand years, they

---

[8] The discovery of "fossil forests" of tropical vegetation beneath the Greenland glaciers was widely reported after specimens were acquired by the Finnish explorer Adolf Erik Nordenskjöld in 1883, popularized, among others, by the French geologist Elisée Reclus.

will be victims of a catastrophe far more terrible than the ice that already frightens you."

"What more is there, then?"

"I've told you: the disruption of the present equilibrium of the seas of our globe, such as is produced alternately from north to south or from south to north every 10,500 years. To begin with, the slow and gradual return of the Ocean toward our northern hemisphere; then, the exposure by the retreat of the waters and the slow disintegration of the southern ice-sheet, which will receive an excess of heat instead of an excess of cold for many centuries; and finally, when the center of gravity of the liquid mass has overtaken that of the globe, the melting and break-up of the major part of the disaggregated Austral ice, which the swing of the seesaw will precipitate toward the northern hemisphere, like a formidable assault.

"That cataclysm, which will not await the maximum heat of the period, any more than our annual polar break-ups wait for the middle of summer, will be gradually unleashed shortly after the center of gravity has penetrated north of the equator. Then the Deluge that remains in the memory of all peoples and occurred, according to the Bible, in the year 2350 B.C. will be reproduced, but in the opposite indirection.

"A frightful mass of water drawing the gigantic debris of the austral debacle will precipitate northwards and submerge the greater part of the countries of the northern hemisphere, leaving new continents uncovered in the south. And when I say 'new,' I'm in error, since they will be the old Antarctic continents that are returning to the surface—the same ones that were swallowed up, along with the nations they bore: the antediluvian humankind, of which only a few remnants survived to perpetuate the tradition of the cataclysm.

"Who were those peoples, those empires so tragically annihilated? What degree of civilization, of progress, of knowledge had they been able to attain in a period of more than ten thousand years? The memory of it was doubtless lost among the scattered survivors that fate returned to the life of nature and barbarity. What is the significance, though, of the tenacious tradition of Titans wanting to equal God himself, Titans attempting to scale the heavens? After all, might not the fabulous legend conserved by peoples be a veridical but disfigured memory of a high and powerful human civilization, which collapsed in a universal disaster.

"That is what will happen to us in our turn. Advancement, civilization and progress rise up and increase incessantly, only to fall in the end and at a stroke into the inevitable abyss—for there is no doubt about it: the Deluge will return."

A heartbroken sigh was heard, which caused all of them to turn toward the kitchen. It was the worthy Martine, who was also listening, standing in the open doorway, peppering her face with signs of the cross.

"Fortunately, we have sixty centuries ahead of us," said Maître Foulane, smiling. "We can therefore sleep peacefully tonight."

"For humankind," said Numa, "sixty centuries is not such a long space of time, Have you ever considered that five or six dozen lives lasting into old age, placed in sequence, are sufficient to fill in the entire duration that separates us from the last Deluge?"

That rather long digression, somewhat out of keeping with the eve of the family celebration that was in preparation, was concluded with a remark by Marius: "Six thousand years from now," he said, "humans will have realized such progress that they will be able to build a dyke against the next Deluge, or escape it in some ingenious manner."

The ladies got to their feet and prepared to return home, accompanied by the two young men, Madame Honorat leaning on her son's arm and the no less happy Jeanne clinging to her fiancé, who was taking her back to her maidenly dwelling for the last time.

The night, delightfully cool, scarcely brightened by a thin crescent moon rising on the horizon, allowed the constellations of the firmament to scintillate in all their splendor. It was one of those nights that cause poets and lovers to dream and draw the gaze irresistibly toward the profundities of the starry vault.

At all times, lovers have been passionately fond of the sky and its stars. Love is the eternal poem of nature and life, and not only ephemeral terrestrial existence but the innumerable hearths of life that animate the celestial expanses, where sidereal planets without number, the majority doubtless more privileged than our paltry residence, also witness beings living and loving: humankinds that we shall never know, and which, for their part, are unaware of us.

What might those earths in the heavens be like, those worlds, necessarily as varied in nature and aspect as all the different milieux that have given birth to them? What existences, what civilizations, agitate and develop there? Perhaps, in the infinity of their number, there is an earth parallel to this one, where a humankind very similar to ours, a sister species, lives! But who will ever penetrate such mysteries?

Why did these strange reflections, in which the vagabond ideas of his friend Numa returned like an obsessive echo, assail Marius' mind at that particular moment? But we have already said that the Marius of that day was not the usual Marius. When solemn moments approach, which decide an existence, all the cords of the soul are tightly stretched; thoughts and sentiments attain a power of expansion that raises them far above the ordinary theater of everyday life.

Our friend was touching one of those culminating points in which the soul rises up and overflows. He had never felt such a tender passion and, simultaneously, such a delirious emotion, as he did that evening, beside the child who remained as silent as him, and was doubtless, like him, deeply plunged in some indescribable interior vision.

They reached the Honorat house. It was necessary to separate, and it was in a troubled voice, as he let go of his fiancée's hand, that Marius simply said: "Until tomorrow"—but in a tone so emotional, and with such a strange expression, that the young woman allowed a slight interrogative disturbance to penetrate the farewell that she returned.

"Until tomorrow, then, my child," said the mother.

"Until tomorrow, my dear Marius," said Numa, with a final handshake.

II

Still pensive, Marius went back to his own house, entering by the small door to the garden, of which he had the key. At that hour of the night, the place doubtless lent itself to the young man's need to savor a moment of solitude before going to bed, since, instead of immediately going to his apartment, he started strolling at a measured pace along the lateral pathway to which the door that he had closed behind him gave access, wandering back and forth through the black shadow that the house projected—a shadow all the blacker because it extended along the high row of dark yews at the bottom of the garden.

Between the top of that obscure vegetable wall and the roofs of the houses there was room for a fine extent of sky where the scintillating stars seemed to the challenging the pale light emitted by the shining arc of a moon scarcely in its first quarter. It is necessary to believe that Marius continued to delight in his nocturnal meditation, for, pausing in his walk, he sat down on one of the large benches with comfortable backs that modern taste is gradually introducing everywhere, in our gardens as well as on our public promenades.

A profound silence, scarcely disturbed by a distant croaking of frogs, reigned in the surroundings. In the house, everyone was asleep, except for Marius and the brave Houzard, who came silently to lie down discreetly at his master's feet. It seemed momentarily, however, that a few soft notes of music came from some way off, doubtless well-known to the amorous young man, because he pricked up his ears immediately. They were the opening chords of the tender melody from *Mireille:*[9]

---

[9] Charles Gounod's 1864 opera, based on a poem by the Provençal poet Frédéric Mistral.

My heart cannot change;
Remember that I love you.

The fugitive notes were coming from Jeanne's shuttered bedroom, where she too was staying up late—but the delightful harmony only sighed briefly, before the silence—the great silence of midnight—reigned once again in all directions.

High above sparkled the golden nails of the "carts" of Ursa Major and Minor, between which snaked the polar Draco, which turns its mysterious head toward the mysterious region of the sky into which, it is said, our own sun is traveling, drawing its cortege of planets in its wake. It is there that the quadrilateral of Hercules can be seen, beside that of the ravishing Corona Borealis, the astonishing symmetry of which does indeed design a veritable diadem of celestial pearls. Thus, Gemma, or the Pearl, is the well-merited name given to the queen of that unparalleled item of jewelry. It really is a set of jewels, to which no crown of this world can be compared, except, perhaps, the white crown of a bride.

And the delighted imagination of the young man sank into the sweetest of interior contemplations—that of his own happiness—with his eyes on the celestial diadem, which, in his amorous folly, he wanted to see descend to within arm's reach, and surrender itself to him...so that he might give it to her.

And still the gold of the constellations scintillated, the limitless field of which seemed the only backcloth worthy of supporting the magnified thought and the divine reams of the most besotted of lovers.

It was, above all, the gentle opaline radiance of Gemma that held his gaze, suspended by the reverie. He could not take his eyes off it, no longer seeing anything but the beautiful queen, who seemed to be gathering her followers together for some mysterious conspiracy. From different directions, however, like a discreet advertisement for Marius, continual fulgurations were launched—winks, so to speak—that the nearer stars seemed to be addressing to him and exchanging between themselves, like signs of intelligence.

That excessively prolonged fixity of gaze ended up having a strange effect. Thus, the star appeared to light up more brightly, staring in its turn at the imprudent watcher; in a way, it took possession of the gaze that had lingered too long on its fire.

Marius had the sensation of a kind of charm that he wanted to break by looking away, either toward the superb Vega or toward the brilliant Arcturus, but it was in vain that he tried to flee the attraction commenced. Even when he closed his eyes, Gemma remained nailed to his retina, and imposed her magnified and magnetic flamboyance more and more despotically. An invincible torpor gripped the young man, gradually removing the lucidity of his mind.

For anyone who has not experienced the strange hallucinations of hypnotism, the fact that we are reporting may appear utterly incredible, but how many things, each more incredible than the last, have imposed themselves on our belief since hypnotism began to provoke talk and rumor of its miracles?

In the meantime, the spell intensified, and poor Marius became breathless, his face turned to the sky. Suddenly, the luminous ray penetrated into the utmost depths of his being, like a steel needle. Would you believe it? It was now Gemma who was looking, staring, at Marius. The soft and timid gleam of a moment before had become a fascinating and imperious gaze that seemed to be saying: "Come to me! I command it!"

How was it that our friend suddenly lost the sentiment of his situation, to the point that the star no longer seemed to be floating above his head? On the contrary, he saw it, fearfully, sparkling at the very bottom of an immense abyss open beneath him.

At any rate, vertigo progressively overwhelmed him, and he believed that he was suspended above a frightful void. A sudden instinct of self-preservation made him extend his clutching hands with a desperate energy, which feverishly gripped the wooden slats of the back of the bench supporting his head.

But was that not absurd, impossible? What about the law of gravity? What, then, had become of the centripetal force that attaches terrestrial objects to the ground and retains them?

Oh, was it really a matter of the reasonable and the possible? It was doubtless just a horrible nightmare that was about to end.

But no! The unfortunate fellow felt, in his delirium, that the rotating Earth was now suspending him upside-down, over the infinite abyss that was gaping before his eyes, with no other support than his desperate grip—and his strength was running out, and the magnetic attraction of the star was increasing. The perfidious queen of the magic circle was darting her most urgent effluvia at him, and ordering once again: "Come to me!"

The unfortunate Marius realized that he was lost. In his anguish, he saw his entire life, all of his happiness, flying away from him in a supreme vision.

"Help! Help!"

Suddenly, his fingers, at the limit of their strength, relaxed, and, uttering a loud scream, he fell into the immensity...

A sensation of a rapid wind, producing in his ears the sound of rushing water, finally extracted our poor friend from a long, perfectly understandable and excusable faint. One sees people fall ill every day for less.

He was immediately conscious of his terrifying situation, and wondered how many instants still separated him from the most horrible death. To prolong such an agony was not desirable. It was better to get it over with as quickly as possible—and yet that death did not come. The seconds succeeded one another, and he fell, still falling face forwards, once again having the diabolical star before his eyes—without, moreover, feeling unduly uncomfortable.

In such an extremity, the length of time that goes by reanimates calm and relaxation in the mind of its own accord.

He was able to think and say to himself: *My poor Marius, if you're still in this world, something supernatural is happening here that you don't understand.*

Soon, the vertiginous shock of the commencement of the fall was gradually transformed into the smooth sensation that a bird must experience in cleaving through the air toward its objective. After having counted the seconds, it was long quarters of an hour that appeared to succeed them.

In the end, it even became monotonous. Marius pulled himself together completely, and began, in order to kill time, to remember appropriate stories, including that of a prodigious jumper of whom he had heard mention in Marseilles, who leapt so high and remained in the air for such a long time that he began to get bored.

If only he knew how long this fantastic voyage would last!

It was definitely time to try to figure out where he was. The poor fellow attempted to look around, which he had not yet dared to do.

The first thing that struck his gaze when he raised his head was, some distance headed of him, the most astonishing landscape imaginable: a landscape in which a curious distribution of light separated a region bathed in light from a vast area that remained in shadow, faintly illuminated by a kind of moonlight. From where he was, Marius could see the most magnificent succession of high mountains with tormented summits and profound valleys that faded away on the horizon—a horizon cut out from an almost black sky by a clear, sharp line.

It was the lunar region that was directly in front of Marius; it appeared that it really was the moon, obligingly keeping company with him, since he was traveling in such an extraordinary fashion himself. Perhaps he would reach the end of the insensate journey there.

If that were the case, what would become of him in a land so different from his own? That prompted our friend to remember all the knowledge he had acquired and everything he had read concerning the abode of the Selenites. He would, therefore, be able to check the marvelous tales told be travelers who had preceded him to that country, so little known as yet, who had doubtless exaggerated the reality somewhat, as is usual for the enthusiastic temperament of bold discoverers of distant lands.

"The travelers that had preceded him?" you say.

Certainly, my dear reader. Come on, try to remember.

Without going back as far as Lucian of Samosata, who witnessed the great battle waged between the armies of the sun and moon, comprised of hippogriffs, fleas as large as elephants and other curious monsters, he remembered Astolpho, whose story Ariosto told in the *Orlando Furioso*, and who, accompanied by St. John, traveled to the Moon in the same chariot the prophet Elijah had once used. Among other curious items that he found in the valley in which they landed, there were all the things that we lose of our own accord, including reputation and common sense, which remain there in tightly-sealed bottles, in order to guarantee those extremely volatile substances against evaporation. Astolpho collected his own, as well as Orlando's, the latter being in dire need of his at that moment, and returned without difficulty, bringing the bottles back intact.

Marius had also read about the adventure of Don Domingo Gonsales, a gentleman from Seville, who, according to the report made by the worthy Bishop Godwin, had been able to domesticate a flock of geese, to which he had attached a gondola in which he traveled through the air. Although the voyage to our satellite that the latter carried out in that fashion was involuntary, entirely due to a caprice of his team, which took off from the peak of Tenerife and flew straight to the moon, he nevertheless reaped the glory of the enterprise, and eventually came back to inform us that there are men on the moon who grow to thirty feet tall; that they express themselves exclusively in music; that they sleep during hot days that last fifteen times as long as ours and stay awake during long nights brightened by the light coming from the Earth;

and, finally, that because everything weighs so little out there, the giants in question can travel through the air, steering by waving fans.

Another of the most interesting explorers was Cyrano de Bergerac, whose flew by means of a machine of his own invention. He, too, saw giants on the Moon, who, far from flying through the air, walked on all fours, but were nevertheless very intelligent and even humorous individuals—as Cyrano had occasion to learn to his cost, for they captured him and trained him to do somersaults and pull faces to amuse the public, deeming a man of his species good for nothing else. That did not prevent him from making a host of curious observations, which he passed on to us in his turn, such as the aptitude of the Selenites to satisfy their nutritional needs with odors alone, and their custom of paying for everything in intellectual currency—which is to say, with poetry of their own composition, varying in quality.

Marius, who was already anxious regarding the means by which he might make himself understood by the inhabitants if he happened to run into them, recalled that Cyrano de Bergerac had also observed that the local language consisted entirely of music, but only in the educated classes, the lower orders expressing thoughts solely by means of signs and contortions. He felt reassured in either case, for our friend was a passable musician; and as for gestures, was he not from the Midi, where sign-language always accompanies speech, and is sometimes more significant?

There have been explorers who traveled even further than those just mentioned, who did not come from sublunar regions, as witness the Micromegas whose marvelous story was told by Voltaire. That native of Sirius, who height extended to eight leagues, traveled from star to star with the sole aim of learning. On Saturn he found dwarfs who were only two thousand meters tall, and took one of them with him, who was none other than the secretary of that planet's Académie des Sciences.

When they arrived together on the terrestrial globe, Micromegas scooped up some water from the Baltic in the palm of his hand, in which something seemed to be moving. When that something was examined through a stone in his companion's necklace that served as a magnifying-glass, it turned out to be a ship undertaking a scientific expedition to the North Pole. That was a good opportunity to talk about science and philosophy, of which the Sirian and the Saturnian promptly took advantage, entering into communication with the microbes by means of tiny tubes, which permitted them to have a fairly long conversation with the terrestrial scientists.

The conversation ended with the peremptory affirmation of a learned ecclesiastic who declared that the entire universe had been created solely for mankind—on which the two friends laughed wholeheartedly at the pride of the human insects.

To get back to the Moon, in addition to the eye-witness testimony of those great voyagers, respectable authorities have also offered pronunciations with regard to what occurs on the night-star, which was once both the goddess Diana and Proserpina. In the first rank is Fontenelle, who imagined the Selenites worshiping the Earth floating majestically in their sky, in the same way that some terrestrial peoples revere the moon—which places the inhabitants of both lands in a position of reciprocal adoration.

Did not the great Kepler himself, in a moment of relaxation for his powerful genius, speak in his *Astronomical Dream* about the subvolvans, the Selenites who see the Earth turning, and the privolvans, those on the far side who are deprived of the beautiful spectacle of the Earth illuminating the nights of the subvolvans—who, without being any more irrational than terrestrial humans, might believe that the star in question, thirteen times large in surface area and more luminous for them than the moon is for us, was made expressly to illuminate them and provide them with amusement in being present to their eyes?

All these facts and extraordinary stories, to which Marius hardly gave any thought in other circumstances, came back to mind now in a very timely fashion. If those different accounts were added together, the result was, in sum, that the moon—which astronomers declare to be denuded of any element supportive of life, and hence utterly inhospitable—was probably better than the reputation they have conferred upon it. Other scientists have declared that, although the face we can see is devoid of water and air, the other is quite different, because the centrifugal force of the world's movement, which is only exercised on one side in this case, as on a stone whirled by a slingshot, draws those fluids and the life that depends on them to the side that is entirely unknown to us.

At any rate, Marius would soon know what the truth of the matter was, if he succeeded in landing safe and sound in the almost-virgin territory to which he was getting closer and closer.

There was only one difficulty, which was also in contradiction to the laws of gravity, which ought to have been drawing the unfortunate castaway toward the lunar globe with ever-increasing speed because of the inverse-square law. The trajectory that our friend was following was, by contrast, carrying him away, manifestly and without deviation, from the orbit of the moon, which was therefore not exerting any force on the body that was traversing its sphere of attraction with impunity. It was becoming probable that Marius would pass beyond it: one more ordeal for the unfortunate, who saw the saving plank on which he was already counting for salvation escaping him—a highly problematic salvation, however, since it would apparently involve a necessarily-fatal fall on to the rocks whose thousand asperities he could see. But was that not preferable to the frightful fate of being swallowed up forever in the abysms of infinite space?

While such dark thoughts were agitating him, in the same way that he had begun, instinctively, to move his head, Marius tried to move his arms and legs. He perceived that an approximately regular movement of his four limbs had effects reminiscent of aerial swimming, as had happened to him in dreams many a time, when he had felt himself flying through the air like a bird.

Marius was a good swimmer, but his discovery could only have very limited effects, for his vertiginous course only permitted him to veer slightly to one side without him being able to break away from the insurmountable current that was bearing him away. Nevertheless, the ability to alter his course by an appreciable angle was something, and in the present circumstances, it might perhaps enable him to reach one of the lunar mountains, whose peaks he was about to skim, to clutch some point of support and hang on tight.

He therefore started swimming vigorously, and in less than five minutes, he had altered the line of his projection sufficiently to see the rocky summits of Mount Tycho, the largest of the ancient lunar volcanoes, at very close range.[10]

If our swimmer had had the time, at a moment of such confusion, to contemplate the landscape that was unfolding before his eyes, illuminated by splendid earthlight, he would have admired the incomparable beauty of the immense luminous streaks radiating from the mountain, which seemed like as many enormous rivers with silvery reflections, emerging from the central crater through gaping fissures, to extend to the horizon not in capricious meanders, like our terrestrial rivers, but in straight lines, traversing mountains and valleys. He would have thought that he saw then that those astonishing rivers have immense fissures in the ground for beds, and are formed by prodigious flows of a metal that solidifies without losing much of its natural gleam, and he would have understood that the crust of the worldlet must have been well and truly smashed up in ancient times by the force of internal explosions, after which that molten matter, rising up from the

---

[10] Because it was widely assumed at the time that the Moon's craters had to be volcanic in origin, Alhaiza was by no means the only author of interplanetary fantasies to misrepresent Tycho as a huge mountain.

interior, had come to fill in all the furrows left by the enormous starring thus produced.

What are our paltry volcanoes and timid earthquakes by comparison with the sequence of frightful cataclysms that our satellite saw when, following the explosions of Copernicus and Aristarchos, the eruption of the region of Mount Tycho might have rendered possible the complete dispersion in space of the lunar globe, entirely reduced to dust?

But that was not what was occupying Marius' thoughts for the moment. In the matter of hypotheses, in fact, he was only considering—coolly enough, however—that of a possible landing, if the word "possible" is applicable here. In consequence, he was making superhuman efforts to get closer to the summits—which he was, however, fated never to reach, for it was elsewhere that destiny was driving the unfortunate victim of the perfidious Gemma's spell. It was much further away that our hero was expected.

It was in vain that the ethereal swimmer, with courage and desperation, multiplied the most skillful and most energetic strokes, the lunar globe and he soon crossed paths, barely a thousand meters apart, and then that distance began to increase again, the former advancing in its eternal orbit around the Earth, the latter hurtling on, ever more rapidly.

Although hope and insensate efforts had previously absorbed all of Marius' faculties, preventing him from fruitful study of the landscape that the moon invariably turns toward its hierarchical superior, the terrestrial globe, it was now bleak despair that overwhelmed him and rendered him almost indifferent to the spectacle, absolutely new for a Terran, presented by the unknown, sunlit side of our satellite.

He went past rapidly, but not so fast that he could not distinguish its essential features.

It was not as if there was any great difference in its general configuration: more craters of all sizes, more mountains and surfaces that were only lacking names akin to the familiar names of the seas of Nectar, Fecundity and Serenity, the lake of Dreams, and so on; in sum, a selenography quite similar to the visible one. What had changed, however, was a particular background coloration, undeceptive reflections that advertised true seas, this time of water, either in the depths of extinct craters or on plains where there was verdure vaguely reminiscent of ferns, reeds and rushes. That evidence supported, therefore, those who supposed that the remnants of lunar life had taken refuge, with all the indispensable elements, entirely on the side to which centrifugal force draws the fluids, of which no trace remains of the side that we can see.

Perhaps, with good eyes and closer attention, Marius would have seen the waves and tall grass stirring in places, and some undulating monster appear, reminiscent of the rudimentary forms of a life that had returned to its initial sketches on that prematurely-aged star—for it too must have had its epochs of prosperous life, as various whitened places seem to testify where contours are outlined that have every appearance of being ruined walls. They are doubtless the last vestiges of an ancient lunar civilization, for nothing advertises the continuing presence of intelligent life on the strangely divided globe, whose Earth-facing side could not be approached by living beings without mortal danger. The result of that is that, while we can no longer see the habitable part of their world, they can no longer see ours. Theirs is, at any rate, a dying world, which, although it still retains internal forces seemingly capable of determining minor superficial changes from time to time— including eruptions like the recently-observed flamboyance of Aristarchus[11]—is certainly not far removed from being an ambulant cadaver.

The state of mind in which Marius found himself at that moment ought to render us indulgent of the scant attention that he devoted to the serious study of the lunar hemisphere that in totally unknown to us. In any other circumstances, it would

---

[11] Aristarchus, one of the brightest points on the moon's surface, has always been a prolific source of observations of "transient lunar phenomena," which are still being reported and discussed today.

have been absolutely unforgivable for him not to have made reliable notes and accurate sketches of the lands of the privolvans, for such an opportunity would not come along again anytime soon.

Although he had an excuse, however, we ought to recall that other voyagers more scientifically-minded that Marius, as were the famous Barbicane, the president of an American Gun Club, and his two friends, whom the audacious Jules Verne sent to visit the Moon in a cannonball, were just as inattentive, and told us little more when their return to Earth produced a worldwide emotion and interest that continues to endure.

Will it be necessary, then, for us to discover our satellite in its entirety, in an accurate manner, to wait until the critical moment when—because, according to the calculations of astronomers, the distance separating the moon from the Earth is always shrinking—the fatal moment arrives when it will end up falling on our heads?

In any case, it is not poor Marius that will inform us more amply on that interesting subject, even if he returns to us some day—something that we do not know yet, for he was now being carried with increasing speed away from that inaccessible lunar landscape. Nor was it apparent that he would succeed any better in encountering and landing on one of the other planets of the solar system—which, moreover, remained invisible to him in the bright light that was dazzling him. He scarcely obtained a vague momentary impression of one vast disk close by—that of the immense Jupiter, majestically enveloped in thick clouds, as befit the god of thunder that it had been for such a long time.

Even the daylight soon began to fade away gradually, however. The voyager crossed the ultimate limits of the solar system, limits doubtless more remote than is commonly thought, for even beyond Neptune, the pale faces of two or three indubitable planets, unknown to their terrestrial sister, went past him one after another, like fleeing meteors.

What human courage and what hope, however tenacious it might be, could resist such a situation? The previous ordeals of physical and moral strength were followed, in Marius, by the resigned fatalism and total self-abandonment of a man who thinks that he is conclusively doomed. Could he not see, in the far distance, in a nimbus that was not very luminous but was nevertheless visible, a small celestial company that could be measured by a hand-span, and which represented for the unfortunate exile the entire solar system—that world, in a corner of which he had been so happy and, where he had left behind everything that he loved? Then too, in front of him, more scintillating than ever, there was still the fateful star, Gemma, and her menacing circle, which seemed to have swelled further, and to be opening up her gaping abyss, as if to capture the unlucky human more securely.

Soon, he was reduced to complete mental prostration, for the physical numbness caused by the extreme cold of space penetrated to the marrow of his bones and extinguished all remaining sentiment. He was no more than an inert mass, a lethargic body continuing its plunge into the limitless extent...

How long did our friend's unconsciousness last? We cannot say, and nor could he. But that death-like annihilation was to come to an end. A time came when a benevolent heat warmed up his frozen blood, and a life that had remained dormant reappeared in the insensible body. There was no immediate awakening, but in the limbo of long-extinct thought, tremulous glimmers began to ignite, and vague images stirred that soon took on the fugitive consistency of dreams—of a dream that was at first enchanting, in fact.

A delightful landscape gilded by the sun, surrounded him. In the distance, there was the horizon of a blue sea; close at hand, there were woods bathed with shadow. Attracted by the gentle seductions of coolness and mystery, the young man had gone into the wood, beneath the thick foliage, when he saw advancing from one side, with the majesty of a goddess, a woman of celestial beauty, whose white clothing was intermittently illuminated when she passed through the narrow sunbeams filtering through the leafy crowns of the trees as she walked through the dark green undergrowth. The delightful apparition stopped a few paces away from him, while staring at him.

O joy! What a surprise! It's her, it's his Jeanne!

And the dreamer, mad with love, falls to his knees and holds out his arms to his beloved…but why that cold gaze, that indifferent expression? Does his Jeanne no longer recognize her fiancé?

Heavens! She opens her mouth to proffer haughty words. She turns her head away and passes by. It's too much!

So Marius opens his eyes, and, recovering consciousness, perceives that he is emerging from a deceptive dream, from a chimerical anguish, instead of which comes the heartache of another anguish, this time far better motivated: that of the reality of his situation.

Then, a spark of revolt and anger against unjust destiny ignites in his eyes. He is doubtless about to see the implacable Gemma again, with her infernal circle.

But no, the malignant star is no longer there. What there is instead is the bright light of a splendid sun, no longer fleeing behind him but above his head, attracting him, drawing him toward its fire!

What has happened to him, then, during his long period of unconsciousness? How is it that the force that was previously drawing him away from the Earth is now bringing him closer to it? Is that really the solar system in front of him?

He cannot doubt it, because, in spite of the light inundating him, the strange and unique plant Saturn appears in the distance, surrounded by the corpuscular crown that we call its ring. It is, therefore, necessarily a fact that, in the course of his fantastic voyage, he has described an immeasurable curve that is now bringing him back to his point of departure—or it might be the case that, having been launched like a arrow into the sky, he is now falling back again, exactly like a projectile of that sort.

The dream he had just now was, therefore, a premonition of his homecoming. He is about to return to the Earth, to his homeland, to his affections, to his happiness!

He tries with all his might further to accelerate his fall toward so unexpected a denouement. He greets with an enthusiastic cheer that first encounter with a world of his own heavens, the immense Saturn that is now deploying its peerless ring so close to Marius that he can see it swirling before his eyes like a vast roundabout. He has only to steer slightly to his right with a few energetic strokes in order to pass through the immense hoop with the agility of an unparalleled acrobat

In the distance, directly ahead of him, a world finally appears that is softly illuminated with a pale blue radiance. Its disk, growing by the minute, soon displays the forms of familiar continents, and the presence of its faithful companion the moon at its side—which our friend rediscovers without having the slightest desire, this time, to stop there—obliterates any lingering uncertainty there might be.

Earth! Earth! exclaims the exile, deliriously, finally on the point of being returned to him homeland.

Soon, he is close enough to be able to contemplate the majestic spectacle of the rotation of the terrestrial globe on its axis. In spite of a zone of light clouds, iridescent with a thousand colors in the oblique radiance of the sun, the outlines of the continents and seas are distinct, with their bays and capes, which sink and disappear successively in the east, while new lands and oceans rise in the west: an admirable scene that the followers of Copernicus and Galileo were the first to glimpse with the intuition of genius, and which Marius was now seeing in reality with his excellent twenty-five-year-old eyes.

He did not linger long in philosophizing about the vicissitudes of science, whose eternal verities are so slow to prevail in the human mind; he did not devote any time to recalling the vain systems of Ptolemy and Tycho Brahe, or even the ingenious theory of the worthy monk cited by the amiable Cyrano de Bergerac, who thought that the Earth rotated because, the central fire being Hell, the damned, desperate to escape the flames, were hanging on to and climbing over the interior walls of the sphere, which was spinning under their efforts like a squirrel-cage. No, he had but one sole thought and one sole objective: to succeed in landing one the beloved globe toward which he was now falling with ever-increasing force without sustaining any damage.

It was necessary for him to make the precise instant of his final fall coincide with the passage of the old continent, as close as possible to France, and, above all, to aim at a liquid surface in order to deaden the frightful impact in the waves of the sea, not far from a coast, instead of breaking his bones on solid ground.

So, in his preoccupation, he did not notice certain significant changes in the regions near the poles, including the fact that the white surface of the Arctic ice had grown considerably, for his eyes never quit the vicinity of the forty-third degree of latitude, anxiously measuring the time and distance that still separated him from the critical moment.

Now or never was the moment to take advantage of the ability he had, limited as it was, to use the swimming strokes with which he had already had the opportunity to experiment—especially the counter-strokes—in a course so vertiginous that it hindered his calculations, not to mention that a burning wind was already setting fire to his face as her traversed the terrestrial atmosphere like a aerolith.

Apply the brakes, Marius, or you're going to ignite like a mere bolide! Pay attention! The Asiatic continent has just filed past in its entirety. Here comes the Mediterranean sparkling down below. Ships can already be seen, sailing for various shores.

The approaching meeting-point between the moving horizontal liquid surface and the vertical fall of our hero's body will certainly be on the margin, but one might make a mistake in traveling so many thousands of miles in a few seconds. Is it necessary to hold back or hasten?

The sea seems to be gaining speed. Beware of the Spanish coast, advancing down below. Quickly! It's time…

By the grace of God!
One, two...splash!

III

Fortunately for our friend, the sea was very deep at that point, and he could hold his breath for a long time. Luckier than the reckless Icarus, who perished in the waves into which he had plunged after his wings were burned by the sun, Marius was to live on. Even so, he returned to the surface three-quarters asphyxiated, and would certainly not have taken long to finish drowning if a small boat, sent from a ship from which his fall had been witnessed, had not come to fish him out in time.

Soon afterwards, Marius was carried on to the deck, and when he recovered consciousness, the tightly-knit group of his rescuers, surrounding the bench on which he was lying, astonished him greatly. He remained silent momentarily, trying to figure out where he was.

He finally realized what must have happened, and the joy of being safe and sound, having returned to Earth, renewed his strength. He leapt to his feet.

"Saved! How about that! Oh, thank you, my good friends. You're the ones who fished me out? You're worthy fellows!" Then, darting a circular glance at the sea, he added: "Oh! The coast's a long way away. Where are we, then, exactly?"

The embarrassed silence that greeted the castaway's first words were a further cause of astonishment for him, which caused him to stop in bewilderment. His listeners were looking at one another—even more surprised, it seemed, than Marius. Some of them were looking up into the sky, as if searching for something; others were scrutinizing the horizon; a few were exchanging remarks in an unknown language; all of them were strange in their appearance and costume.

Marius realized that he was not dealing with compatriots.

"Parlate voi Italiano?" he asked.

No reply.

He tried English. "Can you understand me?"

Nothing.

He went on: "No llegaremos a entendernos? Quer fallar Portuguez?"

Still nothing.

"Warum antworten sie mir nicht?"

The same silence, increasingly embarrassed.

That those questions, addressed in the languages most widespread in the civilized world, should not be not understood by the foreigners surpassed any permissible assumptions.

"Incredible! Amazing!" remarked, in his own language, an individual of severe appearance, who seemed even more astonished than everyone else by the castaway's words and gestures.

"Mes boun Dieu, qu'es aco?" sighed the unfortunate, in the dialect of his nurse.

"What's the matter?" exclaimed the serious individual, in the language that Marius knew best. "I'll tell you, my lad..."

"Ah! I'm finally understood!" our friend could not help exclaiming, looking more attentively at the face of his interlocutor—who, strangely enough, did not seem to be unknown to him.

"What's the matter? It's just that we've never encountered such a mystery. Where have you come from? Where are you going?"

"Where have I come from? I left from Martigues, much against my will, I can assure you. Where am I going? Well, I mean to go back, albeit after a long detour."

"But how were you traveling?"

"Don't ask me. I've been falling from the sky for I don't know how long, Oh, that accursed star Gemma! I nearly didn't make it back, damn it!"

A significant gesture on the part of the questioner made it evident that a sad idea had occurred to him. "But my poor friend, express yourself like everyone else. Why use these ancient languages, which only exist in books? Here, there's only me, Professor Alcor, and my former pupil Namo, the owner of the vessel, who are able to converse in those dead languages.

"Oh! Come on! I no longer understand anything at all, not at all. French is a dead language now?"

"The unfortunate fellow has gone mad," the professor said to his young companion, touching his forehead with his finger. "The shock must have disturbed his faculties."

Marius did not understand the words, pronounced in the unknown language of the foreigners, but he understood the gesture.

"If I'm not mad already," he said, "it's not because there isn't enough here to drive one mad. But I'm believable, after all. Would you like proof of my identity? Look, I still have my wallet on me. Here are letters, family papers. There's money, there's my card: Marius Foulane, notary of Martigues, Bouches-du-Rhône."

As a scientific polymath, Professor Alcor soon realized the authenticity of the documents in question, from the French postmark bearing the date 1890 to the watermarked blue-tinted paper with an illustration by Paul Baudry. His anxious eyes went alternately from the objects to Marius' clothing, whose checkered jacket, matching trousers and split collar seemed as strange to him as everything else. They worthy man put his head in his bands, took a few steps, breathed deeply and then planted himself directly in front of the castaway.

"If I'm not dreaming," he said, "I need to know whether it's you or me, if not both of us, who is out of his mind Come on, let's reason it out—or unreason it out—together. You've fallen from the clouds like a bolide; you resemble a French-man from the beginning of the Third Republic; you speak the language of that time and appear to be unaware of the present date. What is the key to this mystery, then? Come on, Mon-sieur, speak. Tell me your whole story, and have no fear of saying too much."

Marius mastered the astonishment that those words re-newed in him, and did as he was asked with a good grace. He gave details about his family, his homeland, his law studies in Paris; he also mentioned his friend Numa, the son of a brave officer who had died in battle in the disastrous war of 1870, and concluded relating how, on the eve of his marriage to the most lovable of the daughter's of Provence, he had found himself being unexpectedly raised into the sky by an unprecedented accident, obedient to the irresistible attraction of a celestial constellation, and the fashion in which, after the most disturbing of journeys, he had fallen back again not far from his point of departure.

"Now, my dear rescuers," he added, "You're entirely enlightened with regard to what you wanted to know about me, and you'll surely complete the service you've rendered me by taking me to the nearest French port, in order that I can rejoin my relatives as quickly as possible. Oh, my dear Jeanne, my dear father, and my dear Numa—how anxious they must be!"

Alcor, who had shaken his head several times, while reflecting profoundly, during the story of that incredible adventure, still seemed deeply absorbed, and maintained a pensive silence. The anxiety of his features testified to a kind of conflict that was taking place in his thoughts, and he seemed to be sometimes welcoming and sometimes rejecting an idea that was doubtless difficult to credit, for he let a few halting words escape, such as "What if...? No, no, it's impossible...! And yet...!"

Suddenly, coming to a decision, he forestalled a further interrogation that the young man, increasingly intrigued, was just about to ask, with a curt question: "On what date were you lifted up?"

"Oh, I remember it only too well! The very eve of my wedding: the twentieth of June, 1890."

"And do you know what the date is today?"

"Ah! As to that, you'd be doing me a kindness by tell me."

"Well, my friend, the day that is shining upon us is the thirtieth of Messidor in the year 6642 of the Austral Era."[12]

It was Marius' turn to be nailed to the spot, openmouthed.

Professor Alcor, striding back and forth, stopped again in front of the young man, who was literally dumbstruck.

"I shall not examine," he said, "the implausibility of your odyssey through space. We are in the presence of a fact, and one does not argue with a fact. I can even complete the story of your adventure, whose marvelous connection I have finally understood. The perfect concordance of your astronomical, geographical and historical data with what exists, or did exist, at a very remote time of our own annals, leads me to admit that there are two Earths in the universe, two planets and doubtless also two solar systems that are absolutely identical.

"Those two worlds, separated by an immeasurable distance, have realized a fact that is extraordinary, but nevertheless in rigorous conformity with the ineluctable laws of universal physics and metaphysics, which determine that if the conflict of initial forces and eternal matter that have given birth to the formation of a world are duplicated at another point in space in absolutely identical circumstances, the new world will faithfully replicate the same astronomical, physical biological and anthropological scenes, with all its developments consecutively and fatally similar, in the smallest details of organization, progressive advancement and historical unfolding, the same causes necessarily giving rise to the same effects.

"Every seed contains within itself, virtually, all the phases of its subsequent developments, and when two seeds that are absolutely identical to one another, even if they are the

---

[12] The 30th of Messidor, in the Revolutionary calendar, corresponded to the 18th of July in the Gregorian calendar. It is, however, conceivable that the "30" in the Carré text is a misprint, as the third of Messidor (21 June) would preserve a better symmetry.

seeds of worlds, develop in the same conditions, there is inevitably a perfect repetition of the same unfolding of astral existence, from the beginning to the end, including the entirety of humankind, down to the least of its children.

"It is thus established by the events revealed by your adventure, and your presence among us, that you have been precipitated from an Earth similar to this one, which is presently passing through the same physical, vital, human and historical states that our world went through six thousand years ago, for it is evident that your Earth is behind ours to that extent.

"Thus, when you thought you had recognized your solar system on emerging from unconsciousness, it was our system, identical to yours in every respect, that you saw and toward which you continued falling. The sun that warmed you blood, congealed by the cold of space, was not your sun but ours; it was the star that you call Gemma—a name that we also know, as belonging to a pretty second-magnitude star."[13]

The unfortunate man bowed his head, prey to a violent despair. Poor Marius! To have thought that he was reaching port, about to be reunited with his nearest and dearest, and suddenly to find that he had been transported millions or billions of leagues away from everything one loved—what a terrible blow! That, then, was the explanation of all the strange and disturbing aspects of the ship that had picked him up.

Alcor respected that distress. The man he had identified as his former pupil—an amiable and discreet young man who had thus far contented himself with listening attentively to all the marvelous things that had just been said—also found it profoundly moving.

The other people present were the sailors making up the crew of the vessel, which belonged to young Namo, and aboard which he was taking a pleasure trip in the company of his master and friend, the savant Professor Alcor. In brief

---

[13] We now know, although it was as-yet undetermined in Alhaiza's day, that Alpha Coronae Borealis is not a G-type star like our sun but a binary, 75 light-years away.

terms, he did his best to satisfy the perfectly legitimate curiosity of those worthy men, for whom he could not reasonably repeat the laborious explanation that had just been made in ancient French, a language as unknown to them as Zend or Sanskrit would have been to seamen contemporary with Marius.

Namo moved closer to the despairing man and took his hand. "I shall be your friend," said the excellent young man, simply.

Marius returned the handshake and looked at the speaker. "Numa! Numa!" he said, as if talking to himself, either because the memory of his friend's bizarre theories came to him at that moment, or because of the impression that Namo's features made on him.

The surprise and marvelous aspect of such a situation was a welcome distraction from the dire blow that had just struck him. So many questions were crowding his mind that he put aside his grief somewhat. Was it not the most astounding of prodigies to find himself transported several thousand years ahead of his own time, into the environment of another world, where the distant future of his own was presently realized—if it was true, as the astonishing Alcor had affirmed, that the destinies of the two humankinds were identical?

What miracle could ever match that one? A miracle all the more extraordinary, because it retained, after all, a certain logic, and did not violate the laws of nature! So that sea, this ship with the utterly novel appearance, and these men with a strange language and manners, were not of his own time. He was already living in the environment of the Earth's distant future, the Earth being six thousand years behind the world of Alcor and Namo!

He could accept the astral formations and physical laws. Strictly speaking, in limitless space, among the infinity of worlds, there might be two that were similar, but that the material similarity should extend to the identity of the creatures living on their surfaces, especially the peoples, events, historical developments and even personalities, that was too much! That surpassed all the limits of credence.

And yet, if the same physical causes necessarily produce the same effects, why should it not be the same for vital and mental causes, everything proceeding rigorously from cause to effect, from the beginning to the end of the two worlds whose nature and material points of departure were identically similar? What are we, then, we humans? We believe that we determine this, prevent that, go wherever we will, and are the arbiters of our fate. Wrong! All our thoughts, and our slightest actions, are merely the fatal consequences of anterior movements, of causes linked to further causes, acting within us and upon us. Vital and intellectual evolution follow their course in the terrestrial environment as inevitably as physical evolution. It is still an ineluctable chain of events, which has enclosed within itself, since the beginning, the great first cause of the heavenly body that carries us, and sees us born and die.

O fatalism, you are no vain word!

Marius was extracted from his profound reflections by the professor's hand which clapped him amicably on the shoulder.

"Let's not forget any longer," he said, "that supper is ready. The voyage ought to have given you an appetite."

Our thinker ceased delving any further into the abyss of the mystery of universal life, and perceived the one that harsh tribulations and a long fast had hollowed out in his stomach. He therefore allowed himself to be politely guided to the vessel's dining room, the luxury and comfort of which already gave the young man a very favorable opinion regarding the progress and good taste of the people of the world that was an older sibling to Marius' own.

The meal was good, and all that the newcomer could have desired. In spite of the difference in the epoch, nothing had changed in the manner of eating and drinking, and very little in the foodstuffs. The smallest items of crockery and cutlery, however, presented a more pronounced originality of form and ornamentation, especially with regard to their substance, which appeared to consist of new metals, very various in their appearance and color.

"You're not drinking, my friend. Here, taste this Haut-Chétif for me, and shake off a little of that melancholy, which does not good at all." The professor continued: "So, you're telling us that your world had only reached the year 1890 of the Christian Era? Here on Cybele—for that's the ancient name for our world that has returned to current usage—we abandoned that ancient era forty-nine centuries ago.

"First, it gave way to the era of Human Rights, which you already know by the name of the Republican Era, which lasted for ten centuries, and from which we have conserved in our calendar the names so aptly given to the twelve months of the year by Fabre d'Églantine. But that era, purely historical, like the preceding ones, was to be effaced in its turn by a measurement of time of the same order as the astronomical measurements of years and days.

"For nearly five thousand years we have only counted in Boreal and Austral Eras, two periods of 10,468 years, comprised by the entire cycle of the horizontal displacement of the major axis of the terrestrial orbit, which has an exact duration of 20,937 years, each period recommencing with the return of one pole or the other to the point at which the first day of winter coincides with the moment of perihelion, which is the shortest distance between the earth and the Sun. Each of those eras is marked in its second half by a significant transformation of the planet's surface."

At this point Alcor's face darkened, but, without pausing to give the explanation that the singular mention of those periodic changes in the face of the globe seemed to demand, he continued swiftly: "At present, we're living in the year 6642 of the Austral Era, and, in consequence, the Boreal Era will have its turn in 3826 years. Your date of 1890 of the Christian Era, therefore allowed me to calculate immediately the difference in our respective eras. That date corresponds to year 642 of the Austral Era, since it was in 1248 of your era that ours began—including, of course the thousand years constituted by the era of Human Rights. That date removed the era that Terrans are presently going through to a point exactly six thousand years behind the Cybeleans."

"So, if I've understood correctly" said Marius, "and as your knowledge of Earthly matters proves, the Earth's present is the Cybelean past, the centuries that you have passed through since then accurately representing the future of the world I have left behind?"

"There's no doubt about it, my friend; what is already proven by the facts that we have observed is necessarily also true for all the rest. The same people, the same necessities, the same passions and the same motives have produced the same events and the same history, and that will continue until the final destruction of our two worlds, at an interval of about six thousand years.

"In that case," the young man went on, excitedly, "I'm the past and you're the future. There was a Marius identical to me who lived on Cybele sixty centuries ago, and you will be resuscitated, exactly as you are, on Earth after the same interval of time. To you, I'm an ancestor lost in the night of the ages, and to me, you're the offspring of my remotest posterity. I'm an old man and you're children!"

"That's right, my young friend, except that it would be more accurate to say, in considering us from the veritable viewpoint of the collective life of humankind, that the latest arrivals are, on the contrary, the oldest and most mature, because they arrive endowed with the experience and heredity of a longer past of human civilization."

"In sum," the poor Terran concluded, "I find myself as out of place here as the patriarch Enoch would be if he returned to Earth after having left it in very nearly the same fashion as your humble servant, who will surely not understand anything in your world of Cybele."

"You already have firm friends here, my dear Marius, who will take responsibility for acclimating you to your new homeland," Namo replied, as the three men got up from the table and went back to the poop deck, where they could take in a refreshing gentle breeze. Night had fallen, allowing the sight of a sky scintillating with stars.

"Look up there," said Alcor. "Do you recognize anything?"

Marius obeyed and scanned the sky—which was entirely new to him—with his gaze for a few moments. At first, no formations reminded him of the constellations with which he was familiar. Here, Alcor's theory fell down, since the sky was not Earth's sky, and constituted a striking dissimilarity. But was it not admissible, that at such sidereal distances, the cosmic environment of this second Earth might not have any influential difference? At any rate, if Marius had retained the slightest doubt as to the terrible verity, he had an irrefutable proof before his eyes of his exile on a world other than his own.

Suddenly, he extended his arm and said, in a weak voice: "There! There! Gemma! Gemma!"

"Indeed, that is, in fact, Gemma," Alcor replied, initially somewhat surprised. "The Alpha of the beautiful constellation of the Diadem. That's a further item of evidence, which seems to extend to an entire stellar group the similarity that we've already recognized between our respective worlds. So, my poor friend, there's no doubt that our Gemma, which you've just recognized so clearly, is your own sun, while the Gemma you saw from Earth is the sun that will rise tomorrow for us. Now, it's even more evident that our two solar families ought to be perfect replicas of one another. Look at the beautiful red light of the heavenly body rising in the sky over there."

"That's the planet Mars," said Marius, without hesitation, "and that's presumably Venus, which I recognize by its white gleam, and which is doubtless the shepherd's star for you too."

"That's correct."

And Marius, his satisfaction mingled with bitterness, examined those sister worlds with an excellent marine telescope that Namo had just handed to him.

"And there, at my fingertip," said the latter, "is that another one of your acquaintances?"

"Certainly, and I know it even better than our own Saturn," the Terran replied, remembering his mighty leap through the ring. Then, drawing himself up to his full height, he continued: "You know, my friends, to have come from there to here in a matter of days, I must have traveled very rapidly!"

"Damn! It was indeed rapid! When one thinks that the distance separating our two Gemmas is such that it does not even provide observation with a visual parallax susceptible to measurement!"

The time had come to take a well-earned rest, but before separating from their guest, Alcor and Namo told him that the ship would be putting into port, and that the port in question, of which they were citizens, was the great and superb Algiers, which had been the capital of New France for some time, and had few rivals as the world's greatest metropolis.

During that conversation, our friend's attention had not lacked distraction, sometimes caused by the proximity of other vessels that were bright with dazzling light, each illuminating its own course for a considerable distance, and sometimes by the sight of prodigious lighthouses that served as periodic reference points in the open sea, the fires of which radiated like little suns, performing the same function at sea as gaslights do in our squares and boulevards.

Finally, more ample explanations were postponed until the following day, and they arrived at the door of the comfortable cabin that had been made up for the newcomer, and they wished one another good night,

The next day, when Marius found himself on the deck of the ship on which he had found such generous hospitality, quite early and with his mind well rested, he was able to observe at his leisure that in its capacity as a pleasure-cruiser the vessel combined the finest conditions of elegance and interior design.

Other signs of the changed times were recognizable in the general disposition, which overturned the new passenger's nautical ideas completely. There were no masts, such things having become superfluous a long time ago, the wind no longer being anything but a negligible factor in navigation, save for a observation post that was raised up to a fairly considerable height. On the other hand, one was not inconvenienced there by the fumes of coal, which was equally unnecessary, electricity being sufficient for all deployments of force, not by rolling, in spite of the fact that the sea was rather choppy. The latter result was obtained by courtesy of an ingenious system of two inner hulls, one contained within the other, suspended by their extremities along different axes within the outer hull, which maintained a sufficiently horizontal position.

The African coast was silhouetted on the horizon in harmonious lines, and as they came closer, it was possible to see, more distinctly than in Marius' day, the white triangle forming the great city: a triangle whose sides had, of course, grown considerably, especially at the base, by comparison with the relatively small space that the ancient El Djazair of the Arabs has once occupied.

Our friend had visited Algiers once, in company with Numa, during their tour of the Mediterranean. In the presence of the coast, where Cape Mitofou and Pescade Point stood out very clearly, Marius felt less out of place. Something known, something French, was before him, and stirred his heart. It was, therefore, with an almost serene expression that he replied to the cordial greetings of Alcor and Namo, who had just appeared on deck in their turn.

"We're nearing land now," said the Professor. "We'll reach it in less than an hour. Did you know the Algiers of old, my dear Marius?"

"I spent a few pleasant days there in 1884, and I shall take pleasure in seeing the magnificent Boulevard de la République again, the government square and the picturesque Arab quarters. But I'm already forgetting that all of that must have changed a great deal on Cybele."

"You can expect that. From a distance, a certain amount of illusion is possible, but when we've arrived, you won't recognize anything any longer, unless you rummage through the drawers in our museums in which the plans are kept of all the phases that the great capital has passed through since its humble origins. In the time corresponding to yours, the Austral Era had hardly begun, and the sea was still close to its lowest level on this side of the globe, but many centuries have already passed since the ocean began its invasion, reclaiming possession of its ancient bed and gradually recovering the old coastlines of which you might have seen visible traces in those curious marine grottoes that must overlook the Algerian coast from a considerable height on your world. Now, it's at the very place from which your Boulevard de la République used to overlook the old port that we'll be coming into dock."

"Oh yes, I remember. It's doubtless the displacement of the center of gravity of the oceans that has brought about the changes in the epoch that you've reached. And the temperature of the regions must be sensibly lower than it was in my day."

"What! You already knew that?" In a slightly pained voice, Alcor went on: "Then you're not unaware, either, of the frightful threat that hangs over this world, which is approaching the terrible moment..."

Alcor did not continue, and the interlocutors exchanged silent gazes.

"And when is it anticipated?" Marius asked, after a long pause.

"Calculating the precise moment is difficult, especially when we lack precise dates regarding anterior diluvian catastrophes. It's probable, too, that various causes, either related to the globe itself or to the cosmic environment through which it is incessantly moving, might hasten or delay the critical moment. Already, however, it's no longer in centuries that we count the time that separates us from the frightful collapse. Who can tell whether might not soon be eye-witnesses and victims of the terrible cataclysm ourselves?"

The last turn taken by the conversation cast a chill that Marius tried to shake off by questioning his new friends about the transformation and history of the Algeria in which so much was said to have changed.

"The Algiers you're about to see, my dear Marius, is no longer the still-barbaric town that you knew. Today, it's one of the principal centers of global activity. That's partly due to the climate, which is now, as you recalled a few moments ago, significantly less hot than it used to be—which is to say, les enervating and more amenable to activity.

"There is, in fact, a certain thermal zone that is better suited than any other to the collective development of the human faculties, and gives them a boost. That is why, toward the end of the last Boreal Era, after the diluvian cataclysm more than ten thousand years ago, nuclei of civilization began to appear in India and Egypt, where the then-moderate climate activated the surge of their peoples. Then, as the relative warming of the northern hemisphere became more pronounced, those principal nuclei were displaced, successively reaching Asia Minor and Persia, Greece, Rome and then, finally, central and northern Europe.

"You have left your planet, my friend, at the moment when the first symptoms of displacement in the opposite direction were about to be manifest on land. Oh, the displacement is gradual—so slow that many centuries will go by before your Paris, or even St. Petersburg, begins to collapse, but the return of sovereign vitality to the peoples occupying the southernmost regions is no less certain for that. That's what has happened on Cybele. You'll learn in our historical records that from the thirty-fifth century of our Austral Era onwards, the whole of northern Europe was beginning to be nothing but another Siberia, less and less habitable, and that our dear France only preserved its supremacy by moving its capital and centers of action all the way to the shores of the Mediterranean.

"I've always suspected," the Provençal put in, unexcitedly, "that Marseilles would get there someday."

"It was indeed Marseilles that replaced Paris," Alcor continued. "The reign of the new capital of France was grandiose. Her favored situation on the inland sea became the crossroads of the foremost peoples of the world; her unequaled fleets radiated throughout the entire world. The preponderant role that devolved to the French people, which was shared almost equally between the two Mediterranean shores, made the incomparable Marseilles, with her four million inhabitants, the most admired metropolis in the world for nearly two thousand years. It was within her walls that the great Federal Congress met, which had already made the ancient divided Europe into one great country, politically and indissolubly united under the respected title of the European Confederation, several hundred years before.

"And since it's a citizen of Martigues who is listening to me at this moment, I'm sure that it will be agreeable to you to learn that the pretty little town bathed by the waves of the little bosphorus that connects the immense Étang de Berre to the sea—which was already showing its ambition, if history is accurate, by adopting the title of Little Venice—your birthplace, my dear Marius, would have nothing to envy in the future destiny of proud Marseilles. The key to an incomparable maritime basin, from an epoch in the near future of your contemporaries, Martigues had the honor of becoming the principal sentinel of French power for a long time. It would soon be the formidable guardian of the most invulnerable military port there ever was, able to send forth its fleets as easily into the Ocean, by way of the great sea canal, as into the Mediterranean via its natural bosphorus.

"But let's not stray too far from the question you asked me. You must be eager to learn the principal features of the history of the Algiers that is before us now, and which will welcome us in a short while.

"You have been the witness to the beginnings of prosperity for the most beautiful of the conquests made by French arms. Algiers already promised much in your time, and it has kept its promise, as you can see, abundantly. It was not the case, however, that its early days were free of difficulties, and that the prosperity that had made such a good beginning was not compromised by unforeseen developments.

"The France of '89 had set out to change the eternal destiny of Ahasuerus, in return for which it was not Ahasuerus' fault if he did not succeed in putting France entire in his pocket. In the same way, it transpired that when a moment of national disaster came, it was given to a worthy son of Israel and Themis to introduce into the French family with a stroke of the pen all his cousins in Algeria, solely to gratify scribblers of legal documents.[14] So nothing was any longer seen anywhere but Jews caviling and black men quibbling. No infant was every such a simultaneous joy to his mother and father.

"Oh, but that did not last long. For whom had France fought and shed blood on that African soil for an entire half-century? For Judah. For whom had the colonist sweated and nearly died? For Judah. For whom had architects and masons built so many beautiful buildings? For Judah. The second half-century had not gone by when all of Algeria was Judah's. Fortunately, a few just laws and a little firmness soon reckoned with the eternal parasitic race that had always and everywhere obliged peoples to take exceptional measures.

---

[14] In the 1830s, when the French colonized Algeria, the Jews who made up about 20% of the population mostly supported the conquest, which they regarded as a liberation from their former Muslim masters. Initially, they retained a measure of independence, but the French began to reorganize their communities and legal system in the 1840s, when French Jews set out to "civilize" the Algerian Jews, resulting in a long period of complex three-way conflict, which did not end in 1870 when the Algerian Jews were granted French citizenship as a result of a decree issued by Adolphe Crémieux (born Isaac Moïse). These circumstances might help to explain the somewhat resentful animosity that an Arab-descended Frenchman was able to feel toward Jews in general.

"From then on, Algeria resumed the glorious course of its destiny and never ceased to increase in strength and wealth. From century to century, the great African city increased its importance, to the point at which, having become the second capital of the double France with two shores, a time eventually came when, for the same reason that Marseilles had been favored to the detriment of Paris, the capital of the nation, which could only maintain its rank by an incessant southward movement, moved to the Algerian shore.

"That came about necessarily when not only the rigor of the temperature but also the gradual invasion by the sea of all the continental plains brought ruination to so many rich countries. Proud Marseilles herself ended up being attained. With each passing century it was necessary to build higher, and always to increase the height of the walls that defended her against the ever-more invasive waves. A day came when her dykes could no longer save her. A sudden irruption covered the most beautiful quarters of the marvelous capital. The sea took them, and kept them."

"But what you're telling me is frightful! A Marseilles without the Canebière!"

"From the time of that catastrophe, which occurred less than four centuries ago, the first rank reverted naturally to Algiers. In any case, the new France had long surpassed the old France, devastated and vanquished by the elements, in importance and population. Such is the situation occupied today by the great city that we can already glimpse."

"So that it's now the turn of the old France to be the colony?"

"No, she is still the beloved mother who has numerous children in the five continents of the world, and is still cherished and revered by all of them. As for our new capital, you're about to judge whether she is unworthy of the motherland that gave her birth."

The great city now appeared increasingly distinctly, and as soon as the range was short enough, a prodigious mass of houses, palaces and grandiose monuments struck the eye, impotent to find its bearing in such a profusion of domes, towers, steeples. The immense perimeter of the bay was entirely covered by buildings. The principal focal point was, however, still the site of the ancient city, where the same amphitheater, much more extensive, displayed a host of tall monuments amid innumerable terraces, splendid monuments scaling the mountain, while their cliffs sparkled in the sunlight, varying the gleam of metallic reflections with diverse nuances, very harmonious in their effect.

Among all the edifices of the capital, however, dominating them all from the immense platform that occupied the flattened summits of the ultimate heights, an unexpected monument rose up, majestic and titanic. Imagine a Parthenon multiplied tenfold in its dimensions, serving as the pedestal for a Panthéon of corresponding proportions, surmounted by a prodigious golden cupola surrounded by twenty-four colossal figures with the profile of sphinxes, the enormity of which, at such an altitude, was frightful. Marius learned that it was the Great Temple, the architectural marvel of the epoch, and, so to speak, the palladium of the new French.

They were passing the first jetties protecting the harbor when a scruple occurred to Marius.

"I thank you, my dear Namo and Alcor, for all that you've done for me, but allow me to ask you for one last favor, which is to inform me as to the local customs regarding foreigners, so that when we go our separate ways..."

"Go our separate ways!" exclaimed Namo. "Do you think so, my friend? No, no, I forbid it. I will not let you expose yourself to the misadventures and difficulties of the novitiate that awaits you."

"But I don't want to be a burden to anyone," Marius persisted, "And I hope to find work as a clerk in the Algerian notariat."

"Free yourself of any anxiety and scruple on that delicate subject. There will be better things for you to do in Algiers than some banal employment. Do you not understand the inestimable value that you will have in a scholarly city like ours, in your capacity as a messenger from a younger sister of Cybele—or, which amounts to the same thing, a revenant from the past times of our original homeland and our ancient race? You'll be a professor of history and ancient languages, and your lessons will be much in demand, I expect. So I beg you now to give me the pleasure of being your first pupil—and believe me, it's me who will remain obliged to you. Then, as a friend, I intend to keep you under my own roof, where you will be completely at home, as my dear Alcor already is. My mother, who, with my younger sister, constitutes my whole family, will welcome her son's friend joyfully."

"You certainly have the most serious rights to the professoriat," said Alcor, supportively. "Even the masters will come to check their knowledge against the testimony of your living memory. You can settle many obscure and controversial questions relating to your times. You'll be an irrefutable model of correctness in your language and of good pronunciation for the reading of our classics. I shall be the first to have recourse to you, more than once, my dear colleague."

There was no time to reply. At that moment the ship docked and they prepared to disembark.

IV

If the city that Marius had known had undergone an astonishing transfiguration, the same was true of the port, with its numerous basins, its communication channels and its quays, which occupied a very considerable extent—corresponding, of course, with the importance of the capital and its immense maritime commerce. Marius had underestimated rather than overestimated the reality in estimating that it surpassed the proportions of the ancient port by as much as the latter had surpassed the little pirate cove of the days before the conquest.

After a very short lapse of time they were on the quay, and the three friends were then carried away by an elegant carriage devoid of capricious horses or importunate steam, in the direction of what had once been the Place du Gouvernement, and which was now the Place de la Concorde of the new nation: a monumental square, with its palaces of national representation and various public administrations, which occupied three sides of the vast quadrilateral, leaving the fourth entirely uncovered, where tall rostral columns faced the sea. In the middle of the opposite face was a prodigious triumphal arch, at the enormous base of which a broad and magnificent ramp began, which rose straight to the summit of the city, overlooked, in the background, by the immense golden dome of the Great Temple.

From the middle of the square, the view was magical, and one thing that added considerably to the astonishment of the newly disembarked man was seeing that the ramp linking the top and bottom on the mountain was moving. Technology had made progress, and now roads could be seen to move of their own accord, or at least, in the case offered to Marius' eyes, there was a broad strip of the immense inclined plane that descended incessantly, while another similar strip always rose up, in a movement punctuated by occasional pauses.

Those moving causeways were full of people who were traveling comfortably toward the high city, or pouring forth therefrom in waves to the level of the broad arteries that led from either side of the large square to the extremities of Algiers. The principal highways and a few major streets were provided with moving paths of the same kind, with stations at intervals and subsidiary gangways. Marius, already prepared for anything, told himself that, in sum, the new things he found were in the natural order, like those that would have astonished a Phocean of old suddenly transported to the Marseilles of the century of railways and steamships.

Progress and social advancement developed over the centuries had made this New France a land of superior civilization, in which a man of Marius' era was bound to feel an impression of diminution, akin to the weakness of a child. At first sight, everything conveyed an impression of the nobility of the people in question: the richness and elegance of the buildings, the dignified and confident facial expressions, the ample and beautiful forms of costume as well as the orderly appearance and extreme cleanliness of the streets, equipped everywhere with high lateral arcades, where countless mechanical vehicles of every sort were circulating, gliding over the ground without jolts and almost soundlessly. The only horses to be seen were a few being ridden entirely for pleasure.

The dominant style of the monuments, and even the simple houses, was visibly related to the light, graceful and ideal forms characteristic of Arab art. In all directions there were colonnades of an admirable linear purity and external ornamentation of the most picturesque effect. Everywhere there was a bright harmony of colors and sculptures that never went so far as to weary the gaze. There again, the employment seemed to be dominant of the metals that Marius had already noticed, the consistency of which was admirably suited to the airy style that was admirable at first glance.

Some of the buildings seemed to be so delicate in their detail that one might have thought them entirely appropriate to serve as elegant aviaries of rare birds. That comparison only sprung to our friend's mind, however, because two winged forms, too large to belong to birds, alighted on a large balcony, folded their wings as one might close an immense fan, and then revealed a human couple returning from an aerial excursion. The young man opened a glazed door for his companion, which closed on them both—and that was all.

"What's that?" Marius asked.

"It's nothing," Namo replied. "Doubtless a couple of lovers coming home after frolicking and conversing in the open air on this lovely morning. You don't have flying equipment where you come from, then?"

"We only have the bicycle as yet."

"I have such apparatus at your disposal, my friend. The mechanism is very simple. I'll explain it to you."

"I'd like nothing better. I don't know how it happened, but, since my arrival on your planet, I've entirely lost the superb impetus, the unparalleled force that launched me through space without the need for a mechanism of any sort. By the way, my dear Namo, can you tell me why I see nothing but bronze, platinum, silver and so on everywhere? Metallurgy must have made great progress."

"Someday, my friend, we'll visit our national foundries together. You'll see there how we extract molten metal from its very source. Instead of giving ourselves infinite difficulties, as of old, in decomposing rebellious minerals, we simply draw from the interior of the globe the natural cast iron that constitutes its incandescent subterranean mass, as the specific weight of the planet clearly indicates—a mass whose total is far superior to that of the superficial crust, which shows that the heavy metals are in the depths, at distances from the surface that vary according to their nature, only requiring to be pumped.

"Why did it take us so long to draw upon the great subterranean cauldron that is only separated from us by fifty kilometers of the terrestrial crust? It's always the simplest things that one thinks of last. Anyway, now that inexhaustible supply of molten metals flows at our discretion into the molds of our various industries, they serve for all purposes, the most base as well as the most noble. Naturally, their ancient commercial value has been entirely depreciated, to the point that their monetary usage is only preserved for small change, which is made of gold, and fiduciary bonds remain the sole representative elements of all transactions of any importance."

"As serious progress goes, that's serious progress, and my century, already so proud of its discoveries and its industry, is not yet there. Aerostats and railways must also have been improved, of course?"

"Railways? Great gods, what are you talking about? Nowadays, one only sees pneumatic tubes linking all the points of the globe. Tubular carriages crammed with passengers, a detonator, a thrust of the piston, and it's done. The travelers are delivered to their destination, and a single individual could, in fact, show himself at the most extreme points of a continent on the same day. It's that rapidity which has conserved the existence of our ancient communication tubes, which would otherwise have been compromised by aerial transport—for the aerostats you mentioned just now have acquired all the practicality and manageability that they lacked at their outset. Look, there's a public airship passing overhead. You can see how easily it alights at its station to set down passengers and take others aboard."

"And to think that among us, the direction of balloons is regarded by the most level-headed people as a utopian dream. I'm eager to know how the problem was resolved."

"If we weren't so close to home I'd satisfy your legitimate curiosity, but we'll have to postpone to another conversation an explanation that, although not very complicated, still requires a certain elaboration."

The carriage was, in fact, slowing down as it approached a beautiful entrance, though which an ornate courtyard could be seen, with an elegant fountain at its center and aquatic plants, reminiscent of the most beautiful patios of Andalusia.

Namo was the first to jump down briskly from the vehicle, and was received in the arms of his mother, who was waiting, having been forewarned, and advanced to meet him. After the first moments of effusion, he introduced his new friend, who was immediately welcomed very graciously, without his strange appearance and costume appearing to attract overmuch attention.

In the same way that Marius had been struck at first sight by the singular resemblance between Namo and the friend he had left behind on Earth, it was now the mother's features that reminded him astonishingly of the excellent Madame Honorat, who would also have a small part to play in the regret of his exile. A strange sequence of hazards and coincidences, as inexplicable as everything else in Marius' new existence! It was the same face, but with a slightly different expression, as if heightened by a natural nobility, a dignity of attitude that the Terran was not accustomed to encounter in the fair sex, which inspired for the woman in question, who was still beautiful, a profound respect and a keen sympathy.

For his part, the professor had his fair share of the affectionate felicitations, and immediately took charge of installing the new guest in an apartment adjacent to the one he occupied himself, and which proved be entirely ready, in a house that always offered the broadest hospitality to the family's friends and visitors.

While the two of them were going up the stairs that led to their floor, Namo received another woman in his arms who ran to meet him, happily and hastily. It was his younger sister Junie, who Marius could not see but who uttered an audible cry of joy that had the strange, incomprehensible and insensate power to stir the most intimate fibers of his heart.

"Here you are, at home, my friend," said Alcor, introducing the young man to lodgings that were very well-furnished and provided with everything that could satisfy the habits of an ultra-civilized wellbeing. "All that remains is to substitute for the effects and minor items that your luggage would have contained had you not undertaken this great voyage so precipitately. I'll take care of those little details, and in the meantime, Namo's wardrobe will met your most urgent needs. I can hear Mirta our excellent housekeeper, coming now, having been sent to us. She is the providence that watches over everyone in the house, and she will give you her most devoted care."

The professor stepped out of the apartment to intercept the person who was about to enter. "My dear Mirta! Before anything else, I'll ask you to fetch one of my pupil's suits, which will fit his friend of similar stature very well."

While the housekeeper retraced her steps, he continued: "You wouldn't be able to keep your present costume, my friend, without being the object of continual indiscreet curiosity. Dress like us, therefore, when you've washed yourself— you might as well do it now as later. And with that, I'll leave you for a few minutes, for I have to tidy myself up as well."

Shortly afterwards, there was a knock on the door, and Marius went to open it.

"Heavens!" he said "Martine, is that really you? Come here so I can embrace you—but what am I doing? I'm mistaken again."

The young man stopped dead in the midst of his effusion, before the astonishment of the worthy woman, who, not understanding such a warm welcome at all, doubtless told herself that it was the custom in the foreigner's homeland to embrace people like that. It was a fashion that had its merits, after all, and which was inoffensive to her, as a woman capable of understanding the universal language of sentiment, and who immediately felt touched, returning sympathy for sympathy. As for explanations they were cut short, by reason of the impossibility of exchanging the slightest conversation other than in sign-language.

What a strange young man, all the same! the housekeeper said to herself, when she left the new house-guest alone.

It was not without a certain voluptuousness that Marius extended his weary limbs in a warm and reparative bath—after which he put on, not without a certain amount of preparatory fumbling, the ample and majestic garments of the inhabitants of his new homeland.

The ensemble was somewhat reminiscent of Oriental fashions. If the robe was Persian, the headgear was quite similar to the large disk that protects and graciously ornaments the heads of Indians.

When he saw his entire person thus changed, the mirror reflecting an image that seemed quite different from his own, he could not help smiling. *I'd never dare to show myself on the Canebière like this*, he thought.

On that note, Alcor came back in and sat down on a divan, showing a visible satisfaction with the outfit and deportment presented by the Terran transformed into a Cybelean.

"For today, my dear Marius, I think we would do well to leave our friend Namo in the intimacy of his family. Since you're ready, we can go out, if you wish, to dine in the city, and we'll easily find employment for the rest of the day."

They went out, and after walking for a while through the streets, so animated and luxurious, in the midst of people of commanding presence who could all have been taken for happy and fortunate individuals, they sat down in a public restaurant of engaging appearance, where the dishes were all the better for being seasoned by an excellent appetite.

The names of the dishes were not the same as of old, but the cuisine had not varied all that much. The progress realized by the old French cuisine was one of those that can only collapse and go backwards when one attempts to improve it further.

"Could one ever believe," Marius said, "on seeing us sitting together like this, so similar to everyone else, that such an enormous interval of time separates our respective generations? Certainly, although freshly disembarked, I've already been able to observe many changes, to admire astonishing progress and to observe customs unknown in my homeland— or, rather, my own time, my own epoch, for I'm getting increasingly accustomed to consider myself as a revenant from the past—but all in all, the difference isn't as enormous as one might have imagined. You work, you build, you trade—in sum, you love—in much the same way as us."

"Well, do you think that the inhabitants of Memphis and Babylon differed much more from the people of your time? The same needs, the same motives and the same fatalities of nature give individual life a cycle that is renewed indefinitely. It's true that inventions, discoveries and intellectual progress continually augment the mental and material capital of society, in which existence becomes progressively easier and mores less and less barbaric, but fundamental human nature doesn't change as rapidly. The mind and the heart are almost identical in all the epochs of history. Old Homer is as true today as he was in his own time and yours. Virgil, Lamartine and Hugo are still our poets, because they have struck the profound and true chord, the natural expression of the human soul at all times. Along with the scientific and material progress, it's still the same humanity that continues through the centuries."

"There's also a purely moral progress that epochs make, such as the abolition of slavery, the proclamation of human rights," said Marius. "There's a genuine advancement of civilization, of social organization."

"Far be it from me to deny the moral and civilizing progress of peoples," Alcor went on. "I'm only envisaging here the generalities of human life to which you referred a little while ago. You'll also observe that the world hasn't remained stationary from the viewpoint of ideas and mores. Civilization has continued to progress. You'd search Cybele in vain today for the barbaric countries and savage lands that once occupied such a large part of the globe. We've also made progress in the matter of social and political relations, as you'll be able to judge in due course."

"In the meantime, the most urgent thing for me, I think, is to go back to school and, before anything else, learn the language of this new France, in which I've arrived as ignorant as a small child."

"We'll take care of that," Alcor replied, rising to his feet.

The rest of the day was employed in rapidly visiting the finest quarters of the city, using, by turns, the mechanical vehicles, omnibus-airships, moving roadways and so on that Marius had already glimpsed, and which easily met all the populous city's needs for locomotion, without the public ever becoming annoyed by overcrowded stations and vehicles that were always full.

Our tourists then saw a number of superb edifices: temples, museums, schools and theaters, which, albeit to a superior degree, nevertheless continued to respond to the same needs of worship, science, work and entertainment as before—things that are as ancient as society itself.

As a wise cicerone, Alcor had reserved the best for last; at dusk, without his young friend expecting it, Marius suddenly found himself confronted by the immense upper square, the leveling and extension of which were themselves the result of genuinely cyclopean labor. Facing him, in all its superhuman majesty, was the Great Temple, which, in the middle of that vast open space, loomed up into the sky, while the gold of the incomparable dome that formed its prodigious summit was sparkling at that moment with the red gleams that the sun, already descended beneath the horizon, was still sending forth.

The marvel of Ephesus or the temple of Olympian Jupiter in Athens could not have approached the unparalleled work of art that was thus revealed in its totality. In the presence of that immense quadrilateral of innumerable columns more than a hundred meters high; before the crushing mass of its frontons and vaults, supporting another upper edifice whose giant arcades and enormous pillars the eye could not count; at the sight of the colossal bronze figures in the form of winged sphinxes that sat upon the final entablements, still enormous in spite of the frightful height and surrounding the base of the prodigious cupola, the mind was numbed and reason tottered.

So far as Marius was concerned, it defied all comparison, surpassing any acquired notion, any possible conception of style and proportion. It was nothing but a sublime and ultimate synthesis of all the passed creations of human genius, over-loading the thought of a brain sixty centuries behind the times.

Alcor, who understood that, remained silent beside his companion, who seemed to have been struck by an invincible intimidation before a spectacle that was grandiose to the point of terror.

That first, overwhelming impression, however, soon gave way to another, just as profound but doubtless more comprehensible to the young man, whose eyes had just lit up with a glimmer of ecstasy: from the troubling heights of the severe edifice, his gaze had finally descended to the base, to the section where the giant doorway seemed to be pouring out an avalanche of marmoreal whiteness, formed by masterpieces of statuary, arranged on a long succession of stairs and plat-forms that gave access to the Great Temple, glorious propylaea worthy of the sublime monument.

The capital of a people that had become profoundly reli-gious again required a sacred place capable of bringing to-gether the innumerable hosts that assembled on the religion's major feast-days, and the Great Temple had been born of that noble need, with all the accompaniment of splendor to which religious art has give birth in every epoch, the measure of the height of the ideal and sentiment that different people are able to attain. In the presence of that superhuman work of art, it was possible to sense the power of the religious ideal that reigned over New France.

"On certain days," Alcor said, "not only the temple and its interminable upper galleries, but also the parvis and the entirety of the vast space that you can see, are insufficient to contain the people who want, at such moments, to constitute a single body and soul."

Alcor then told his companion that the ancient usage of bells had given way in the Great Temple to something resem-bling colossal harps with giant strings of fine metal—harps whose melodious appeals could be heard several leagues away, producing the most harmonious chords. In addition to that celestial music, the monstrous sphinxes that were visible

79

near the summit of the edifice had the gift of speech, of pronouncing words articulated with extraordinary distinction, and capable of throwing their thunderous voices to the utmost extremities of the city—but it was only on rare occasions that the marvelous mechanism was brought into play. Only the four great festivals of the year, corresponding to the seasons, and the occasional exceptional announcement of some great event, had the privilege of triggering and unleashing the tempestuous breath that carried the growl of those formidable voices into the distance.

"All this shows me, my dear Alcor, that religion has not ceased to be honored by humans, and that it has not been killed by the materialist philosophies that put it on trial in my time and pronounced its final condemnation."

"Your epoch did, indeed, correspond to one of those phases of the transformation of the religious sentiment that see the decrepit forms of worship collapse, without which the new form cannot be born, to take up the ineradicable sentiment once again—for everything dies and is reborn in human evolution, including religions. Notice that I say *religions*, which are only a kind of vestment, and not *religion*, which is the sentiment itself, in its purity.

"Christianity was not the first religion to appear on the Earth, and it would not be the last. Without mentioning the Masonic institution that, appeared in its final phase, to want to take over a place left vacant, with its vain simulacra and its baubles,[15] or a serious Buddhist movement that took brief possession in Western Europe of a spiritual elite seduced by the noble morality of the Buddha, and raised temples to Brahma even in Paris. Other, more elevated forms of worshiping the divinity were yet to succeed one another before the superior conception that has constituted our religious ideal for many centuries could take shape. But you need have no doubt that it

---

[15] The Freemasons were another of Alhaiza's pet hatreds, against which he railed in the pages of *La Rénovation*.

is the same universal God of all times that we still revere in this temple."

"Oh, my dear Alcor, how glad I am to hear you express thus what I seemed to feel myself, without being able to explain it clearly. In fact, it is only that promise of an imminent renovation than could bring hope and light into the confusion of ideas and sentiment of the people of my era. So many scientific errors are mingled with so many moral truths, and so much weakness is displayed beside so much grandeur in the Christianity that drove some to despair and others to revolt, that doubt, incredulity and irreligion are gaining ground increasingly in my France and Europe, everywhere provoking abasement of character and the violence of material appetites. When shall we finally see the elevation of souls reborn, along with religious peace? Hasten, then, my dear master to tell me what this religion is that the generations of a time as advanced as yours have in common?"

"I cannot summarize an entire doctrine in a few words, my friend. I shall simply tell you that the divinity which, through the religious and philosophical systems of an ever-progressing humanity, was already becoming more and more detached from a narrow anthropomorphism in your day, has risen with time to the pure abstraction of a principle—or, rather, an immaterial being—endowed with supreme intelligence, will and power, existing eternally beyond and above a material principle, similarly eternal, the energy of which reacts within certain precise limits while submitting passively to the action of the first, in the eternal dualism of spirit and matter.

"In that, I am not telling you anything new, except that the ineluctable truth barely glimpsed at the beginning of human thought shines today with a pure gleam, and has rejected the heavy alloy of gross superstitions and overly complicated symbols, to take on an allegorical transparency that charms the mind without leading it astray, and elevates souls toward duty and virtue without frightening them with chimerical threats.

"The indissoluble unity of the principle of life that extends from a blade of grass to a human being, and which, being nothing but an emanation of immaterial being, thus being part of that being, is for us a fundamental dogma, coming immediately after that of the very existence of the supreme principle. From that stems a form of worship that is merely a sequence of aspirations and actions of grace, rising toward the Being of beings, the ultimate term in the vital hierarchy, the ultimate goal of increasingly perfect manifestations assumed by the life that worlds produce, and which climbs everywhere toward its pure immaterial source.

"That gives rise in its turn to the respect and love that we have for everything that lives; I might almost say to a kind of Sabaism[16] that enables us to understand the universality of the similarly-living worlds that surround ours, in the homage merited by everything emanating from the Great Being, from the God that is the eternal father of all existence. You shall see in our great religious festivals what role we have been enabled to allocate to all the forms in which the universal ubiquity of the great divine principle is manifest."

"Isn't that pure pantheism on a large scale?"

"Yes and no. Yes, it's pantheism insofar as the universality of a God must embrace all of living nature; no if you mean that the universe itself is God. Our God is outside and above matter, which is not God. He is, if I may employ an insufficient word for want of anything better, a person endowed with will and power. He acts upon the material and universal substance, which he penetrates or from which he withdraws at will. Plato had already referred to him as 'the demiurge operating on the substance that exists independently of the demiurge, and limits that power in its turn.' It is not, as you can see, a pure pantheistic doctrine. We remain true deists, while understanding living nature in the person of God. Our Naturalist religion does not cease to be an absolute monotheism. Of the two eternal principles, the immaterial alone is intelligent,

---

[16] The religion of the Sabians, or Shebans, was thought in Alhaiza's day to constitute a kind of sun-worship or a more general astrolatry.

willful and active; the substantial in merely passive and reactive. Only the former is God."

"Ha! You've just pronounced a word that is creating some noise at present among us—but I suspect that your Naturalism is not the same as that of our Naturalist school."

"I believe, in fact, that I remember something bearing that name in a moment of decadence or reaction against the ancient ideal; the said school made an art of only painting and describing the soiled and ugly aspects of society—a morbid and sterile art of the impotent and misguided, which only seemed to shine briefly because there was an eclipse of true art and ideas. But don't worry, my dear Marius, the word Naturalism, which you have obfuscated, will soon resume among your contemporaries its nobler meaning of the worship of nature as a whole, with all the surges of the ideal that only nature of that kind can inspire."

While the two friends were conversing thus, night had fallen without Marius noticing, so bright was the light spread over the entire city, as if by another celestial star, by the luminous globe that was now resplendent at the tip of the immense spire that rose from the ultimate summit of the Great Temple.

"It's getting late," the professor suddenly remarked, "and it seems to me that we've earned our supper."

The ramp descending to the Place de la Concorde was fast-moving. A few minutes later, Alcor and Marius were back in the lower city.

Facing the sea, elegant establishments offered their attractive tables to the public, bathed by a fresh marine breeze that had succeeded the heat of the day. Several of those tables sheltered beneath arches of verdure, and it was one of those that received our strollers, a trifle weary at the end of a busy day. A light collation was served to them while the conversation resumed, returning to the marvelous Great Temple, by which Marius was still gripped.

"The public festivals must also be marvelous," he said to the professor, "if their deployment and apparatus can crowd such an immensity."

"You'll be able to witness our great festivals," Alcor replied, "and you'll see a spectacle of which your era can have no notion—not that every epoch has not seen great religious pomp and immense crowds assembled, but the notion of vital hierarchies did not exist in the past, or, at least, was barely suspected, while since then, the power of multiplications of a precisely edified and ordered life has been revealed and affirmed.

"You'll understand what I mean better if you recall the various collectivities that all human societies have known, in which an organization dictated solely by natural laws already furnished the image of distinct and personal creations living a life of their own quite distinct from that of the simple individuals comprising them. A collective being—a people, an army, a caste, an institution—does indeed possess, like all living beings, qualities that are, in a sense, specific. It has its causes and necessities of existence; it is born, it feeds, works toward particular goals, engenders, struggles and dies. These collectivities have, in sum, real personalities rising above simple human personality.

"Well, that which was already naturally born of the ascensional forces of social life, a savant art has been able to control and improve. In addition to the permanent collectivities that constitute the vital mechanisms of our national organization, that art, unknown to the past, gives us the ability to create new edifications, temporary but nevertheless alive, which emerge from the laws and perspectives of the superior life, which the contention of an isolated mind cannot perceive unaided.

"You'll understand, therefore, what attractions these festivals have for us, in which everyone has a designated place and role, and from which rapidly emerge thoughts, aspirations and spontaneous impulses toward the great extrahuman unknown, which, from the synthetic being in which an entire people has been dissolved, durable impressions redescend into the soul of each of the participants."

The conversation stopped there. The strange novelty of the religious festivals of Cybele stunned the Terran's mind somewhat, and it was only after a long pause that the two men got to their feet and made their way back to the friend's house that would now become Marius' dwelling in his exile—which, it appeared, was likely to be permanent.

V

The irremediable situation into which an implacable destiny had thrust our friend was not one of those to which it is easy to resign oneself. How could an entire happy past, which promised a no less happy future, be effaced from his mind and his heart, especially at the moment when he had been just about to attain the supreme happiness? In spite of having so many good reasons to reckon himself the unluckiest of men, however, he nevertheless experienced a certain satisfaction in returning to the apartment that had become his, and finally feeling that he was at home, in a tranquil refuge to which he might retire, and steep himself in his memories at will.

One going into it, he noticed, not without gratitude, that people had been preoccupied with his wellbeing, and that during his absence a friendly hand had added several new items to the furniture that the comfortable abode already possessed, including a small bookcase exclusively stocked with rare and precious examples of old books, or new editions of selected classic works going all the way back to the Cybelean antiquity of which Marius was a terrestrial contemporary, and whose languages he spoke.

It was evident that Namo had passed that way, and taken a considerable part in the careful installation of his friend, while the worthy Mirta had taken care of all the petty details of a bachelor household. An excellent bed, ready made up, awaited him—but not for long.

Marius abandoned himself without further delay to a complete and perfect rest, such as he had not enjoyed since the fatal night that had cut his existence into two such dissimilar and irrevocably disjointed parts.

We do not know whether agreeable dreams came to bring him the solace of some sweet illusion during his slumber, but what we can say is that, in the extraordinarily abnormal situation into which our friend had been delivered, there was now a confusion in his mind between dream and reality. So many unusual adventures, and so many supernatural events succeeding one another in quick succession, were enough to trouble the best equilibrated of minds, and to confound any notion of truth and falsehood, possibility and impossibility.

It must also be said that since the mysterious influence of the star Gemma had acted upon him, a very particular and indefinable state of being had given him a mental disposition such that he could no longer tell whether he was awake or asleep. Either his dreams presented the same clarity of images as the realities of the waking state, or that latter state no longer seemed to him to be anything but a sequence of dreamlike illusions.

Furthermore, he could not avoid the two worlds with which his past and present were associated sometimes becoming confused in his memory, and by the very fact of the phenomenal duality of existence, it happened more than once that he confused the two sets of individuals most closely associated with his personal life, and even identified his old and new friends on Earth and Cybele with one another. The ancient philosophical adage that "life is but a dream" had never been applicable more truthfully than to Marius' new existence.

It was in that state of suspension between illusion and the notion of the reality of things that our friend opened his eyes the following day, while the cheerful light of a sun that was already high above the horizon darted beautiful golden rays between the curtains over the carpet of his room, which invited him to get up—which he did, while retaining the laxity of thought that ordinarily follows great fatigue and long collapses.

As soon as he was dressed, he went to the apartment of his neighbor Alcor—but the professor, having risen much earlier, had gone out some time before. Too new in the house to dare to introduce himself on his own, he remained where he was, leaning on the balustrade of an interior gallery that looked down over the entire habitation.

Beneath him was a rather large courtyard paved in marble and decorated with rare plants surrounding the graciously-ornamented central pool—the cool patio that he had glimpsed on arrival. Three of its sides were occupied by the main building and two wings forming right-angles, and on the side that was not built up there was a superb grille, a masterpiece of artistic wrought iron, in which a door opened giving access to a vast garden, the far side of which was abruptly interrupted by a beautiful row of somber yew-trees; then, further beyond, rose the majestic green foliage of other trees of taller species.

That garden, the enclosure of yews and the larger trees behind, all the way to a strip of blue sea visible in the distance, bore such an astonishing resemblance to the scene that Marius had always had before his eyes in his paternal dwelling, that he could not help being forcefully struck by an instinctive desire to go down into it, which he soon obeyed.

Shortly thereafter he was sitting in the shadow of a clump of plant-trees and sycamores. The place formed a cool and delightful solitude in which one could savor the full value of the warm hours of a summer's day.

Suddenly, a slight rustle of braches caused him to turn his head.

Poor Marius! It was more a case of losing his head entirely!

Slowly advancing from one side, at a pace imprinted with an easy nonchalance, was a ravishing young woman clad in light morning clothes, who, in that mixture of sunlight and shadow, brought him the divine apparition of...my God! Of Jeanne herself, of his adored Jeanne!

It was, as you will have guessed, Namo's own sister, Junie, whom Marius was seeing for the first time.

At the sight of the stranger, the young woman started in surprise; then, timidly and discreetly, she hastened her steps toward the house, leaving the poor young man trembling, and nailed to the spot, understanding his error but with his heart bruised by the shock.

Oh, this time it was more than he could bear. His hands rose to his face and he wept, for a long time.

Some time had passed when a familiar voice was heard. Namo was approaching.

"I've been looking for you, my dear Marius. I'm so completely accustomed to you that I could already sense your absence. And then, you know, my mother and my sister are impatient to make your more ample acquaintance. I've told them about your astonishing adventure, and you're not unaware that heroes—for you are one—always please women. But you seem downcast, my friend. More of those vile black thoughts? I can certainly understand how much reason you have to deplore such a distant exile, but it's necessary to resign yourself to it, damn it! We'll do everything possible to soften that exile for you here. We'll find you distractions, useful occupations, relationships that will connect you and attach you permanently, in accordance with the elevated life that you will lead henceforth. Come on, is that agreed? You're no longer sad? You're smiling? Come along, so I can introduce you to the ladies."

Linking arms with his friend, he drew him away and took him to a small intimate drawing-room, still dominated by the love of flowers and oriental artistry, where the two women were sitting at present: the imposing Nora, who had already greeted him the day before, and her charming daughter Junie. At the sight of him, they got to their feet and took a few steps, in an almost fearful manner, their astonished eyes staring at such an extraordinary guest.

At that moment Marius could see nothing but that second Jeanne, whose gaze burned him and troubled him so profoundly that he could not say a word. Fortunately, the ladies' ignorance of Terran language and the evident impossibility of making himself comprehensible to them, excused him from speaking and saved the situation. Namo divided himself, speaking for everyone, explaining once again to his mother and sister the principal features of his hero's marvelous adventure.

Curiosity, perfectly natural in the presence of that exile from another world, was not the only sentiment that showed in the faces and the mannerisms of the two women; also legible there, in addition, was sympathy, and a real compassion for the mental suffering that a human being suddenly abstracted from his homeland and affections must be experiencing.

In fact, it was evident that the unfortunate fellow was suffering cruelly at that very moment. The desolation painted upon his entire person touched the amiable Junie. With an impulse as spontaneous as it was sincere, she took the young man's hand, and, although her words could not be understood, her large and expressive eyes told him, at least as clearly: "Be brave; we're here to help and console you."

It would not have needed as much to excite the young man madly. He replied to that gaze with another, in which there was such expression that the young woman took a step back, and the impulse of a moment before instantly gave way to a glacial reserve. She immediately became a Jeanne more than indifferent, a proud and reserved Jeanne, the stranger that she really was to him.

How was it that Marius had forgotten himself to the point of confusing, even in the depths of his heart, the image and the reality? How was it that he had of let the unknown young woman see the sentiment that filled him for the woman to whom he had pledged his entire life, the absolute love that one only experiences once and can never be recommenced?

At that moment Alcor came in and created a fortunate diversion. The conversation was prolonged for a few minutes more, during which Marius strove to tear his eyes away from the object causing his disturbance; then the men went out in order to go to the study, where Namo and the professor were accustomed to work together at certain hours of the day.

The presence of their friend did not impede their habitual labor, and they did not even appear to notice somber preoccupation of the poor lover. The latter, moreover, did his best to conceal the emotion that was still agitating him, and appeared to be absorbed in reading an incunabulum that still endured, while the books of his own century only existed in frequently repeated reproductions that had replaced volumes fallen into dust less than a century after being printed.

The voluminous library the filled the room contained veritable treasures of erudition extending over all epochs. But that science, the history of Cybele, so full of interest and so tempting for a latecomer like Marius, would only become accessible to him when he had finally learned the language and script of the present day.

Alcor was already occupied in composing an alphabet comparing the two scripts for the Terran's benefit, with indispensable annotations, as well as an elementary grammar composed inversely to Cybelean scholarly texts, for the exclusive usage of Marius, who was in a unique position analogous to that of a pupil who had to study modern French by means of versions of the ancient and new language.

"You'll see that progress will be rapid, my dear Marius," the professor said to him. "Our writing is as simplified as our language. You'll see that the French that we speak today is the result of a long process of selection from ancient European languages that entered more or less profoundly into the canvas of Old French. We can even begin by observing in your language the penetration of different neighboring idioms whose locutions were imposed upon you, including entire phrases, either by virtue of legitimate necessity or by simple puerile infatuation.

"Time and the increasingly strict logic of ideas subsequently, on the one hand, eliminated all the scoria and superfluities, and on the other hand, reformed the syntax of the language, always favoring brevity and clarity, without any prejudice to the abundance of expressions and all their potential nuances. I'm only speaking about our own language, of course, for our era, advanced as it is over yours, has not yet realized the desire to have one manner of speaking for humanity entire. Language is too much the work of various and changing societies for it not to be continually transformed as they are, remaining the sensible translation of ideas, sentiments and fluctuations of each great human family.

"The European group, once so profoundly divided, had long been subjected to a slow fusion, like the provinces of a single nation, and has now produced a common idiom of which Old French has furnished the base, which is spoken here and in all that now remains of the ancient European Confederation. On the other hand, English and Spanish, after similar transformation, still divide the two Americas; Russian has extended its empire over half of Asia, while Chinese and Hindi share the rest, and German, having disappeared from Europe, was saved by emigration, as you shall see, to the Australian continent, of which it retains a share.

"To get back to the language that interests us most, you have already been able to observe that the same root monosyllables reappear constantly, except that their combinations are always different. The unlimited variety of words by means of the complex transpositions of simple elements is the fundamental mechanism of our language.

"That return to a set of common to Indo-European languages has had one curious result, which is that the mutual convergence has, if not exactly reconstituted Sanskrit, sat least given a meaning intelligible for everyone to all the roots that come from it, to the extent that the Vedas and the Mahabharata have once again become books that all of us can understand without overmuch effort."

"You're frightening me, my dear Alcor. I'll never succeed in making sense of such an amalgam of all the languages of old Europe."

"It will come to you quite naturally, my friend; you'll soon be able speak it with no more difficulty than you put into thought."

"God willing, I'd like nothing better."

The housekeeper came in to say: "Come down; we're waiting for you."

That first family meal put the firmness of our young lover to the proof again, but this time he had the strength to master his emotion, and Junie, for her part, appearing to have forgotten the singular impression that she must have sensed that morning, showed herself to be the gracious and amiable individual that she usually was.

Understandably, Marius continued to be the subject of attentive and curious remarks, and the conversation revolved almost entirely around him, but he did not take part in it, for good reason, also being preoccupied by keeping watch on himself, sticking firmly to the virile resolution he had made no longer to search the depths of his heart for the image of his beloved, and making a complete abstraction, in the presence of Namo's sister, of the features and the voice that were merely a deceptive copy of the real object of his profound love.

He had not reached the end of his ordeals, however. As they got up after dessert, a visitor came in to whom everyone gave a warm welcome, at the sight of whom the young woman could not conceal a slight disturbance, while a more vivid crimson colored her cheeks. This was too much! A sentiment that he had not yet known in earnest, as surely as unjustified as the one that had attracted him to Junie—an atrocious constriction of the heart caused by jealousy—suddenly gripped Marius.

Who was the visitor in question? None other than Monsieur Camoin, his almost-forgotten rival in Martigues, Jeanne's unfortunate suitor—and here, no doubt, Junie's fortunate fiancé. That was immediately obvious.

How, after so many repeated assaults of the same inconceivable fatality, could his courage and reason not totter? Did not the poor lover had reason enough to believe himself the victim of a frightful nightmare? Did reality ever produce such blows? And yet, it was necessary yet again that he yield to the evidence and tell himself that this living proof of his Jeanne's infidelity was not his concern. Even so, was such a spectacle not a torture?

His heart sick, his head reeling, Marius could not stay where he was; he was suffering too much—and he went out as if he were running away, to go and shut himself in his apartment and bury himself there at his leisure in his agonizing regrets and his bleak despair.

When people inquired about him during the day, he begged to be left alone, offering the excuse of a violent headache—a plausible pretext that could serve on Cybele as well as his homeland, and which, in any case, was only half a lie, for it was all too true that the day had been a day of great mental suffering and physical prostration for the poor fellow.

Night finally bought a little calm to his brain by cooling the fever that was agitating it. Marius got a grip on himself, and sensed that it was necessary for him to shake off some of the torpor that still held him motionless in the darkness that had begun to fall without him noticing it.

He went out of his apartment, went to the end of the gallery, and climbed the steps of a staircase he found in front of him. He then found himself on a vast terrace that overlooked a part of the city, and revealed a beautiful extent of sky strewn with stars.

As if moved by a sudden attraction, he looked up, and his gaze was arrested by the soft scintillation of one of them, which he immediately sensed to be, not the fatal Gemma of before, but the other Gemma: the sun of his own homeland, his Jeanne's sun—the sun of his true Jeanne, who loved him there, lost in the distant radiance of a star in the shy that extended at present above his head.

At that thought, an irresistible impulse caused him to raise and extend his arms toward that point lost in the immensity. Deep sighs inflated his breast. Finally, he fell to his knees, his hands still extended toward the star that retained his happiness, his life, his everything, appealing to his Jeanne, insensately, as if she could see or hear him.

That was not sensible, evidently—and yet, was it not something to have before his eyes the very place where the object of his worship lived, and to address to it his most intimate aspirations, however impotent they were?

It was obviously something, since that overflow soothed him, as prayer soothes and restores serenity to the souls of believers.

So, he was often to return thereafter, in moments of depression, to the same place, to wait for the first glimmers of his Gemma, in order to offer his devotions to it like a true pagan. Once or twice, he was surprised in that attitude by the worthy Mirta, who was always here there and everywhere about the house, and who never wearied of repeating to the dear lady of the house: "What a strange young man! What a very strange young man!"

The next day, therefore, a relative calm had returned to him. He was rational again. Since he no longer had any reason to be astonished by the continual strangeness of his new existence, one surprise more or less should not have affected him to such a degree. True, the latest coincidences that had been revealed had awoken his most secret trouble so dolorously that he had been unable to master his emotion, but after all, was it not madness for him to love this Junie as he loved Jeanne herself, and given that, how could he be jealous in regard to a woman other than the one he loved? A vain resemblance could not deceive him, to the extent of deceiving his love!

Has rationality ever been able to reason with the impetuosity of the heart, though? Marius felt that he would not be able to tolerate for long the image of that inversion of his ideal; so deceptive was the image in question that he would always suffer from the spectacle of that derision of his own lost happiness.

Namo came to see him and to enquire about the inconvenient migraine.

"Oh, I can see that it's better. That sudden indisposition was very untimely, precisely because I was about to introduce you to my future brother-in-law, our friend Cam—a very learned and amiable fellow, a young magistrate with a bright future, and who, on the basis of what he has heard about you, is also very eager to make your acquaintance."

It was not without a violent effort of self-control that poor Marius replied that such an intimate friend of the family would also be his.

On Namo's heels, a beautiful spaniel had come in, of which Marius took no notice until it stopped in front of him, contemplating him.

"But that's Houzard that I see! Come here, my good dog, my worthy Houzard!"

"Hou!" replied the animal, with an amicable nod of the head.

That's the full set now, Marius thought, recognizing his dog's twin. *All the way to my poor Houzard! Although it's not really you, I'm glad to see you anyway. Come on, my good Houzard!*

"Hou! Hou!" the animal repeated, continuing to look at Marius in a benevolent and intelligent manner.

"That's our friend Hou," said Namo. "You can hear him telling you his name himself."

"Dogs can talk now?"

"Not entirely, but well enough. They always make themselves understood perfectly, and the cleverest know enough French for nothing essential that we say to escape them. Some of them can even read, or, at least, decipher certain written words. Six thousand years of further progress have had the effect of raising the intellectual level of elite animals."

"Damn! If that's the case, I expect the dogs of Cybele have their own newspapers and engage in politics. We have no lack of intelligent and well-educated beasts at home, though. At this very moment in Madrid, I was recently told by a friend who had returned from Spain, there's a kind of dog named Luna,[17] known throughout the city, which is his own master and has been able to create a position for himself that many a poor man would envy: sociable habits, aristocratic tastes—one encounters him everywhere in high society, pampered by

[17] The reference is to the breed commonly known as Spanish Water Dogs.

women and spoiled by children, with whose games he joins in, always welcome in the big houses of his choice, to which he invites himself without ever lacking in decorum. He's an example of a terrestrial dog, almost a socialite, who can stand comparison, I think, with the animals of Cybele."

"Your Luna does indeed seem to me to be a very interesting animal, but what you cite to me as an exception is an everyday matter here for all animals of the same rank. Apes, dogs, horses, elephants and others have all been improved to the point that they already participate to some degree in Cybelean humanity, while the domesticated animals whose destiny is to serve as food have, on the contrary, seen an idle intelligence devoid of utility atrophy ever more completely.

"Everything thus works out for the best. The quasi-vegetative soul of cattle, sheep and poultry excites less pity for the sad fate of those animals. As for our auxiliaries, however, the companions of our pains and pleasures, they have gradually acquired the right to our regard, and they merit the protection of our laws, which extend to them and punish the murder of those inferior brethren. The mental distance between them and us has diminished, and we owe them more affection as the attachment of those devoted servants has risen to a degree unknown in your time.

"In the effort of those poor brains scarcely emerged from darkness there's already a veritable notion of worship, and it's humans that they revere as gods. Thus, one no longer sees beasts of burden maltreated as they once were; there are, in any case, machines that can replace them advantageously. Intelligent servants and devoted friends until death, that is what our dogs, horses and apes are. You'll encounter the last-named animals in many houses fulfilling all the functions of well-trained valets, for domestics in the sense that the word was once understood no longer exist, and a person who becomes an intimate auxiliary of another, or of a family, becomes, so to speak, a member of the family.

"As for our friend Hou, he's capable of rendering many services. For example, he knows all the quarters and al the curiosities of the capital by name, and he's like nothing better than for you to employ him as a guide. Isn't that right, my worthy Hou?"

"Well, that suits me," said Marius. "You'll be another Houzard for me, my good dog, but with the difference, to your advantage, that back home, Houzard follows me, whereas here, it will be me who follows Houzard."

"Hou! Hou! Hou!"

"Yes, I know—your name is Hou. Understood. And I, my worthy Hou, am named Marius, and you'll see that we'll make a pair of good comrades."

That polite introduction was translated by Namo for the intelligent animal, who then understood completely, and immediately testified to his master's friend how desirous he was of employing his modest talents in his service as soon as possible.

Many a time thereafter, in fact, Marius ventured into the great city without fear of getting lost in the company of such a reliable guide. It was marvelous to see the prudent animal guiding the young man everywhere he had been commissioned to take him, choosing the best routes and making him take his place, if necessary in the vehicles appropriate to the various journeys.

With his master, the dog would certainly have chatted a little on the way—which is to say, exchanged a few simple ideas forming part of the scholarly baggage of any educate dog, but with Marius, Hou could see that he would be wasting his time going into explanations. If he happened to make a few remarks during the journey it was only with some other animal of his acquaintance, no longer with the actions in bad taste and familiarities worse than inappropriate that are still commonplace among terrestrial dogs, but, on the contrary, with decent and polite manners, courteous gestures and slight modulations of the voice that really were an authentic language, with which six thousand years of uninterrupted progress had endowed the canine people.

"Well, I take it that you're not going to stay shut up in your room again today, my dear Marius, when a little fresh air will do you so much good?"

The best relief that the exile could find from obsession with painful regret for the past and the no-less-dolorous ordeals of the present was, indeed, the distraction and interest that the innumerable marvels of Algiers might offer him, the surface of which he had barely brushed in company with the professor. This time, it was Namo who proposed a new excursion to him, agreeable and instructive—which he accepted gladly, for he would not have dared venture out alone so soon into the midst of people and a way of life so new to him, even in the company of the faithful guide to whom he had just been introduced.

"Would you like to make a tour of our national museums?"

"Let's go."

And the two young men set off immediately, accompanied by the faithful Hou, who had politely asked permission from his mater in advance.

In a very short time they reached the Museum Palace, for in the new Algiers no one knew what it was to lose time traveling; there were always twenty ways for someone to reach a destination quickly and comfortably.

After the Great Temple, the Palace was the largest of the capital's monuments. It had been designed not only to permit access to large crowds, but above all to make the endeavor concrete by bringing together as many objects and documents as possible in a single collection, in the most succinct order and the most natural classification, in such a way as to summarize and rapidly present a picture of each branch of the productions of human genius.

To achieve that, the initial procedure was chronological, every century having its special section and its artifacts being distributed in an order that was the same in every case. One could see faithful life-size representations therein of people of every race, with the clothing, weapons, ornaments and tools of their epoch; objects, either authentic or reproduced, of the arts and industries of the time, such as agriculture, construction and navigation; musical instruments; texts of various means of fixing thought in graphic symbols; and finally, figurative scenes of the principal episodes of the century. All of that was completed by numerous paintings, maps, rich albums and innumerable volumes for those who wanted to study an epoch, or a particular moment of past time, in depth.

Such an accumulation of documents and historical riches would have embarrassed the most intrepid researchers, without the admirable classification that rendered knowledge easily accessible to all. It sufficed for simple curiosity seekers to stroll attentively through the palace to pass in review the general history of humankind. As for artists, scholars and amateurs who were particularly interested in architecture, navigation, ceramics or panting, they had only to restrict themselves to the specialized collections that grouped the arts that were the object of their preference together. The chronological order of their distribution, strictly observed everywhere, served to aid the memory and facilitate research.

On this first occasion, the two friends visited a few of the rooms, which were so numerous, vast and well-stocked that it would have required weeks to visit them all, even at a rapid pace. For that day, of course, it was only a matter of obtaining a first glimpse. Later, Marius would return often, to examine at leisure and admire in detail. That succinct visit was nevertheless sufficient for him to make a considerable number of interesting observations.

It did not take him long, for example, to observe one very significant fact, which was that the civilizing evolution of different peoples presented broad features of resemblance in the same periods of development, allowing for time and place. Each cycle saw one civilization end and another commence, which followed a similar path in its turn, especially in remoter epochs when people did not mingle much and evolved in isolation. As they got closer to the present, however, it was evident that societies at every level penetrated one another reciprocally, and the observation lost its value from then on.

What also offered a keen interest was the ability to follow step by step al the developments and the entire progress of an art or a style, in models chosen from among the most characteristic, from its debut to its apogee, and finally in its decadence. A considerable number of the objects were veritable relics conserved from the past, but the majority were only faithful reproductions, thanks to which the series were completed, and which rescued from oblivion a quantity of masterpieces of sculpture and painting, especially, whose originals had been destroyed by time. Thus, one could still admire Raphaels and Michelangelos, more fortunate in that regard than Apelles and Praxiteles, whose statues were among the most precious relics of centuries gone by. Marius even had the pleasure of recognizing the Venus de Milo, now more the eighty centuries old.

At the sight of these collections, it was easier to understand that a style of architecture, for example, is not something arbitrary or capricious, but the spontaneous expression of the artistic sentiment of an entire civilization, and the work of successive generations. That expression sprung forth in its entirety and without admixture before a massive pyramid or an indestructible pylon, which defied the centuries; or a colonnade and fronton with pure and harmonious lines, as Greek genius was; or the Oriental poem of light arcades standing out in the midst of dreams of azure and gold; or before mystical sheaves of slender stone stems reaching toward vertiginous vaults and forming aches there as if regretful of not being able to rise higher into the sky.

In troubled epochs that had only been able to employ, or combine discordantly, elements borrowed from the creations of the past, however, no distinctive expression came to mind to characterize the works with an ideal imprint, and that was precisely the case of the epoch to which Marius belonged. His self-esteem suffered slightly in consequence, but he confessed that truth without hesitation to his companion.

The latter took him rapidly through several halls before pausing again, for it was necessary to skip on ahead to find another full and entire manifestation of a homogenous and veritably creative art. That was the age of pure metals, which developed entirely new edifications in which the consistency of materials and the variety of colors to which they lent themselves so well permitted the realization of the boldest concepts and the most delirious caprices that artistic imagination might dare: walls of magical lacework, aerial dreams of turrets and spires of gold and crystal, iridescent in sunlight, medleys of chimerical flowers and artificial vegetation in which nature was surpassed—all of that revealed a genuinely new ideal, which simultaneously combined power, beauty and an indefinable aspiration toward the extrahuman, which anterior ages had not known.

The two friends had left behind the history of the centuries that were Marius' past and present, and he had paused rather gladly amid the faithfully-costumed figures, objects and souvenirs of every sort of his own epoch. Everything that he saw now represented items of the future of Cybele's younger sister. The monuments, products and works of every kind whose nature and utility he understood immediately were succeeded by things of which he had no notion, and for which he required explanations with which Namo never ceased to furnish him, with unfailing kindness. The instruments and weapons with which he was familiar—primitive locomotives, awkward cannons, etc.—were succeeded by mysterious machines, and by the awesomely destructive and infallible weapons that had rendered warfare impossible.

Science had progressed even further than art. Reserves of new forces were in the service of humankind, permitting the mot gigantic projects. The great magnetic current that runs incessantly from north to south over the entire planet had been utilized by means of veritable barrages that accumulated unlimited supplies of disposable energy. On the other hand, after picrate and dynamite, the increasing force of explosives had not ceased increasing, and the regulation and utilization of all the degrees of expansion had become feasible.

"You have reached panclastite, I believe, my dear Marius. That was far from being the last word in the force that explosive substances can develop instantaneously, Other products, each more energetic than the last, continued the list of those terrible substances, all the way to the memorable nihilite, capable of blowing up the Atlas mountains, or even reducing the entire world to dust. It's thanks to that unlimited force that we were able to piece the terrestrial ball and open the way to the molten metals it contains, which we employ for so many purposes.

"Human labor, as you see, is no longer the difficult and humiliating toil of old. All these machines carry out the work, people employing their force and application while they assume the less taxing roles of direction and surveillance, with more leisure and mental freedom, entirely to the advantage of their intellectual and moral elevation. Even the manipulation of numbers, always so absorbing, is carried out by ingenious and reliable mechanisms. Every office and workplace is equipped with an apparatus like this one, which not only provides solutions to the most complicated calculations, but all information regarding dates, places and operations of every sort."

The young men, still moving forward, found their progress interrupted by a group of people surrounding a musician, who was extracting from an instrument made entirely of metal a harmony that was doubtless delightful to their ears but which surprised Marius considerably, for the music only conveyed interrupted sounds to him, incomplete sequences that seemed to be coming from a mutilated harp lacking several strings

When he made this observation to Namo, the latter replied: "I think I understand. Your remark lends support to the opinion expressed by some of our anthropologists, who claim that the sense of hearing was less well-developed in olden times than in modernity, because humans have undergone physical improvement. It's not the music, it's just that your incomplete ear can't grasp certain sonic nuances, Our senses have made progress in other ways too. Do you know that most of us can see the colors of sounds, the vibrations of heat, and even the radiation that living bodies emit, and that a single glance can, in consequence, indicate a person's age, state of health and physical or intellectual vigor? It's unfortunate for you to be deprived of that aptitude. You can't imagine what a marvelous and magical spectacle a person presents, when placed in darkness—the multicolored flames that appear to be running over our entire bodies, and the phantasmagorical aureoles that radiate around certain individuals."

A little further on, Marius stopped in front of marbles in which the veins, although natural, presented astonishing designs: not simple seams due to chance, or even fossil shells, which are so frequently seen, but the form of objects produced by human industry.

"What's that?" he asked.

"Ah! That's right; in your time the Ocean hadn't yet laid bare the great austral lands—in exchange, alas, for all those it is invading in our hemisphere. Those marbles come from the land at our antipodes, which contains the human fossils that were sought in vain on this side of the globe. It's not merely urns, helmets and weapons that ancient sediment, since petrified, has conserved in its strata. Let's go further and you'll see many other things."

The first object that Namo pointed out with his finger was a tablet in which a human head, facing forwards, was clearly designed. But that was nothing compared to the macabre scene represented by an immense slab, against the black background of which several white skeletons stood out, incomplete but perfectly recognizable, groups together—huddling so to speak—in a disposition that immediately reminded Marius of the human cluster in Girodet's famous painting entitled *The Deluge*.[18] It was a sad and lugubrious

---

[18] The Painter Anne-Louis Girodet (1767-1824) was in the forefront of the French Romantic Movement. "Le Déluge"

subject, too appropriate to meditations which Namo did not want to dwell, for he did not delay in drawing his friend in another direction, where a spectacle that was no less astonishing, but evocative of very different ideas, had attracted a large number of spectators.

It was a small ring set in semi-darkness and surrounded by a balustrade that held the public back. Above it, disposed along the tubular walls of a kind of inclined shaft, immense crystal lenses were suspended, the whole constituting a veritable telescope, of monumental proportions but nevertheless mobile, which was projecting astonishing images on a vast screen extended within the ring. It was at that dark area that the gazes of the silent and pensive spectators were directed.

To begin with, it was necessary to wait for the eyes to adjust to the minimal lighting of the location; then a kind of landscape became sufficiently perceptible and distinguishable, which was a direct image taken at that very moment of the planet Mars, at which the gigantic eye of the incomparable instrument was aimed. Obviously, the problem had been solved of the visibility of images magnified far beyond the dimensions at which, for want of sufficient light, all perceptibility had ceased, and the screen before their eyes had the virtue of making extinct features sensible and reanimating them.

However the curious magic mirror worked, the most marvelous spectacle was now offered to human eyes placed hundreds of millions of leagues away from its true theater. It was a polar landscape, recognizable by the fantastic forms of enormous icebergs that might have been mistake for their peers on Earth or Cybele. Marius would rather have seen red-colored forests and vegetation, or the canals that were said to connect the seas and great lakes of the planet in question, which were doubtless traveled by Martial fleets, but that would have to wait for another time.

---

was exhibited at the Salon of 1806 and became a popular source of prints representing details taken from the vast scene.

That was enough, for the present, and it was while talking about the recent progress that had established real links between the various members of the same planetary family that the two friends began to make their way back to the house.

"Yes, my friend," said Namo, "not only can we see what is happening on our neighboring planets, while they can see us, but we also exchange a certain amount of interesting correspondence with them by means of projection, either of bright light or black shadow, which sometimes design symbolic shapes and sometimes even ideographic signs.

"Following on from tentative experiments, the latter have ended up expressing meanings comprehensible to the various inhabitants of the planets in the system. We know, in consequence, that human and animal life on Mars, Jupiter and Venus—where, for example, all life is winged—bear no resemblance to us and the other living forms of Cybele, except in the matter of intelligence, which is perhaps similar for all beings, whatever place they occupy in the spectrum of universal life.

"Furthermore, the radiations of the different celestial bodies have been analyzed by our astronomical physicists much more completely than your scientists can decompose their light, and they have been able to discover much more therein than colors, spectroscopic lines and waves. They have even identified animate effluvia of astral existences, which give us an exact expression of the degree of vital expansion of each of them.

"The physical individuality of a planet is thus completed for us by its mental personality, and we have been able to classify our celestial companions according to their particular character, in complete knowledge of causes, not chimerically, as your chiromancers did, who found—no one knows why—the Moon whimsical, Mars brutal or Venus loving.

"We have that, and many other things, to distract you and help you to shake off your melancholy, Monsieur Inconsolable."

VI

Meanwhile, the rumor had spread through the great city, by virtue of one of those supernatural phenomena that defy all science and confound all reason, that an inhabitant of a sidereal planet similar in all respects to Cybele, but its younger sister by several thousand years, had arrived in the capital, where he had been welcomed by an honorable Algerian family. Such an implausible event was assumed at first to be a joke, but the rumor gradually acquired consistency and authority, and however marvelous it seemed, people became convinced that it was true.

The imminent approach of a terrible cataclysm was then preying on all minds and disturbing a large number. Some people wanted to see the miraculous visit of an inhabitant of the remotest skies as the advent of a divine messenger endowed with the power to ward off frightful misfortunes; others, by contrast, saw the envoy extraordinary as a sinister prophet announcing that the end of the world was nigh. The newspapers got hold of the story, and they too competed in irrationality with regard to a matter that defied all explanation and before which it would have simpler to bow down and keep silent.

True scientists and philosophers—those who were sufficiently learned to know that, in the final analysis, we know nothing—accepted the fact, since it was one, for what it was, and only sought, as practical individuals, to extract some advantage from the presence of the Terran similar to their ancestors on Cybelean antiquity. They judged him inestimably useful for clarifying the history of those remote times with new information of every sort. They knew from Alcor, who was a member of several scientific societies, that the Terran was an educated and companionable man, for his era, and considered that such a precious document ought not to be neglected for a moment longer. Alcor found himself besieged with demands from all directions to produce his prodigy.

As a clever man, Alcor did not fail to profit from the opportunity to obtain for his young friend a special chair at the Great College, thus acquiring a very honorable official status for him. It was, therefore, with the support of that good news that he came to Marius one morning to propose that he introduce him to the scholarly bodies of the capital. An assembly composed of all the eminent men in Algiers was in session, feverishly awaiting the arrival of the Terran, whose entrance caused the greatest sensation.

To tell the truth, the prodigious individual initially caused a certain disappointment. They had expected at least to see a distinctive physiognomic type, but there was nothing of the sort. The man was in conformity, down to the slightest details of his individuality, with the perfect identity of the distant world from which he came with the world of Cybele. He was of the pure Caucasian race of Europeans in general, a race that had set foot and multiplied in all five continents of the world. There merely seemed to be something slightly different in his appearance, doubtless stemming from the fact that among the new French a belated but finally complete mixture with the indigenous race accomplished several centuries before had abundantly conserved the noble Arab blood and produced a type similar to the Spanish type.

In the midst of all those learned individuals, who knew Old French, Marius soon found himself at ease, replying with the most perfect grace to the sometimes-bizarre questions addressed to him from all sides. The precision of the information he provided about Algeria during the early days of the occupation, as he had known it, and about France, still similar on Earth to what it had been on Cybele sixty centuries before, caused the entire assembly to marvel.

His Algerian memories were precise enough for him to be able to indicate the exact locations that had been occupied by the Mosque of Abder-Rahman, the Tomb of the Christian, the Palace of the Seven Deys and the equestrian statue of the young Duc d'Orléans,[19] and thus to rectify doubtful questions that had divided archeologists and had caused impassioned floods of ink and words to flow.

One thing, above all, of which they did not tire, was hearing him speak about the ancient political, social and religious questions that Marius had left his contemporaries of Earth to debate without him, as present concerns. The Paris about which he spoke at length and enthusiasm, albeit as a slightly prejudiced provincial, had been quite forgotten by present generations. The subsequent splendors of Marseilles had effaced it from history somewhat, and Marseilles too had had its day.

An ineradicable tradition, however, attached to the name of Paris a kind of aureole of unparalleled glory and heroic virtue. Had it not been the venerable cradle of the revolution that, breaking with the ages of arbitrary power and unbridled violence, had conceived, proclaimed and caused to triumph through the entire word the new tablets of the law known as human rights? The stains of the time, the inevitable accompaniment of all human endeavor, had long been effaced and washed away by the long martyrology of the apostles of human rights. Had not that epoch of renovation been the point of departure of an era that counted for much in the annals of human progress?

The first century of that glorious era, in particular, had been the abridged preface of the progress to come, which was to overcome many obstacles and withstand many assaults before seeing the realization of that which had appeared to its instigators in a lucid vision. The man that the assembled Cybeleans had before them at present still belonged to that revolutionary epoch, which had lasted for more than a century

---

[19] Ferdinand-Philippe, Duc d'Orléans (1810-1842), the eldest son of King Louis-Philippe, fought in Algeria against Abd El-Kader in 1835, and returned in 1839 to help complete the conquest of the interior, but his career was subsequently cut short in France when he was killed in a riding accident.

before its agitations had concluded. They could, therefore, hear him testify to the virtues and devotions of those heroic times.

To begin with, Marius responded to that unanimous expectation by celebrating the fathers of the Revolution, the proclaimers full of faith in the great principles of '89 in the old style. But it was necessary to turn down that admiration when the interrogation bore upon the years of eclipse, of the periods of moral depression that had alternated with moments of enthusiastic impulses and generous efforts. Marius' own youth had coincided with one of those periods of lassitude and enervation, which were like the inverse of the times of awakening and noble ardor. His personal memories only recalled, to begin with, a dictatorship commenced by treason and crime, about to conclude in an ocean of other shames and other treasons with the defeat and abasement of the homeland. Then came a confused mixture of virile aspirations and audacious turpitudes—a mixture that was still enduring when the course of the story-teller's terrestrial destiny had been interrupted.

"How would you define, in sum," one of the more intrepid questioners persisted, "the political ideal of your present time?"

"That ideal," said Marius, "is easy to formulate: remove yourself from power and position, in order that I might occupy them myself. Our militant politicians scarcely allow anything else to be perceived in their quotidian struggles, of which the abused people have no understanding. To mount an assault on the government and the advantages it procures, that is everything. To conquer it is not easy, and to hold on to it more difficult still, and in the incessant battles that hardly leave a government on place for a matter of days, any weapon is appropriate: every question, every incident, every interest and even every national peril, is only ever envisaged from the sole viewpoint of how it might serve the contending parties for defense or attack. What does the colonial future, for example, or the external grandeur of France matter? What does it matter that a centuries-old preponderance, interests superior to civili-

110

zation itself, are being sacrificed, and Egypt surrendered to England? Is it not necessary, above all else, to topple the Cabinet?

"One is, therefore, alternately in government and opposition. When one is in power, one feels oneself so completely surrounded by snares and pitfalls that one scarcely dares move the Chariot of State for fear of ambushes; and when one is in opposition, one no longer envisages anything but impeding or derailing the aforesaid Chariot, because, if it moves smoothly, the situation will be too favorable for the adversaries who are guiding it. Such are, applied to our temperament, the beauties of parliamentarianism in the English style—for it's necessary to tell you that we are aping the English in everything, and no longer know how to be simply ourselves."

"Was it not your era," asked someone else, "that elucidated the great social and moral questions that were to rebuild society on new foundations?"

"I can't tell you whether the future will do better," Marius replied, naively, "but the principles of the moment do not seem very clear to me, and I confess that personally, I have not yet fixed my preference between communism, anarchism, impossibilism, and puffism, which all rhyme very well with one another.

"There is no lack of newspapers to elucidate, or rather to confuse, so many questions posed at the same time. They cater to all tastes, but those which are most successful are those that, in social matters, stick entirely to matters of petty commerce, having understood that it is not the great but rather the petty aspects of weak human nature that grip their readers most firmly. There are some for the broad public that likes certain things to be said in the raw, and there are others for refined folk whose taste for gamy meat seems to merit the palm of a gourmet. I ought to add that, fortunately, there are also some that are sensible and patriotic, for simple and worthy individuals sickened by all that."

"If you had deferred your visit by a mere half-century," one of the most knowledgeable historians in the audience observed, "you would know that many obscure questions were to find a clear solution. After having seen the political collapse of the Third Estate, of a bourgeoisie that had rapidly become egotistical, corrupt, exclusive and enslaved by money, you would have witnessed the advent of a Fourth Estate,[20] more faithful to the great principles of '89, because its views embraced the entire nation, and by virtue of that, were to realize a more equitable social justice. Nevertheless, rights and patriotism have never been as scorned as you claim, young man, and your time, depressed as it was, was able to appreciate and honor its great citizens, its Hugos and Gambettas, souls as noble and hearts as elevated as France has known."

"And those great men will not have appealed in vain to our sentiments and our courage, I can assure you," Marius replied, swiftly. "Already, certain symptoms of our future awakening are appearing on all sides. Voices are making themselves heard that we have grown unused to hearing. The emergent generation will be better than its elder. It has a better knowledge and understanding of the information and exhortations of men of courage and patriotism opposed to cowardly compromises and egotistical instincts. It is in her schools, above all, and under the salutary influence of labor, that France is getting a grip on herself and renewing for an imminent future the best traditions of her glorious past. One of my most moving memories is the impression made on me, last fourteenth of July, by the procession of our young scholarly battalions. We sensed the reverberation between those children and ourselves of heartbeats in which an echo vibrated of the great impulses that have always characterized the great French race."

"Bravo! Bravo!" someone shouted. And the hands of all the people surrounding Marius extended to grip his.

---

[20] Alhaiza is not, of course, referring to the "Fourth Estate" as the term was then understood in England, and is still is, to refer to the press, but rather to a new social class, perhaps more akin to what is meant by the "intelligentsia."

Meanwhile, new arrivals kept coming from all directions. The doors and windows were crowded with curiosity-seekers, and, to calm their impatience, Marius was asked to climb up on to an elevated platform so that everyone could at least see him. But for Alcor and his friends, he would not have been able to get away from the rising tide of invaders who, forcing all the entrances, wanted to get closer, at any price to the terrestrial man who was presently the topic of all conversations in the capital and the entire country. It was necessary for Marius to promise to come to the National Theater the next day and the following days in order to give impromptu lectures. The great traveler was beginning to experience the inconveniences of celebrity.

In the lectures in question, people wanted to see him dressed in his traveling clothes: garments woven and stitched on a planet lost in the remotest regions of the visible heavens. Those garments were sketched and copied as a curiosity of the first order. Then, at the request of the curator of the Algerian museums, who wanted to exhibit them in a special display case, Marius hastened to make him a gift of his Elbeuf suit and all the rest.

Unfortunately—a regrettable lacuna—his hat was missing, although he could not remember in which corner of space he had lost it. Perhaps—probably, even—it had fallen off at the critical moment when he was flailing desperately in the attempt to land on the mountains of the moon, and the Selenites, on seeing that new kind of aerolith falling on their world, had lost themselves in conjectures regarding the entirely new variety of bolide. In any case, if there were astronomers there, the partisans of the volcanic origin of terrestrial projectiles would be subject to a memorable setback, for the scientists who professed the opposite opinion would have had a fine time demonstrating that the volcanoes of Earth had never, etc., etc...

Marius made it a point of honor to fulfill his new duties as a professor of ancient history and geography conscientiously. While awaiting the time when he would be capable of giving his lessons in modern language, his courses were taken exclusively by people well-versed in ancient French, and who were uniquely concerned with improving or checking what they already knew at a good source. His task was, therefore, easy. He only had to speak for his correct syntax, his well-turned phrases and, most of all, his pronunciation, to yield very profitable examples, for although writing conserves the words of a language that has ceased to live, it cannot perpetuate the accent and tone, any more than its natural mannerisms and wit, which are no longer felt in their true measure by generations elevated in their ideas and possessed of a new language.

Marius did indeed rapidly observe many stylistic errors and numerous barbarisms, although that did not surprise him. It is certain that if Demosthenes or Cicero could return to hear our oral competitions at the Sorbonne, they would find the Latin and Greek of 1890 somewhat deformed and deplorably pronounced. If anything astonished him, it was that after so many centuries, a language forgotten by the people should be retained almost intact by the learned, who deigned to honor it with their attention.

For their part, his students were all ears, in order to lose nothing of the accurate and measured prosody that writing had been unable to retain and perpetuate in all its correctness. They took note religiously of the authentic consonants, and the particular euphony of the nasal vowels in the pure accent of Provence. Instead of pronouncing *divin* and *étrange* as they had before, they now said, like their model, *diveign* and *étreigne*, and although the details was of scant importance, they repeated those rectified intonations to one another and even to themselves in the privacy of their own rooms, coming back to them incessantly in order to become more accustomed to them.

In addition, Marius found, conserved in everyday language, a number of locutions in ancient French, which cropped up occasionally in current conversation, in the same was that the French of his contemporaries often reverted to classical locutions such as *Eureka* or *Errare humanum est*, and he had occasion to criticize more than one that the modern users were employing inappropriately. Thus, having heard one of his new pupils, who evidently wanted to express his appreciation of the Attic salt of a delicate observation, say: "*Ah, cher maître, vous nous faites vraiment à l'oseille*," it was necessary for him to explain and make it understood that the expression in question had completely lost its original meaning.[21]

Marius' position at the Great College was utterly exceptional; a professor in his working hours, he reverted to being a simple pupil when, in his turn, he followed his colleagues' courses. He was beginning to get his teeth into modern French, but not without great difficulties, the majority of which arose from terms that were untranslatable for him because they represented things and new ideas devoid of meaning for the obsolete intellect of a man of his epoch. He was nevertheless able to observe the immense progress that all the branches of human knowledge had made on Cybele, whose records and endeavors went back nearly ten thousand years.

The sciences were not limited to dry nomenclature and the observation of observed facts; they supplied the why of almost everything: why a flower had one particular form and hue rather than others; why one animal lived for fifty years and another only for ten, etc. To tell the truth, there was only one science, all the branches of which were tightly connected and synthesized into a unitary knowledge.

Physics had taken complete possession of its natural domain, and clearly recognized the ultimate boundaries that sep-

---

[21] The literal meaning of *oseille* is sorrel, but it also figures in the phrase *sel d'oseille* [salts of oxalic acid] which Marius' pupil seems to be mistaking for a metaphor equivalent to *sel attique* [Attic salt, i.e. wit], whereas the expression *faire à l'oseille* is actually closer in meaning to such English expressions as "pulling [someone's] leg" or "having [someone] on."

arated it from the immaterial order. Chemistry had analyzed all substances, without exception, and could reproduce almost all of them at will. The Great Work of the transmutation of metals, the dream of the ancient alchemists, was now child's play in laboratories where gold, once so tempting but now greatly depreciated, could be made at will. The philosopher's stone that had driven so many seekers to despair had been discovered long ago. Even the so-called elementary substances could no longer resist analysis, and had been brought back to the sole chemical unity. One word now summarized the entire physical order: matter.

It was necessary to recognize that squaring the circle and perpetual motion still remained undiscovered, although there were some obstinate individuals who still expected to reckon with those problems.

As for medicine, it had realized the greatest progress by renouncing drugs, which had been advantageously replaced by vital magnetic impulsions, and especially by sound precepts of hygiene and diet, for its practitioners had ended up by understanding that animate nature is something other than a chemical retort or crucible.

Among the sciences that had made so much progress since Marius' time there was one that interested him most of all, because of the noise it was generating at that moment on Cybele's sister-world. We are referring to the magnetism and hypnotism whose enthusiasts were predicting the most fantastic futures, and in which spiritists and fakirists already saw the effective and material effects of souls in torment entering into communication with the living. Time had also done its work of purification there, and disengaged from the marvelous in which the imagination delighted, its real and veritably scientific aspect, which was no less admirable and astonishing for having rejected the supernatural.

The more profound knowledge that had been acquired of the infinitely diffuse and yet always material nature of the ether, the ultimate irreducible fabric of universal atomic matter; its aptitude in reverberating in all directions the slightest physical quivers, including the atomic agitation of a brain engaged in the work of thought; and the innumerable ethereal contacts of the hidden vital radiations emanating from all living beings, had provided the sole and ultimate key to so many previously-incomprehensible phenomena.

As had ever been the case, no man had any greater power of domination or suggestion over another than the physically and mentally strong had always had over the weak, without ever achieving complete possession of their personality and free will. But that magnetic action, subordinating an accidentally-passive living mechanism to a more active and powerful mechanism of the same order, impeding or impelling even at a distance by the intermediary of etheric waves, had become an everyday matter, yielding the most magnificent results in medicine, and even in education.

Thus, for example, an arduous problem of which a pupil could not get to the bottom in the waking state, was easily solved by him during the somnambulistic state in which perceptions, although still simply natural, are more profound and more concentrated, and extend over a latent field of intellectual life much vaster than that of ordinary life. Progress had consisted, above all, in fixing by intelligent exercise the cerebral images thus perceived, instead of allowing them to be effaced at the moment of awakening. Mental acuity and sensitivity were thus profitably exploited by a rational and measured practice of genuinely scientific magnetism and hypnotism.

Mathematics had also been taken much further forward than the stage at which Newton and Laplace had left them. Astronomers calculated the most complex movements of the innumerable suns comprising the resolvable nebulae. The Fayes of this epoch had been able to calculate the entire astral past of comets, just as they had been able to determine the laws of the incommensurable vortices that operate in the ultimate depths of the infinite ether.[22] Their science had exhausted all the possible observations.

They had detailed knowledge of many other planetary worlds of whose cortege Cybele was a part, and possessed exact tables, not only of the trajectory that the ensemble of their own system was following into new skies, but also the proper motion of every star in the firmament, with centuries-long records of the birth or extinction of some of them. Finally, the universe, fathomed to new depths by the analysis of universal electric waves and the power of new optical instruments, showed them, in distant luminous figures far beyond our starry nebula, strange and mysterious contours that gave rise to the suspicion of something like an immense organism: a living being; an unimaginable body, whose molecules are the immense globular masses that we call stars.

The catalogue of the various aspects of human science was so vast that the greatest intelligences could scarcely claim mastery of an infinitesimal part of it. A human life was only sufficient, at the most, to assimilate completely one small twig of one of the branches of one specialty. Lovers of knowledge and general syntheses naturally resorted to brief summaries that were within everyone's compass, and still had difficulty in embracing more than a few.

It was no longer a time when a Pico della Mirandola could emerge victorious from a scientific tournament in which he could challenge *de omni re scibili* the scholars of his era, and confound them all by means of the universality of his knowledge, which he could express in twenty-two different languages. Even he, history claims, was taken by surprise by an unexpected question posed by a simple married woman, who knew better than he did how a certain cheese, which was one of the delights of the gourmets of his day, was manufactured in the vicinity of Rome—which shows that even in the

---

[22] The reference is to Hervé Faye (1814-1902), an astronomer who achieved fame in 1843 when he discovered "Faye's comet."

relatively ignorant epoch of 1486 A.D., one could not know everything.

What the astronomers of Cybele had calculated only too well was that since the year 5235 the winters of the northern hemisphere had begun to exceed in length the Antarctic winters, that the weight of the boreal ice-cap was already displacing the globe's center of gravity measurably northwards, and that the moment was approaching when an abrupt shock was about to precipitate the frightful disintegration of the dislocated austral ice-sheets.

While the coasts and lowlands of the northern hemisphere had been gradually invaded by the ocean for a long time already, the Austral lands, increasingly liberated, were beginning to rise up, and their beds were emerging in many places as the level of the waves diminished. The Polynesian islands seemed to be trying to join up everywhere; chains of submarine mountains were reappearing, raising their summits, bizarrely crowned with walls of coral, ever higher; the small Australian continent was spreading out like a patch of oil, extending its shores further into the ocean every day; finally, closer to the pole, the lands once glimpsed by Ross and Dumont d'Urville were visibly growing, and the immense extent of another continent was beginning to surge forth, whose coasts would one day advance into the Indian Ocean all the way to the fortieth parallel.

For the same reason, America and Africa were extending further southwards, and the island of Madagascar was growing in its turn, now only separated from the African coast by an arm of the sea no wider than the strait separating England from the European continent had once been.

That land of Madagascar had, over the centuries, become a third France. The mildness of its climate and the fertility of its soil had furnished an environment more hospitable to colonization than any of our old homeland's other distant possessions, and a great State had been created there, which had eventually become independent but had never ceased to maintain close relations with the metropolis, and had busied itself in its turn extending French ideas an influence in the hemisphere of the future. It goes without saying that for many centuries, the sympathetic shadow of the gentle Bernardin de Saint-Pierre had no longer been weeping over the Île de France that had long been a prisoner of the English but had eventually returned to the maternal bosom.

As, on the other hand, England had founded throughout southern Africa, partly spoiled by the Portuguese, a great empire that had also become autonomous, destiny had continued to bring the two rival races closer together, with the difference that this time, it was an insular France that neighbored a continental England, and continued a fecund struggle of civilization and progress therewith.

It was not only England and France, however, that had carved out domains on the other side of the globe. The majority of the other European peoples has been able to find room there, and so, when the period began in which terrestrial destinies would recommence, old Europe would be renewed and perpetuated at the antipodes, in those of its emigrants who would survive the inevitable cataclysm, just as the black yellow and white races, which probably represented as many interdiluvian types, had survived previous cataclysms.

To begin with, South America was broadly sufficient to perpetuate Spanish, Portuguese and even Italian descendancy, for the Italians although they were late arrivals in the content, had been able, thanks to a strong current of emigration sustained for a long time, to create a sizeable independent population in the Patagonian region now encompassing and surpassing the once-inhospitable Tierra de Fuego. The Dutch had also brought serious reinforcements to their brethren in the Transvaal, the increased territory of which formed a free enclave always valiantly defended in the midst of the great Anglo-Saxon states of southern Africa. For their part, the Belgians had colonized several salubrious high plateaux in the central region of the Congo, and there was no one—including the Russians, Scandinavians, Austro-Hungarians, Greeks and even the Swiss—who had not acquired a few Oceanian archipelagoes, driven by an imperious national desire for conversation, all that to the great scandal of Albion, which had long become accustomed to believe that she had exclusive property rights over the exploitable regions of the planet.

It was, however, Germany most of all that had done great work and prospered. As the lead had been taken almost everywhere by the other European nations, it was necessarily into the territories of others that she had initially directed her enormous emigration. She had since conquered, it is true, immense possessions in equatorial Africa, but what she could not conquer was the climate of her new empire, which was capable of devouring as many Germans as came to settle there. Thus, her innumerable emigrants were forced to see their fortune elsewhere.

Toward the end of the twentieth century A.D., the prosperity of Australia had particularly attracted to that immense and fertile region the principal branch of the German emigration stream, which had previously been dissolved in the United States and had become the root-stock of the Yankees. First there was a slow infiltration, entirely to the advantage of the first Anglo-Saxon occupants, among whom the newcomers had been dissolved and denaturalized, as usual.

At length, however, the ever-increasing infiltration became an inundation, and there came a time when the Germanic race, absorbed as it was, became absorbing in its turn, to the point that the Anglo-Saxons found themselves seriously threatened in their integrity, their language, their autonomy and, in sum, their national existence. From then on, a muted rivalry had been established between the two elements; then, finally, a veritable conflict had broken out between them—a conflict that, without making use of murderous weapons, had nevertheless been replete with ardor and tenacity.

It was evident that the definitive victory would go, as ever, to the big battalions, especially in this case, where numbers were both the end and the means. Between two races as prolific as the German and the English, a war of population was bound to take on gigantic proportions as soon as nationalistic spirit was engaged and the future was at stake. So, the most heroic enthusiasm was seen to be ignited in both camps for a truly glorious warfare that produced citizens instead of destroying them. It must also be said, in praise of the female citizens who bore the brunt of the struggle even more than their husbands, that not one, in either camp, weakened in the face of difficulty or shirked her duty. Once hostilities had been declared, none would ever have fraternized with the enemy or married a man of the opposed nationality, thus augmenting the chances of the rival population.

What emerged from that feverish zest is indescribable. No one any longer asked fathers how many children they had but how many dozens. The staff of the offices registering births was literally overwhelmed. If the Germans advanced, the English, for their part, held firm, and the victory remained or a long time in suspension between the belligerents, but reinforcements never ceased arriving for the former, and those fresh troops, continually renewed, were finally to decide a hotly contested triumph. It was in vain that the English called upon the old guard—which is to say, older households—to return to the fray like young troops. The drums were beaten at silver weddings, and even golden weddings, calling for truly Homeric exploits worthy of admiration, but the god of battles had decided in favor of the newcomers. As soon as it was beyond doubt that the Germans would hold sway, their valor redoubled, while dejection entered into the opposed camp and weakened courage.

The day came when what remained of the English in that immense territory capitulated, or emigrated to New Zealand, the other great British territory nearby, which was only half-assured. There was no risk that the vanquished would seek to recover the lost ground; for a long time they trembled at the thought that the terrible German women might advance further, to populate the large islands that were their last refuge in the region.

And that was how Australia, in its entirety, became a German territory in perpetuity.

By contrast, in the other hemisphere, the scene was depressing. In contrast to the past, the old and new continents no longer had large continuous territories in their northern parts. The greater part of Russian and Siberia, and almost all of Canada, had given way to open sea, and it no longer needed a Nordenskjöld to accomplish the exploit of a circumpolar navigation. Even the territory of the United States had been invaded by gulfs that extended deep into regions that had once been covered by flourishing cities.

One of the curiosities of the epoch was the colossal Statue of Liberty that still stood in front of the place that had once been New York, no longer materially the same, for the bronze had been replaced several times, but a faithful reproduction that had religiously perpetuated Bartholdi's creation. Its appearance had changed considerably, however, and the statue, whose immense pedestal was no longer visible, now seemed to be walking on the water.

It goes without saying that Europe had not been spared; not only Russia, of which little remained but the great massifs of the Caucasus and the Urals, but Prussia, Denmark and the Low Countries had disappeared. Scandinavia formed a large island hollowed out by numerous fjords. Great Britain was considerably reduced and France had seen her rich northern provinces swallowed up, leaving only a few archipelagoes visible, still inhabited for the most part. Vast lagoons rendered other parts impracticable, which the sea still seemed to be sparing, and Parisian soil was seeing the recommencement of the labor of forming new marls and sandy terrains that would eventually figure in the number of geological strata of that soil, so often transformed, but in which the quarrymen of the future, in their excavations, would discover many things very different from marine or lacustrian mollusk-shells or prehistoric flints and pottery.

The sinister preoccupations that haunted the minds of all the populations of Cybele were, naturally, keener on that side of the planet than the opposite one. They knew what definitive height the Great Northern Ocean would attain after the cataclysm. At present, the casuistic Voltaire would have had difficulty making fun of scientists with regard to the seashells that were found mingled with mountain rocks, and seeing them as nothing but oyster-shells left behind by excursionist lovers of good food.

Everywhere, on the heights, people were laboring to build new immense Towers of Babel with formidable walls and surrounded by protective works capable of withstanding the assault of the supreme tide, the waves of the last hour, the degree of whose fury it was impossible to calculate in advance. They lived, therefore, in mortal dread, having nothing sure in prospect but the few hours notice that electricity would give them of the moment that the frightful Austral disintegration had taken place. And when that terrible news finally broke, what a frightful picture would be painted of the universal stampede!

What was about to be annihilated permanently by the abrupt displacement of the liquid element was the apogee of civilization that had been realized by a hundred centuries of human endeavor and progress.

Now that Marius was able to read books and journals more fruitfully, and to interest himself in the affairs of his new homeland, he was able to get the measure of what was happening around him, and what the superior civilization amounted to of which the most optimistic philanthropists of his own time had dared to dream—a civilization so ancient that it extended back without any great social changes for several thousand years, virtually proving that there is a certain form of social organization that best responds to the necessities and natural dispositions of human societies, outside of which there is only retardation or retreat. That is why, once realized, that state of relative perfection, relative to public order, had remained almost stationary, the need for political change no longer being felt.

The great empires of old only continued to exist, so to speak, as geographical expressions. Everywhere, gradually, petty republics of familial administration had been organized, which formed various confederations satisfying broad general interests, and the greater of lesser extents of which often went back to historical causes, to the commonalty of a similar past. Thus, the New France was composed of thirty little free States, and what remained of ancient France only accounted for half that number. The capital, Algiers, outside of its own territory, only had a limited political role, somewhat akin to an honorary presidency.

The governmental mechanism simply consisted of a central authority governing and administering under its responsibility, the instructions of an assembly that was aware of all the services and all the interests of the country in general, the whole being under the control, without appeal, of a grand council of censors who represented the nation itself, which did not legislate but had full powers to impeach abuses and even remove incapable or culpable governors from their positions. The best form of government was thus found to be a directive power—the brain of the nation, so to speak—its emanations always, however, being refined in an elite of capacities regularly renewed without assaults or jolts, rather than in an overly direct representations of the public, in the impulsions of an inferior order of popular masses.

Between the state of things that Marius had known in his own homeland and the one he found now there was continual matter for comparison and reflection, and that inexhaustible subject was one of those that most frequently came up in the conversations that he had almost every evening with his neighbor Alcor before the time came to go to bed.

"How is it," Marius asked him one evening, raising his eyes from the newspaper he had been reading, "that I never find any account of some stirring debate, any of those brilliant speeches that give so much luster to the tribune of our assem-

125

blies and constitute the great attraction of politics? To tell the truth, my dear master, I believe that in the matter of orators, it's still my time that wins the palm."

"Eh? What need do we have of insidious words and clever rhetoric, when the truth or the necessities of any situation are obvious to everyone, when there is no one to indoctrinate or seduce? You will notice the absence of many other illustrations for which we have no use. It's necessary to go back a long way in our old annals, almost to your time, to find virtuosos of dispute, almost all of them professionals, apart from a small number of great speakers and veritable Statesmen: the discoverers of formulas and infallible governmental panaceas, flatterers of ignorance and the worst prejudices, making a force out of popular credulity; those economists who balanced the budget of a country by overwhelming the country with enormous debts; the so-called progressivists drawing their luster from their art of bringing the least ripe questions to a premature settlement and instituting least well-prepared reforms; and the rabble of political highwaymen who only saw the lucrative side of the management of public affairs.

"I can understand that our affairs, which proceed without noise, and our newspapers, which merely give a genuinely enlightened public the straightforward account of the facts that the public in question demands, must seem monotonous to someone who has been accustomed to the resounding thunder of the tribune and journalism. Like political disorder, however, the papers of coteries created uniquely to rouse and manipulate opinion to their whim, or, even worse, corsairs of the pen selling their services or ransoming cut-throat calumny no longer exist here. Universal political and social education is too well-founded for anything contrary to great national interests to attempt to prevail.

"Everything happens here in a calm and orderly manner. As the government no longer has any prizes to win in parliamentary conflict, those conflicts no longer exist. In addition, as our representatives are selected by lot from among eligible citizens, the lottery makes better choices among honest and patriotic individuals without ambition than your scandalous public elections—although, as a result of that principle, it happens quite often that opinion designates some capable individual who is forced to yield to the desire of his fellow citizens and to occupy a position that he has not sought.

"The public is no longer a base and coarse collective entity made to be abused, cynically despised by those who flatter it the most. The public is improved, moralized and enlightened, and nothing that affects it can be hidden from light of day, so even the cleverest are forced to play an honest game. We live, my friend, under a regime of obligatory honesty, a regime of strength and health for the great living organism that a society, a people and a State veritably constitute.

"All that is because every citizen not only knows his rights but, above all, because he carries out his duties, thus realizing the desire expressed by one of the noblest minds of your time when he said: 'The task of our fathers was to conquer right; ours must be to inform and propagate duty.' The shade of Jules Simon ought to rejoice that his great lessons have borne such fine fruit.[23]

"Politics is not a profession, nor is journalism; both are within the range of everyone. All the great social and national interests have their own organs, by means of which they manifest their mode of existence, their endeavors, and their demands, if they have any. If necessary, a simple workman is able to put down his tools and take up the pen, to treat a subject of his competence in his professional publication. That means that our daily press is no longer the licentious industry of so many papers of old, free of all restraint as of all control.

"Here again, as always, refinement happens automatically, without the liberty of writers being compromised, for in the new intellectual milieu, everything born that is not viable perishes of its own accord without the lies or obsessions of bold

---

[23] The statesman Jules Simon (1814-1896) pleaded the case in question in his most widely-read book, *Le Devoir* [Duty] (1854)

advertisement being able to abuse a public that is a good judge and remains the master of its impulsions.

"To get back to the gift of eloquence that you believe to be lost, reassure yourself. It still knows how to move and charm, but it is necessary to search for it elsewhere than in busy assemblies where there are no new principles to proclaim not any reaction to combat. Without mentioning the eloquence of the pulpit, to which our religious beliefs open the vastest horizons, there is no shortage of great scientific discoveries, or gigantic and passionate enterprises to excite the enthusiasm and inspire the sacred fore of our orators.

"You will not find them in our courtrooms either. The spirit of justice is too deeply embedded in our mores for the simple knowledge of any crime or a disagreement not to impose its immediate redress on everyone, with the same spirit of equity. The profession of advocate has disappeared with the progress of general education, plaintiffs and accused persons being perfectly capable of defending their cause without those costly intermediaries, who no longer influence any tribunal. You will not see today one of your eagles of the bar striving for hours in the attempt, often successful, to have a confirmed criminal acquitted, to win the indulgence of the judges for some large-scale embezzler or some manufacturer who has made money selling homicidal gods, or even speculating, as has been known, on the homeland's means of defense, at the price of the lives of your soldiers and the defeat off your ill-equipped and barefoot armies.

"The old Themis no longer threatens the powerless with her false balance and her heavy sword, and we have even cured her of that famous limp that caused her to drag her feet for such a long time. Justice is free, and hence disinterested and expeditious. That which was stolen and thrown away by the arsenal of its old laws is now believable, to the extent that the word justice only has one accepted sense now: that of its literal meaning. Thus, although it would doubtless scandalize your terrestrial magistrates, it punishes the crooked business-man who ruins a hundred families more severely than the starving man who steals a loaf of bread, and it is no longer tolerant of the adulterator of food, the thief of health, a thousand times more guilty than the thief of money. It is not that the new law is harsher; on the contrary, it is full of indulgence towards those who have simply gone astray, but it has become inflexible severe for the incurably perverse, to whom it applies, if necessary, the capital penalty of definitive disappearance, which sheds no blood but removes society's irredeemably gangrenous members permanently."

It was often the case, of course, that Namo often came to his friend's apartment to take part in these instructive evening conversations. Less well-versed than the professor in the mores and customs of the nebulous past that corresponded to Marius' time, he was often surprised by the remarks, objections and occasional resistance of the latter, who usually ended up yielding to Alcor's superior reasoning, but nevertheless sometimes felt slightly humiliated in what we might call his Terran patriotism—for was it not the terrestrial globe in its entirety that, at the distance at which he found himself, now appeared to him as his unique homeland: the homeland that one always loves, such as it is, with its inferiorities, its faults and even its ugliness?

"Up to what point will you follow this path of limitless progress?" he asked his two friends.

"We shall always make progress in the sciences and the arts, in which the last word is never said," Alcor replied, "but as for political and social order, it was concluded many centuries ago. The governmental form best suited to civilized humankind, and the true solution of the social problem for which the search was so long, we have had for five thousand years, during which it has had ample time to prove itself. It is not like science, where an unknown always remains. There is, inevitably, a state of affairs that corresponds better than any other to the rights and reciprocal interests of people in association, and that best foundation, once finally encountered, can only be changed to its detriment. Thus, social stability has been realized, just as, at an inferior level, it was accomplished long ago by the societies of bees and ants, and you see no longer see in us, my dear Marius, anything but diehard conservatives."

VII

In the house in which Marius had already been a guest
for a long time, he had had the opportunity to get to know,
among the friends who visited from time to time, a woman
who was received there in the most perfect intimacy, as if she
were a member of the household. That was Nea, formerly
Junie's governess and still the young woman's dearest friend.
Nea was a young woman, whose beauty was a trifle cold and
severe, more imposing than attractive, and to whom Marius
paid little heed the first few times he saw her, but whom he
liked a great deal when he got to know her better.

Nothing about her betrayed the desire for pleasure that is
so natural to her sex, without, however, appearing to distance
her from relationships of an easy familiarity or even a frank
amity. On the contrary, she was very approachable, and in her
presence one experienced the penetrating charm of a nature
full of generosity and knowledgeable intelligence. In the midst
of the liveliest conversation, however, one would not have
dared addressing to her any of those gallant attentions and
banal compliments that men customarily permit themselves,
even toward the most reserved women, because they know
that they were usually welcome.

With respect to the woman in question, with her pensive
expression and a clear gaze that could read minds, any frivolous thought seemed out of place. She was not one of those
charming and futile individuals that one can treat a little like a
child; her character was equal, if not superior, to the virility of
soul that Marius, like all his contemporaries, considered to be
the exclusive prerogative of his own sex.

There was doubtless in Nea a slightly unusual elevation
of nature that probably placed her above the level of other
women, but it soon became evident to Marius that the women
of Cybele were very different from their terrestrial sisters of
his own epoch, and that Nea was not so very exceptional, even

in a certain particularity that was only later to be added to the numerous observations of which Marius never ceased to make ample provision—a particularity that we shall identify before he did, because of its capital importance.

It pertained to a relatively new factor on the world of Cybele: a marked decline in the rate of procreation. Was that due to a deterioration of a human species aged by sixty centuries? Was it not rather a natural adaptation of reproductive faculties to the new conditions of a population arrived at the fullness of its possible development on the terrestrial surface? That would have been in perfect conformity with spontaneous adjustments observable in the general history of life. So long as the environment had lent itself to the expansion of the species, procreative forces had been prodigal; now that the expansion was complete, the faculties were limiting themselves to the maintenance of a normal level. Not only had the fruits of marriage become rarer, but certain individuals found the secret ardor that had sometimes been so importunate in the effervescent epochs of the species becoming dormant, or even extinct, within them. The evils to which excess of population gives rise, which had once caused Malthus to utter the first cry of alarm, had been avoided by the foresight of nature itself.

Many things were no worse for that. A little rarity renders bonds that had once been squandered infinitely more precious, even refining the sentiment of love by making children, upon whom death had ceased to levy the horrible taxation that had once stolen the greater number of them, more lovable and more desirable than in the times when they were not surrounded by so much care and attention. Even those who had renounced the joys of paternity nevertheless entertained paternal sentiments toward the young, the hope of the fatherland.

It was to this latter category of citizens that the excellent Alcor belonged, who, in remaining celibate, did not incur the reproach that he would have merited in other eras, when advanced races had the mission and the duty to expand over the planet. Every principle has its limits, including that of the expansion of the human species, in spite of what certain statisticians think, for whom a country can never have enough people and who, forgetting that humans cannot do without air, space and even solitude, aspire for humans something akin to the crowding of grain in our crop-fields. Those limits had been reached a long time before Alcor's epoch. The planet had as many inhabitants as it could reasonably accommodate.

To tell the truth, if it had only been up to Alcor, the New France would have counted one household more, but the only woman he had ever loved had had even less inclination to marriage that him—and that woman was Nea. Nor was that example of renunciation a new development in the world. There has never been a lack of women refractory to the yoke of marriage, but whereas the fault usually lay in love itself, which entangled them in its game and often left the most deserving to remain apart because they could not follow their hearts, love was less guilty in this instance, as we shall see. In most cases, nobler causes restricted its domain, giving the human orchard a number of infertile flowers, and it was often the most beautiful of those flowers, those whose blossoming absorbed their own reserves for the future, which ceased to bear fruit.

Two natures as well-endowed as Alcor's and Nea's, brought together by the circumstances of life, and being able in consequence to get to know and appreciate one another, could not have remained indifferent to one another. A solid link of affection had been established between them, which was a little more than friendship and a little less than love: one of those unions of heart and intelligence free of any other bond; unions once very rare between a man and a woman, but which had become frequent on Cybele. Thus the life proceeded of the two beings, made to understand and love one another platonically.

Fortunately for the future of the human race, not all women were like Nea—but the condition of women had changed in comparison to the state of affairs with which the Terran exile was familiar, and which habit had caused him to accept as something natural. It was not in his former entourage that he would find points of comparison unfavorable to Terran women. Would his Jeanne not have merited first place among the worthies young women of Cybele? But he was not unfamiliar with the society of his time and when, apart from the small number of the fortunate and those who found the solid support of a husband's arm, the image appeared to him of the misery of so many Frenchwomen, dragging out the wretched existence of pariahs, a flood of bitterness rose in his heart now that very different social conditions had opened up to his sight.

What, then, were the titles of superiority claimed by the old French society that considered itself at the head of civilization, really worth? Odiously miserly in rewarding all women's work, disgracefully insulting toward the unfortunates that its own rigors caused to fall, unjust even toward the forsaken who took refuge in convents, what did it expect to become of its women? Yes, everyone knows that men are at the feet of the idol who reigns by virtue of beauty and sentiment; that is agreed—but the truth is that they only place the idol so high in order to topple it thereafter, and when a woman has fallen, no hand is extended to her honestly thereafter.

On Cybele, there were no more pariahs of poverty or obligatory vice, and no more capitulations to hunger, since the progress of time had made room for everyone at the banquet of life. Dignity and self-respect had elevated mores and character. With independence, there were no more shameful compromises, no more degrading steps. Women, estimating themselves at their true value, had promptly taken the place that belonged to them by the right given to them by their noble maternal functions and their superiority of sentiment.

In the world that was new to Marius, as in the one he had left behind, wherever one searched for hidden causes, one found women, but women ennobled, and not debased slaves. Love reigned more than ever, except that it had more worthy inspirers. Women, who had only ever known and listened to their interior impulses, good or bad, which had once caused so much unhappiness, no longer incited men to anything but good, and no longer drove them to any but the right path;

while remaining the gentle sex, they now merited, by their nobility of soul and their intelligence, having become the initiating sex and the true guide of humankind.

The equals of men in power and knowledge, better than men in their hearts, what wives, and above all, what mothers, those regenerated women made! The true center and key of the family, the benevolent influence of a woman extended over the entire life of a man. As a child, he owed her everything; as a husband, it was from her that he incessantly drew his moral strength; as an old man, who else but a daughter could warm his old heart and still spread some joy through his final days?

That advancement, that considerable elevation of public mores, dated, above all, from the moment when the material progress of civilization had rendered existence easy for everyone and brought veritable, healthy liberty—that which, with independence from the primary needs of life, permitted the natural expansion of character and sentiment among men and women. When, with that, a freely-lavished education accessible to everyone had developed individual value without distinction of fortune or rank, how could the general level not rise to the perfect equality of rights that, in the new environment, placed a man of merit devoid of other wealth on a par with the most fortunate; that only saw dependents and courtiers among the avid and the ambitious; that led to social relationships based on human respect involving reciprocal and sincere regard?

It ought to be said that the society Marius had before his eyes belonged to the somewhat proud Celto-Latin race, which does not suffer scorn and has always been able to value human dignity in all conditions of life, instead of appreciating people entirely in terms of the money they possess.

All of that was gradually revealed to Marius, day by day, giving him a high opinion of his new fellow citizens.

"I confess," he said to the professor one evening, "that this world surpasses mine in everything, and by comparison one could deem it perfect—and yet it seems to me that it lacks something: the discordant note, the suffering, if you wish, that helps one appreciate by contrast the few joys that life still has in reserve for even the most disinherited of creatures. You're too happy here."

"That's because you're judging us from your terrestrial point of view," Alcor replied. "You still feel here as you felt on Earth, and have not yet been able to harmonize yourself with the sentiments that agitate the people of Cybele. It's as if you were to say that the Frenchmen of your own era needed, in order to feel alive, a little of the insecurity and deprivation of their prehistoric ancestors. What represents satisfaction for a savage is not the same for a civilized man, and what would have seemed to fulfill the most chimerical dreams of the debutants of civilization is simply the everyday currency of civilization at its full. Isn't everything relative? You can take it for granted that, even in the most elevated regions of a life of ease, there is never any lack of worries, chagrins and passions to drive people further on in search of a more complete happiness, which always draws further away as one pursues it."

In the meantime, though, what philanthropist of Marius' epoch would not have considered to be generous but unrealizable utopias everything that the latter saw in practice as everyday matters, so long-established that the people of the day could not understand that they could ever have been different?

Thus, the ancient and burning question of poverty had long been resolved. There were, strictly speaking, no more paupers devoid of all resources and at risk of dying of starvation. Without their being a strict communism of the State, the national or local government, the services of primary necessity—bread and fire being as indispensable as air—were available to everyone, and public refuges were available everywhere for people without their own homes.

Everywhere, existence was assured in its strictest elements, without the fortifying struggle for the other needs of life giving way to idleness and parasitism in consequence. On the contrary, that security given to the ineluctable necessities of the human condition prevented the irremediable falls to which so many deserving strugglers once succumbed, forming a kind of safety-net in which those vanquished by life could get back on their feet and recover the courage to launch themselves once again into a career.

Then again, how many elite souls, pure minds detached, so to speak, from material considerations, unskilled in matters of interest, whom the rigors of old once brought down irredeemably, shone here with a steady gleam: scientists, artists, poets, going through life in their dream, which could be accomplished without being interrupted by the anguishes of hunger!

Where the foresight of the administration—which bore no resemblance to the fallacious system bearing that name in Marius' homeland—invested its most delicate care was in the beautiful and comfortable retreats open to the elderly. In the same way that childhood has rights to the protection of all, it was deemed that the weakness of old age merited the same support. Workers whose strength was exhausted, or people of any class betrayed by fortune and arrived at the end of their career, entered one of those retreats—rural, for the most part—as a matter of right, where they found assistance, care and protection, as well as roles to fulfill appropriate to their aptitudes, not only in the community that welcomed them but outside, in councils, assemblies, ceremonies and private or public celebrations, where the presence of old people had become, in that eminently familial society, an element of experience and a necessary sanction, as well as a respectful homage to old age.

While proletarians afflicted by old age and infirmity after an existence of hard labor had once had to take responsibility for themselves or, too often, to become a burden impatiently supported by unworthy children, they now saw the doors of a new and easier existence opening to them. Here, by contrast, old age became for many of the less fortunate the happiest period of their life, in the midst of a peace, security and well-being that they had not yet known—an existence that was extinguished very gently. The exit from life, like the entrance, was no longer a suffering, and even the prospect of an imminent death did not take anything away from the joys of the present—a present that, after all, might last longer, for what age, no matter how advanced it might be, cannot reasonably see another ten years of future? And ten years of a peaceful and happy life is something worthwhile.

It is also necessary to say that an entirely new state of mind had been added to the assured and ameliorated material life: a serenity of soul liberated from any concern of interest; an elevation of thought already anticipating the imminent liberation of the immaterial element of human being; a dignity of conduct and attitude that showed old age in its most beautiful aspect and recompensed society for thus ensuring and honoring that final years of its old people's existence.

As for those who were still in the ranks of the combat of active life, the struggle for existence was no longer for them the merciless war of barbaric times in which society represented little more than a hazardous assemblage of individualities in reciprocal conflict, instead of a veritable careful collective entity with an organization equally benevolent to all its members, in which laws and public order, violently established and maintained, were based on rights that were too exclusively personal and not in the general interest—inclusive, of course, of individual interests.

Thus, for example, the question of national labor was understood inversely to the days of old. It was not the products of labor that were envisaged as the essential goal; it was the work itself, and its distribution—which is to say, the existence of its nationals and the continual circulation of wealth that primarily preoccupied the economists who had abandoned a deceptive free trade.

The strong individuality of a State did not permit the elements of its vitality to be sacrificed to the deceptive advantages of external commerce, which too often only enriched the few while exhausting the precious wells of indigenous labor. It had finally been understood that a national existence, like any other living thing, cannot subsist without regular alimentation, incessantly renewed, without a nutritive function supplied by the industrial and commercial class. In times past, sad experience had shown that a State that allows itself to become a tributary of external industry and products, without balancing that tribute with an equivalent exchange, is a State headed for ruination, doomed to perish. Anything is preferable to that continual impoverishment by foreign suction, even absolute isolation, for it is necessary above all to live.

The question of external commerce was one of the great concerns of governments, an question always complex and difficult, in which it was vitally necessary, without being deprived of necessary foreign products, to preserve national production and not to follow the errors of the economists of free trade who added together every-increasing imports and ever-decreasing exports and celebrated, as a proof of prosperity, an ever-increasing total traffic, to the benefit of foreigners and the detriment of national fortune. But since there were no longer any but small States, the difficulty of reconciling those two sorts of needs was much less serious than in the days of large heterogeneous empires. The very nature of the resources of a restricted territory limited the kinds of industry and indigenous products, and, thrown back on the different branches of commerce in imports, every state then acted with regard to others with the same logic and the same interest as a mere individual can in his household, who lives in accordance with his means and will eventually ruin himself is his annual expenditure continually exceeds his income.

That continuity of interests also provided the security of workers, who were no longer exposed to suddenly finding themselves out of work and deprived of wages because a product arriving from a distant country was on offer at a lower price. The progress of the industrialism that had once classified workers in special and tightly closed categories, outside of which there was nothing for them but a fatal loss of work and sustenance, had caused such great public misery as to serve as a lesson, and the question of providing work for everyone had become a vital issue. One no longer saw, for example, agricultural populations condemned to disappear because the products of lands on another continent, which cost nothing and were exploited mechanically, debased the profitable territorial wealth of an entire nation by lowering prices to the exclusive benefit of a few rich speculators.

It had also been recognized that low prices of the most essential things did not constitute economic progress, when the people deprived of remunerative work could not return to circulation money of which they were increasingly deprived. Does not the general advantage, on the contrary, reside in a legitimate price acquitted by all the products of labor, and spreading ease through all levels of society? The equitable remuneration that is maintained by an intelligent moderation in production, since it is excess production that creates gluts and crises, not only profits labor but also capital, which is then employed, circulating and no longer remaining immobile, unproductive and depreciating, to everyone's cost.

An insignificant difference in the sale price of a product is often sufficient to obtain a considerable one in the resale price, permitting the wages of the worker to increase. When unbridled competition leads by degrees to the lowering of everything, ending up no longer putting on the market anything but degraded products, objects lowered in value and in merit, the intervention of protective industrial laws provides a remedy, in guarding the equitable social division of resources provided by labor and thus satisfying all interests—for everything in that regard is a matter of sharing. It is not at the bottom, however, but at the top that the question of national order has to be tackled, and in order to solve it, only the State—a State worthy of the name, that is—had the necessary power and authority. To leave the market to its own devices, which has too long been mistaken for true liberty, has given all the advantages to iniquity and fraud, sacrificing honest and dutiful labor. Hence the scandal of unmerited fortunes at the expense of the poverty of the greater number; hence unsustainable disequilibrium and increasing disorder within nations.

It was the excess of that disequilibrium, threatening society with collapse, that, after cruel suffering and intolerable abuses, had finally obliged legislators also to tackle the delicate question of capital, which, departing from the just principle of property, had ended up under the old laws creating an absolute domination of money, drained and amassed entirely in one direction by virtue of the natural attraction of capital to capital, while entire populations struggled with difficulty against the primary necessities of life. That extreme situation had inevitably been produced at one time by reason of the considerable progress that had revolutionized the economic conditions of societies, by the enormous proportions that commerce and industry had attained and the irresistible force of large capital at work, gradually crushing everything established on smaller bases.

The nature of the evil had finally indicated the remedy, in the form of the legal limitation of the right to individual property, brought about by progressive taxation imposed on acquired personal fortunes above a certain level, at a small proportion to begin with but subsequently multiplying to the point of making it impossible for too many millions to accumulate in the same hands. The tyranny of capital was thus destroyed, or at least considerably attenuated, while the inevitable subsequent movement of money profited the labor that saw the movement in question.

The new situation required new laws: truly reparative laws that broke the omnipotence of money men devoid of a fatherland, and, by the same token, re-elevated public mores that had been too long debased; laws entirely in favor of the middle class, in which the sinews and honor of a nation reside, and which was reconstituted healthier and more energetic than ever, after having nearly sunk between the two extreme states of excessive wealth and profound poverty to which the domination of capital had led. Nothing, in any case, was hindered by the fall of the financial oligarchy, for association continued to render the costliest enterprises entirely practicable.

How far it was from the time when States burden with excessive debt, at the mercy of a few financiers, had balanced their budgets by means of expedients, when they were not irresistible drawn toward collapse and bankruptcy! State finances had become, on the contrary, an immense reservoir incessantly filled, from which money was returned directly to the people in the form of considerable public works, and also in enormous expenditure on public festivals and ceremonies, such as had never been seen before—something akin to the natural distribution of fecund waters that evaporate and rise up from the ground only to return as benevolent dew.

It is true that everything concurred in alimenting that ever-increasing wealth of States that had no more ruinous administration or absorbing armies, and whose public coffers were filed by the increasing receipts of progressive taxation, which it was necessary to employ at any price if they wanted to avoid a veritable inundation of capital.

As is evident, it was not precisely the regime of which Auguste Comte had dreamed when he made capital the providence of the worker and banking a kind of priesthood, but that powerful mind was rich enough in great and noble ideas for him to be mistaken on that occasion without discredit, in forgetting that those who make a profession of finance are generally financiers—which is to say, men whose role tends to one single and unique goal: the incessant accumulation of capital, always absorbing with an attractive force that increases by reason of the capital already centralized, without paying any further attention to producers, whose fruits are trampled by a blind mechanism, pressured to render even more than they can give.

The role of Providence was thus filled, not by the champions of personal interest, but by the superior organ of society, by a power that guided with a view to absolute general order. That which private interest and individual initiative could not attempt, the State undertook, whenever there was some great national advantage to be gained, or even, sometimes, a public sacrifice or a useful but costly experiment to be carried out.

It was thus that, among others, one of the most curious enterprises of the epoch was realized. In an era when a scientific agriculture that had subjugated the entire vegetable realm and utilized even the most ingrate regions of soil, and which even did without soil in order to fabricate artificial crops in special factories, in certain places, prompted by some strange caprice, vast spaces rigorously protected from human action had been returned to nature: free domains in which plants and animals did not take long to go their own way and resume characteristics very different from those imposed by centuries of methodical culture.

People who were admitted into these enclosures brought back therefrom an extraordinary impression, something like a rejuvenation of thought, a remembrance of sentiments that steeped the mind and heart once again in the forsaken springs of primitive life. It was as if those ultra-civilized individuals, after having exhausted all the forms of art, had only been able to encounter new beauties and awaken new and profound sensations by returning to the point of departure, in discovering simple Nature.

They had left that simple Nature so far behind that it had been completely forgotten. There was no vegetable or animal species that had not been transplanted everywhere that it might encounter viable conditions, and thus been profoundly modified by innumerable and bizarre varieties, which never ceased to astonish Marius and throw all his knowledge of natural history into disarray. The products of culture had been multiplied tenfold on Cybele since the backward times that the Earth was still going through. People knew how to utilize and direct all the natural elements, by distributing humidity or heat everywhere that it was required, and mastering the scourges that had once been the terror of rural populations. Thus, in the electricity that made thunder and hail, they had been able to recognize an inexhaustible source of life, seek it out instead of fleeing from it, and distribute it in the soil, where its effluvia animated intensively everything that was sown there.

Understandably, such agricultural riches, not to mention the other products of human industry, had been able to facilitate existence and spread well-being everywhere; thus, societies progressively less constrained by the anxiety of assuring the primary needs of life had taken giant steps along the road of social improvement, the first indications of which had scarcely been sketched out on Cybele's younger sister. A nation was now an entity organized in a superior manner and solid in all its members. Human collectivities were regulated by much broader laws, much more extensive needs and much wider views than in the distant times of ancient particularism, when the wisdom of a Lycurgus had demanded that, repudiating all wealth, every citizen should build his humble dwelling with his own hands.

The organic characteristics of the social entity, becoming increasingly accentuated in a centuries-long development that is reminiscent of the successive improvements of animal life, had not, it is true, ever been entirely unknown, but while those characteristics had been barely suspected during the initial phases, they had been confirmed and completed since, and everyone understood the extent to which they were merely units within one or another organ of the great national entity composed of all the citizens of the same State. It was an effective and tangible reality, no longer the vague tendency that had once left the field free for many more or less perspicacious interpretations.

Already, anticipating that distant future, there had been the praiseworthy attempt of the Saint-Simonians, setting out to furnish an example of a perfect community in which each member had to fulfill the collective function best suited to his natural dispositions. The error of those hasty precursors, however, was, firstly to misunderstand their epoch, and secondly to overshoot the envisaged target by too complete an effacement of the human personality, which needs to be maintained in its entirety, with its own individual life, even when adapted as perfectly as possible to the role that it fulfills in the much larger and very different existence of the great social organism.

Certainly, when, for his part, a Fourier pursued his Phalansterian idea and also determined the place and precise role that each individual had to play, in accordance with natural aptitudes, in the perfected society of his dreams, he had likewise been guided by the profound sentiment of social mutuality and collective organization inclined by passionate attraction, making all the members of a community into a solid and harmonious whole. His great imagination had doubtless gone astray, though, when he formulated his celebrated theory of the four movements, which gave exactly eighty thousand years to the existence of humankind: six thousand years of struggle and strife comprising its childhood, seventy thousand years of social unity and happiness its youth and prime, and four thousand years of decadence making up the final phase of human destiny. And yet, there was the dominant idea therein of solidarity, extending as far as the concept of humankind considered as a unique individual traversing, like all living things, the various natural periods of growth, adulthood, maturity and final deterioration.

The deadly contagion of English ideas in politics had lasted too long. England had been allowed to remain a collection of ambitious and egotistical individuals tolerating one another as best they could—but perfect societies had finally been formed whose well-balanced and infallible mechanisms were often beyond Marius' comprehension but nevertheless commanded his admiration.

What he saw, in the meantime, was that, just every animate being is really and literally only a collective of other beings, which are born, live and die as so many individuals—an association of microscopic laborers agitating, struggling and producing in the special roles devolved to each of them in the milieu of the organic ensemble of the veritable social edifice that every living being represents from that viewpoint—so the highly organized societies of Cybele constituted immense

145

collective entities, in which individuals tightly knitted together, while each conserving a personality of their own, felt dependent on another inclusive individuality: a life higher than the narrow personal existence that was almost everything for the people that Marius had left on Earth.

VIII

When the desire took hold of curiosity-seekers to take their mind for a stroll through ages past, it was a magnificent tableau of general history that was presented to the human race of Cybele, whose written annals went back more than a hundred centuries. It is time to say that Marius, thanks to Professor Alcor and before even being initiated into modern language, had been able to satisfy the legitimate desire that he had testified from the very beginning to acquaint himself with the principal facts of forgotten epochs, the greater number of which represented the future of his own Earth, lagging six thousand years behind the exactly similar history of Cybele.

The moment when Alcor, equipped with a large volume, had offered to instruct him in that prophetic past had left an ineradicable impression on him. He had seemed to see him as another Janus, holding the book of destiny in his hand.

The haste that Marius was in to learn, before anything else, the events immediately following the epoch in which he had lived, especially in his own country, is understandable, and it was with a patriotic anxiety that he saw the book the professor was holding open at the page where the fateful revelations commenced.

At the time when his terrestrial existence had been interrupted, everyone had already been able to see that the disequilibrium into which the inordinate preponderance of Germany had thrown Europe could not last long. Black clouds were already rising on the political horizon, concealing thunder and lightning. Between those menacing symptoms and the moment when the storm would burst, a few more years might pass, but the long-contained tempest would only become more inevitable and the conflagration more terrible. That was what everyone anticipated, including Marius; so, the first question that he addressed to the professor was clear and precise:

"Who won?"

But Alcor, as a methodical and conscientious historian, insisted on beginning at the beginning. He recalled the arrogant pretensions of Germany, so convinced of her future; the effacement of other States subject to an irresistible ascendancy, or even making themselves humble satellites of the foremost military power in Europe; the isolation of France, which kept quiet but collected herself, worked, strove and reconstituted her strength.

The people whom Bismarck had thought irredeemably crushed and ruined soon picked themselves up, more energetic and redoubtable than ever. After having been defeated by superior numbers and armaments, they reorganized an army that was also formidable in its numbers and armaments, and the army in question was not only their force and security, but more than that.

In those times of profound commotion, in which an impure mud had been seen rising from the depths, which troubled the very summits of society, while waiting for that mud to sink back into its sewers, one thing remained intact, and that was the French army, a school of duty, patriotism, disciple and abnegation. The army was not attained by that filth, and preserved the future within while it guaranteed the present against any and all enemies without. It was Bismarck's turn to fear.

That overrated great man, whose genius had consisted primarily in disposing of four times as many soldiers as his adversaries could gather, in order subsequently to play the facile role of the stronger, was now revealed in his true light: the living antithesis of the likes of Frederick the Great and Napoléon. An old fox always trembling in his skin of reiterated insolence, he could only seek to make any alliances he could, at any price, even with the humblest States of Europe, in order to oppose France once again with the crushing disproportion of numbers that had previously constituted his superiority.

Germany and the Triple Alliance were soon nothing but a camp where more than ten million soldiers were relentlessly drilled. Thanks to its politics, Europe retreated further every day into barbarity. Bismarck could disappear or be removed from the world stage, but the work of the baneful man still remained, and could only be undone by war. One day or another, Germany would have to pay the sinister debt of blood incurred by the premature birth of a German unity that would have come into the world more viable and better conformed without him.

Increasingly impoverished by unsustainable military budgets, Europe saw the inevitable moment of its ruination approaching, and anything became preferable to the Bismarckian peace, which was worse than war, and even defeat. It was necessary to end it, at all costs, and since France not longer allowed herself to be compromised imprudently, the first pretext to come along would serve for an attack on France.

That is what would soon have arrived if, on the far side of Europe, a powerful sovereign with vast and noble designs had not adopted an attitude at that juncture more worrying for the allies.[24] The danger that emerged in the east suddenly laid siege to those who, shortly before, were deliberating a westward surge, and for more long years, the millions of soldiers continued, weapons in hand, to impoverish and enervate the nations, none of which dared take the terrible responsibility of first giving the word to the artillery.

Just as a sky saturated with electricity that has no issue cannot endure without the thunder finally bursting forth, how-

---

[24] In 1890 the Tsar of Russia was Alexander III, who, although more conservative than his liberally-minded father—whom he had succeeded in 1881—fought no wars and acquired a reputation as a peacemaker; he did, however, believe that the best way to avoid war was to be prepared for it, and made a point not only of keeping large number of troops stationed close to the German border but also of establishing cordial relations with France. The scenario sketched out by Alhaiza was, therefore, plausible at the time, although things actually worked out very differently.

ever, a political situation as stormy as Europe's could not relax without an explosion, and fatally, by inevitable necessity, it would only take the slightest spark to unleash a frightful conflagration. Without the determining cause that everyone anticipated and feared having yet appeared, as in the hours before a storm, a somber presentiment and a mute anguish gripped the breathless peoples, creating a kind of great silence on all sides.

Public life seemed to be in suspense, without anyone knowing why, gazes flickering anxiously toward the frontiers; and no Frenchman was surprised when hasty dispatches suddenly informed everyone that France as at war because a petty prince had taken up arms in the Balkans, and that, at a stroke, on the eastern frontiers of Austria and Germany, those two powers had found themselves at odds with Russia. Something akin to an electric shock ran through the country from end to end. Everyone fund himself on his feet, ready to march.

"Enough, enough!" cried Marius, standing up, his gaze on fire. "Let me go—I feel that my place is no longer here."

"Calm down, my excitable friend, calm down! Have you already forgotten that this is history, six thousand years old."

Slapping his forehead, the young man sat down, in order, so to speak, to drink in Alcor's words, which related briefly the still-memorable fact of the final crushing of the central powers, caught between the double avalanche of the French and Russian armies, overturning everything before them until they came to fraternize in the very heart of enemy territory.

At that point, a general peace treaty was concluded, and imposed on the entirety of Europe, on a larger scale and more beautiful than history had ever known. Rising above all wrath, all narrow ambition and all human passion, the great emperor, the worthy arbiter of the cause of twenty nations, the ally of France whose soul was at the level of her own, convened the representatives of the powers at the moment of victory, fairly assessed their aspirations and rights, and laid the foundations of a new order.

For the first time in the annals of the world, an all-powerful victor was seen to put his sovereign will in the service of the common good; more than that, to turn his omnipotence against himself by founding the liberal government of his people, basing a truly durable peace not on force and arbitrary power but on justice; to proclaim that Europe must no longer be anything but one great family, that each member of that family ought to recover the integrity of its natural frontiers and means of existence; and finally, to communicate to all the noble ardor that animated him. No congress had ever had such a task to fulfill. The old diplomats found themselves utterly disorientated, but the great work was nevertheless carried to a successful conclusion, in spite of a certain amount of inevitable but impotent resistance.

The German empire, the excessive expansion of which had disrupted the necessary European equilibrium, was divided into two distinct states: Prussia to the north and Germany, properly speaking, to the south. Austria, which had for a long time only had an artificial homogeneity, gave birth to two other independent states, Hungary and Bohemia, surrendering to Germany the greater part of its Germanic population and the Tyrol to Switzerland, while Trieste and Illyria formed, along with Montenegro, an Adriatic state of similar size to that of Serbia, augmented by Bosnia, and that of Bulgaria and Rumelia, rendered independent and guardian of Constantinople. To one side, Romania grew by several districts, and to the south, Greece finally annexed Macedonia and Epirus, as well as Candia, Cyprus and Rhodes, along with the entire archipelago—which is to say that nothing remained of European Turkey. This time, the sick man was really dead. Turkey's name and the shadow of its former power only survived in Asia Minor, and coveted Byzantium was no longer anything but the great capital of a very tiny kingdom.

In the midst of such a fine zeal for the principle of nationality, there was even talk of reconstituting Poland. Unfortunately, the same intestinal causes of the fall of that heroic but worm-eaten country opposed the possibility of it ever being able to stand on its own feet, and it was necessary to renounce that generous idea.

The other States remained almost as they were before, except that Alsace-Lorraine and the Norman islands returned to the arms of the motherland, and Denmark resumed possession of Schleswig. Scandinavia, Great Britain, Spain and Italy experienced no significant change, any more than Holland, Belgium and Portugal, whose smaller size did not render them any more unfortunate—quite the contrary.

As for Russia, which had a great and laborious mission to fulfill on the Asiatic side, she showed the most magnanimous disinterest in the face of all hostility, at least with regard to Europe. She was destined soon to recover another territory, that of British India, where she was to reign shortly afterwards. By renouncing in such a solemn manner the testament of Peter the Great, she was the first to set the great example of the spirit of concord that she demanded of all.

In addition, she and her ally, France, crowned the magnificent achievement of universal peace by imposing on it, to the great advantage of liberty, with absolute frankness, the formal neutrality of all the seas—and, in consequence, all the straits and passages that were henceforth to be safe routes protected from the enterprises of the enemies of general prosperity. Thus, the Bosphorus and Suez became common property, and the bunkers of Gibraltar were blown to smithereens, in order that something unprecedented and unexpected could be seen: a continental war turning out to the disadvantage of England, which had shared in the defeat of Germany, whose side she had taken because she believed it to be the stronger.

It was high time for the Mediterranean nations to free themselves from the shame of seeing the two exits from their sea guarded by the cannons of a northern power. It goes without saying that Albion did not fail to show her fangs, but she had to be content with having shown them. The time had definitely past for her always to exploit continental discords to her advantage.

That last great European war had, however, been the most terrible slaughter ever to bloody the Earth. Well worthy of the barbaric times of which it fortunately marked the end, it left an imperishable memory of horror that made a considerable subsequent contribution to strengthening the new political order that a sovereign but prescient and beneficent will had been able to create, at the very moment when it responded to the decisive evolution of societies toward universal peace and fraternity. Time was, in fact, to prove by the happiness and unity of peoples the justice and nobility of vision of the glorious arbiter of that new beginning in the destiny of Europe.

The immense efforts that all sides wasted in continual bellicose preparations were to have other goals. Of the innumerable legions of old, only limited squadrons and internal police forces were conserved. Work and competition took off with a surge that soon gave full flight to all possible prosperity to each of the members of the great European family.

It was not only Europe, but all the continents, that gradually benefited from the new order of things. By the same token, colonization acquired a new impetus and character. It was no longer as predators that emigrants went to occupy countries that were still barbaric; it was as a protector and a monitor of inferior or backward races that regenerated Europe imposed itself, solely by virtue of the ascendancy of its superiority and its civilization, on the destiny of the world. It was no longer the era of a so-called anti-slavery movement dissimulating avid covetousness and serving as a pretext for the most brutal invasions. The Europeans of those times were only obedient to honorable motives and a genuine humanity.

On that terrain too, England was gradually obliged to surrender the considerable advance she had obtained at a time when she alone had free hands; English hunger was restricted to normal rations, and that contributed more than a little to the further accentuation of her jealous exclusivity and irreconcilable egotism. It was necessary to accept the isolation of an increasingly intransigent England, which remained outside the entente that was later to constitute the great European Confederation.

In the twenty-second century A.D. continental Europe, also with the exception of Russia, which was too vast and too divergent in her interests to accept that community, presented the aspect of a single great country in which each component State preserved its individuality as entirely as before, but found in the federative link the precious guarantee of peace, not only internally but externally—for other great rival human families would still have been able to imperil world peace.

In fact, in the same century of the monumental history that Alcor as summarizing in broad strokes for the edification of his your terrestrial friend, mention was made of another war, in which, let us hasten to say, the Europeans were victorious: a primarily naval war this time, fought between the European Confederation and the North American Union, a country that then united two hundred million ever-enterprising Yankees more and more invasive of all points of a planet that was definitely too narrow for human covetousness. In the same way that John Bull had made war on China in order to constrain her to purchase his murderous opium, Uncle Sam attempted to impose, also by force, his trichinous meat, his artificial aliments and his intoxicating beverages. The American Republicans had remained faithful to the great principles that distinguished their ancestors, of which the first and foremost was still: Make money, honestly if you can, but make money.

It is necessary to say, too, that in spite of the memories of profound gratitude that continued to make Russia beloved, the very force of circumstance created dangerous dissidences, and it was feared more than once that the immense empire of the Tsars might be for free Europe another Macedonia conquering a Greece impotent to withstand its assault. The same history taught, however, that nothing like that happened, doubtless first of all because the European family remained united, and secondly because the Russian colossus was eventually to collapse under its own weight and be divided in its turn into a number of distinct States—for such is the tendency of advanced civilization.

The various confederated states of Europe were also to give birth, later on, to increasingly numerous concentrations, until the realization of the perfect national individualities permitted the best development of institutions and human faculties, without prejudice to the federative groupings that gave satisfaction in their turn to great general interests. The system was, in any case, not new in the world; for a long time the wise people of Switzerland had provided a profitable example.

It is only natural that, of all the revelations thus offered by the ancient history of Cybele to the curiosity of the young Terran, the ones that captivated him most were the events nearest to his own epoch. He never wearied of returning to the pages that presented to his mind the image of that renewed France, that pacified and prosperous Europe, united in almost the same fashion as the provinces of a State, in which tighter and tighter links brought peoples closer together that so many passions and ambitious had divided for so long.

It pleased him to consider, so to speak, as compatriots Spaniards with elevated and noble sentiments, artistic and clever Italians, even Germans, for whom he no longer felt any rancor, bringing into the new great family their serious qualities, profound sentiments and philosophical genius—together with the Slavs, the Flemish, the Czechs, the Magyars, the Scandinavians and the Hellenes, all with their particular natures, their merits, and even their faults, pardonable and often likeable, who comprised the members of the foremost human family on the globe, completing one another and being reciprocally valued.

Thus had been crossed one of the principal stages leading to the superior progress whose highest realization Marius had found on his new planet, too distant from his own way of being for him to be able to adapt himself to it completely. How much more comfortable he would have felt in a world that was only a little in advance of his own, and had only realized aspirations accessible to his contemporaries!

It was, therefore, to the chapter that told him about the century of our grandchildren that he returned most gladly. He often took up the world map of the twentieth century, where modifications no less important could be seen on another continent than his own: with regard to the imposing group of the United States, another, a more northerly confederation that seemed desirous of rivaling the immense Republic, and within that confederation, a schism that informed him that the French element of Canada, unable to reach a satisfactory accommodation with the Anglo-Saxon element, and having become prolific by its own efforts, numerous enough and strong enough to demand respect, had been able to take back its independence and constitute a distinct nationality.

On the other hand, for their part, the Indo-Spaniards of Mexico, Cuba and Central America formed a homogenous and consistent union whose vitality was considerable increased, along with that of other American States located further southwards, by the considerable movement through the great maritime highway of Panama, finally wide open and permitting ships to travel in a direct line from the coasts of Europe to those of the Far East.

Asia itself had progressed and reorganized like the rest of the world, as had Central Africa, where the negro race of the tropical regions lived meekly and happily under the governmental tutelage of the European race, now just and humane.

Africa was, in fact, the most extensively transformed of the five continents, with its new population composed of the three principal human races. To the north and south, almost linking up to the east and west by the occupation of the coastal region, the white race ruled; in the center, throughout the torrid region, the pure negro race could still be seen; and between those two different domains, in an extension representing the largest fraction of the African continent, a mixed hybrid race gradually formed, to which subsequent centuries gave the fusion and unity of a distinct race adapted to the climate and combining the aptitudes and qualities of the white and black races.

What Marius always reverted to for preference, however, in order to indulge himself for long intervals, was the edifying political geography of the Old World, which showed him a Europe repartitioned in conformity with its veritable nationalities, overflowing externally via Asiatic Russia, a Spanish Morocco, an Italian Tripolitaine, an Egypt Hellenized as in the time of the Ptolemies, and finally, an increasingly French Algeria—an Algeria that was preparing to become the new France, and where fate had thrown him, Marius...which brought him back to melancholy reflection on his situation as a exile in space and time, sighing in remembrance of the happy days when, near to his Jeanne on his backward planet, he had been ignorant of all the fine things that he had learned on ultra-progressive Cybele.

A historical field so vast and so various permitted the most capricious and boldest flights through peoples and civilizations presenting the most curious connections, and visibly displaying the uninterrupted chain of ever-increasing human progress. That was an inexhaustible aliment for the conversations in which the three friends indulged themselves on a daily basis.

"A mind truly impassioned by human history," Marius observed one evening, "and enclosed in the short duration of an ordinary life, is certainly obliged to regret occasionally that the brevity of existence allows him to see so little of this marvelous developments with one's own eyes."

"Undoubtedly," replied the professor. "That is why there are some such individuals, impassioned by history and science, who sacrifice their affections and their habits and divide between a long sequence of centuries the time and strength devolved to human individuality."

"I beg your pardon, my dear Alcor, but I don't understand what you mean."

"Alcor is referring to the inmates of that we call the Sleepers' Hostel," Namo put in, "in which hundreds of individuals submit to a combination of lethargic and fakiric slumber, awaiting in their cubicles, while carefully monitored, the periodic dates of their temporary awakenings. These people, some of who are nearly a thousand years old, and who are retained by a special preparation in a state of latent life, almost corpse-like in appearance, are only returned to active existence at long intervals of time. They then re-enter society—a society always new to them, it goes without saying—where they find, and not invariably, no other family but more or less distant descendants of their own posterity.

"They do, however, recover their memories of old, their knowledge of the people and things of another time, and their passion for the study of historical, anthropological and socio-logical sciences, and after spending a year or two adding to their former baggage everything that they can learn from the new world that has traveled a long road without them; after having found their footing in a society that educates them, and which they charm in their turn with tales of another age; and after having seen transformed cities, recognizing monuments of their times older than they are, they return to the darkness of their centuries-long sleep for a further interval.

"Establishment of that sort have a skilled staff, who pre-pare the volunteers who present themselves, render them un-conscious and bury them in a kind of cell in the form of a sar-cophagus, where they sometimes wait for fifty or a hundred years for a further awakening, keeping on their person the manuscript of the notes and impressions of their voyage through the centuries."

Marius remembered then that he had heard mention of Indian fakirs who were able to take on a death-like appearance and have themselves resuscitated after a certain time. That method, profoundly studied and subjected to scientific exper-imentation, had produced marvelous results. It was possible to suspend the functions of life almost indefinitely, or, rather, slow them down to an imperceptible minimum, but without completely stopping a molecular circulation of which the ab-solute prevention would have been true death. It was also pos-sible, on the other hand, to reactivate the vital mechanisms and temporarily renew, in the old and the feeble, all the ardor of youth and health, using them up without losing any of the integrity of the vital forces with which the human species in endowed.

For those who submitted to the regime of periodic torpor, from slumber to slumber and rebirth to rebirth, considerable time elapsed, and the eighty or ninety years of a normal human lifespan could be stored up in order to be released in several fractions in the course of a long sequence of centuries.

When we say eighty years, we are only referring to the usual median of human life on Cybele, for the duration of existence, considerably augmented by a perfect wellbeing, and especially by an almost entirely vegetarian diet, as preferred by human nutritional organs, often attained and surpassed a century and a half without it being a prodigy—which it to say that the potential duration of human life had been doubled.

Our friend had nor neglected to read in the periodicals of his own time the story told by the Viennese doctor Honiberger of his sojourn as a guest of the Rajah of Lahore, during which he had witnessed a fact of that order.[25] The doctor had followed, day by day, the scrupulous preparations made by one of those fakirs, his methodical training by abstinence and the gradual slowing down of the respiration, the clearing and drying of the stomach, the obstruction of the throat by means of his backward-folded tongue, and his hypnotization, after which his nostrils, mouth and ears were sealed with wax; and finally, his burial in that extreme state of catalepsy. When, after several months, the yogi—that being the name given to fakirs given to the curious practice in question—had been disinterred, he had every appearance of a cadaver, but after being copiously washed with warm water, and his mouth and nostrils had been unblocked, and he had been armed up by friction, the yogi was resuscitated. Several European witnesses, including Jacolliot, Crookes and many others, also affirmed

---

[25] John Martin Honiberger's memoirs, published in English as *Thirty-Five Years in the East* (1852), did report this oft-repeated anecdote, but he did not claim to have witnessed the prodigy himself.

the reality of the resurrection of such seemingly dead individuals.[26]

Reason should not, in any case, be shocked by these effects of artificially-produced lethargy, when there are frequent examples of natural lethargies often lasting for weeks or months. Is not the prolonged torpor of hibernation a normal and regular routine for certain animals? What is one to think, for example, of the almost indefinite suspension of life in those strange insects, the rotifers, which can retain for an unlimited period the appearance of desiccated husks, but which a drop of water is sufficient to reanimate and resuscitate until dryness makes them into insensible and inert objects again?

What nature had indicated as a possibility for a few living things, science had realized in human beings. After a few successfully-concluded experiments, having oneself put into a state of torpor in order to be returned to active life later became a current practice. Lethargy became fashionable. For the sake of a chagrin or a mistake, a yes or a no, people departed, after having put their affairs in order, for one of those stations of vital repose, and postponed the resumption of their destiny for ten, twenty or more years.

One could entrust oneself in total security to the skilful operators of the establishments in question, where the greatest vigilance was maintained. Every sarcophagus contained a volunteer, bearing an indicative and explicative label, as well as a register in which the friends of the buried individual could write their messages, their good wishes, the missions that they requested them to undertake in times to come, and information of every sort that the interested party would find on awakening. In addition, the body itself was often visited and subjected to expert examination by supervisors, who reanimated the

---

[26] William Crookes did not affirm any such thing on the basis of personal experience, and if Louis Jacolliot ever did, it would only provide one more instance of his notorious unreliability.

subject immediately at the first symptom of any permanent vital arrest.

"The majority of the sleepers in our establishment in Algiers," Marius' young friend continued, "are only there for a relatively short time, but there are some whose express desire is not to be awakened until the last possible moment. Some, doubtless in despair or incurable victims of spleen, have had recourse to lethargic slumber as if they were committing suicide. Others undertake intensive lethargy as a way of showing off, or simple as a game of chance. They want to go further than the common run of sleepers; it's a celebrity, like any other. They've wagered that they can endure an uninterrupted temporary death for an entire century, and have staked their self-respect on winning their bet.

"One sees friends, couples in love, and entire families accomplishing such extraordinary odysseys together, sleeping and waking for the same intervals. Those approach the matter in a more sociable and more entertaining fashion, sharing all the vicissitudes of the voyage. There is no shortage of advanced minds, misunderstood authors who think that they have been born before their time and prefer to come back to produce their work at a later date, when the world is better able to appreciate and reward their merit. Finally, there are patients who have donated themselves out of pure devotion to science, and who remain at the discretion of experimenters.

"Strangely enough, there are people who get a taste for the practice, who become passionate about it, either because the exotic sleep has its mysterious dreams, or because those resuscitated in the midst of a world different from everything they love fall victim to ennui and refer to return to their peaceful chrysalis. For example, some of our more ancient sleepers acquire an exceptional importance when we celebrate the centenaries of our great men. It's rare that one does not see at such celebrations a few resuscitated contemporaries of our hero, sometimes even having known him, and you'll understand how precious and gripping the testimony of those revenants of past centuries becomes at the most solemn moments of the ceremony.

"It's regrettable than none of our lethargics is from the epoch that corresponds to your own; otherwise we would doubtless already have asked for and obtained the favor of introducing you to one of your Cybelean contemporaries. However, a life, even reanimated from such an extreme latent state, is nevertheless only one life, which has its precise limits of strength and function, and it is already very difficult to furnish a career of ten or twelve centuries. We therefore ask you to be content with the next opportunity, which will soon present itself, to see someone resuscitated who is only seven or eight hundred years old."

All these details kindly given to Marius, to which the young man listened attentively, appeared to interest him even more than the other novelties of every sort that he encountered every day—and when he took his leave of them, his two friends remarked that he seemed very pensive and preoccupied, like a man pursued by some obsessive idea.

IX

The active existence into which Marius had entered provided a fortunate diversion from the black thoughts to which he would have abandoned himself entirely had he not been taken out of himself, not only by his professional duties but above all by the great care taken by his excellent friends, Alcor and Namo, to keep on distracting him by offering new aliments to his curiosity.

In spite of everything, however, the daily sight of the amiable Junie, even though he had the courage to encounter her without apparent disturbance, reminded him of his sweet beloved, and continued to maintain the wound in his heart, which would doubtless never scar over. Thus, he seized all possible pretexts to avoid, as much as possible, the infernal torment, neglected by Dante, of contemplating the cherished featured and hearing the beloved voice of his Jeanne, and remaining the impassive witness of the insolent happiness of a detested rival.

However hard poor Marius tried, however, the moments of unconsciousness when he could no longer distinguish the present and the past, Cybele and Earth, continued to recur. When that happened, it was no longer Junie but Jeanne who was there, and when Cam came in, radiant with happiness, all his blood congealed, and he got up and left in a hurry, his head and heart turned upside down for the entire day.

Then, he resolved to leave the house and go to live somewhere far away—but whenever he tried to talk about leaving, stammering poor excuses, a touching word from Namo—who was becoming increasingly attached to him—and, by an inexplicable contradiction, the very thought that he would no longer be able to contemplate the deceptive image that was torturing him, held him back and prevented him from hastening the denouement.

"If it's the desire to see this unknown country that's nagging you," his young friend said to him one day, "we made a plan some time ago to undertake a long voyage that would permit us to test out the navigational qualities of a new airship, which we've acquired, like everyone else, and I'm counting on your coming with us. It won't be on the sea that we'll be traveling this time, as in our last expedition, during which we obtained the joy of meeting you; it will be through the air, and we hope at least to make a tour of Old Europe in that fashion before returning to Algiers.

Such a proposal was by no means unwelcome to the troubled and tormented mind of the young man, and it was with a marked eagerness that he greeted Namo's project and offered to be part of it. Delighted by this enthusiasm, the latter hastened he preparations for the interesting voyage. Soon, Alcor, Namo and Marius were talking about nothing else.

As we know, because menacing symptoms were presaging the imminent collapse of the last major sheets of Austral ice, the dominant preoccupation of the inhabitants of Cybele was the search for the best means of escaping the inevitably cataclysm. Already, the summits of the highest mountains were being crowned with habitations, and populous cities surrounded by high walls, erected in haste, in order to withstand, if necessary, a supreme assault in case the diluvian waves reached those heights. Panic was thus beginning to take possession of all minds.

The strangest rumors were spreading in all directions, emerging from the most insensate ideas, to the point where the plan was proposed of escaping implacable fate by a grandiose and titanic suicide—that of the planet itself, which, by means of a few shafts filled with nihilite, would be blown up and scattered through space as dust. Such was the general exasperation that the project gained new partisans every day. Those lunatics did not hesitate to evoke the heroic example of the other planet that might have been blown up in a similar fashion, the scattered debris of which astronomers now counted piece by piece between the orbits of Mars and Jupiter.

The greater number, however, clung to a courageous resignation, putting their last and most reasonable hope in the employment of the aerial vessels whose use was so widespread. At the last moment, there would still be time to launch forth in airships, carrying everything possible to confront a long sojourn in the atmosphere, until they could land safe and sound in locations that the cataclysm would leave definitively uncovered.

That exciting prospect was equivalent in its measure to the extraordinary catastrophe that was in preparation: one the one hand, the unleashed ocean sweeping the entire extent of the face of the continents, and on the other a compact cloud of aerial ships rising simultaneously from all the points of the globe, carrying into the air a entire castaway human race. It was easily a match for Noah's famous Ark, which had only saved one family.

That was why so many aerial machines were being constructed everywhere, including the large airship of which Namo wanted to carry out a serious trial, presently lodged in a vast hangar built a short distance from our friends' house.

In the course of the scrupulous preparations that an enterprise of that magnitude demanded, Marius had abundant leisure to have explained to him and to understand the theory of aerial navigation as it had once been applied in France—for aerostatics had remained a French invention until the end, a short time after his own epoch, which represented a respectable antiquity for the world of Cybele.

From the day when the progress of science had permitted the condensation of very light gases in the granular form of slight weight and volume, and the possession of accumulators of electric force of sufficient power, the problem of the direction of aerostats had had the necessary elements for its practical resolution. Since then, the progress of science had been able to provide improved gaseous condensates and increasingly powerful motors, but the principle of the propulsion of aerial machines had remained the same. The essential condition of specific weight, once so extensively discussed, was not the absolute prerogative of the lighter-than-air balloons of the lower atmosphere, or of heavier machines; it lay between the two extremes—which is to say, in a specific weight varying from lighter to heavier than the atmospheric environment, modeled not on birds but on fish, allowing for the difference of the density of the fluids in which the fish or the airship had to sustain itself and through which it had to move.

It stands to reason that in order effectively to vanquish the resistance of the aerial environment, subject to so many unforeseen disturbances, the superiority of the weight of the apparatus, considered as a projectile providing its own impetus, is an imposing necessity. With an aerostat merely equal in weight to the layer of air that carries it, the force of penetration remains within narrow limits, its effects annulled by currents whose own speed exceeds that of the impulsion of the apparatus, carrying the latter in a direction different from that of it heading, which is almost always the case. On the other hand, an apparatus of variable weight, but which is obliged to maneuver on departure and on arrival in a vertical direction, avoiding any violent impact, must also be able to travel like ordinary aerostats.

Well, all these conditions were perfectly met by an airship that carried with it, at a minimum weight, a large provision of gasifiable matter—something akin to a powder capable of an immense gaseous expansion. When the little laboratory of the platform sent the gas it produced through its tubes into the body of the balloon, the apparatus rose up; when the mechanic opened the valve, it descended, and that happened at will, ensuring a long potential sequence of vertical movements. As for horizontal impulsion, a powerful propeller placed at the front of the apparatus, moved by the force stored in the electrical accumulators, drew it along with a rapidity soon augmented by a greater power of penetration by means of a slight increase in weight brought about by a release of gas, without provoking a descent so long as the force of projection was in equilibrium with the increase in weight, as it is for any projectile sustained by a sufficient initial force.

166

At the most, it transpired that the apparatus, alternately lightened and increased in weight by the actions of the mechanic, was animated by the undulatory movement so frequent in the flight of birds. Even that slight difference of specific weight between the airship and the surrounding air was sufficient, however, for it, impelled by the considerable power of its engine, to be able to advance easily in spite of winds and contrary currents. As for imposing direction, a vast rudder in the form of a fish's tail, mobile in all directions, gave it complete control, either by inclining to the left or the right for lateral movements, or by reverting to the horizontal and striking the air vertically to make the apparatus rise obliquely and counterbalance, if necessary, descendant movements. All of that was controlled by means of a few levers placed under the pilot's hands, as easily as a ship or a locomotive.

To these principal organs, a few others had been added, less essential but also having their utility, such as wings and ailerons that opened at opportune moments and had the same role as the feathers of an arrow.

Naturally, these new conditions had necessitated an appropriate construction and the adoption of a kind of skeleton, of slight weight, to be sure, but sufficient in its consistency to maintain its fixity without taking account of the balloon, which was supported by its own membranes and was furled once at rest in the middle of the apparatus, like a ship's sail.

The veritably practical direction of aerostats had been realized, as is evident, on bases quite different from those already given Dupuy de Lôme a partial result,[27] and which

---

[27] The naval architect Henri Dupuy de Lôme (1816-1885) was commissioned by the French government to design a navigable airship, and he did, indeed, produce one in 1872, named after himself, powered by a 2 horsepower engine and capable of carrying eight passengers at a speed of 10 kilometers an hour, but it remained very vulnerable to atmospheric disturbances. Arthur Krebs and Constatin Renard subsequently produced another model for the French army, *La France*, in 1884,

Krebs and Renard had taken up with greater precision, but without being able to obtain a real solution to the problem.

Needless to say, the airship that was about to receive our voyagers was constructed on the best and latest model of the epoch, in which must effort had been put into improving those precious machines. Thanks to its colossal dimensions and the gas it employed, even lighter than hydrogen, it could carry numerous passengers and a considerable cargo of provisions of every sort, as well as its own fuel supplies, for a long sojourn in the air. A certain comfort was ensure by the elegant cabins and the intelligent equipment of all the supplements that garnished its large platform—which, for the role of salvation that it might one day be called upon to play, formed an extremely comfortable life-raft.

Everything had been anticipated in order that nothing essential should be lacking aboard, even in extraordinary circumstances; in the same way that a ship careful of the security of its passengers is equipped with lifebelts, Namo's airship, which already bore the name *Espérance* in golden letters on its prow, carried flying equipment known by the name of aerovols, which, without mentioning their utility in case of peril, would permit the travelers, if the whim took them, to make brief excursions in the vicinity of way-stations.

That other solution of aerial transportation was necessarily based on a different principle from that of the airship. Here, it a was the bird, or rather the insect, that had provided the model, and the considerable deployment of force necessitated by that mode of transporting a body much heavier than air through the atmospheric milieu had only been rendered possible by a very great improvement of electrical accumulators, which had become capable of storing extraordinary forces activating a mechanism that imparted an extreme agitation to

---

but it had similar limitations (although it was reputed to have inspired Jules Verne to write *Robur le conquérant*, tr. as *The Clipper of the Clouds*). Even so, their efforts meant that in 1890, the prospect of further progress seemed highly likely.

large artificial wings—an agitation similar to that employed by beetles or moths.

The person strapped into the aerovol, and thus sustained in the air by the automatic movement of the wings, steered by means of broad manually-operated vanes serving the same purpose as paddles, while a slight movement of the feet made a weight rise or descend along the longitudinal stem of the apparatus, to which it was fitted like that of a steelyard, thus giving the body the various inclinations one wanted to adopt. Then, if by chance some unfortunate accident afflicted the ingenious mechanism, the security of the aerial swimmer was guaranteed by a parachute that he wore artistically folded on his head in the form of a helmet, which opened automatically, preventing a fatal fall.

Marius who had long been subject once again to the ordinary laws of gravity, sometimes took pleasure in that aerial sport, which reminded him a little of his fantastic evolutions while the malign attraction of the unforgettable Gemma had been exercised upon him. Nothing, in any case, was more hygienic and vivifying than going forth to spend a few hours drinking pure air at altitudes that had once been the inviolable domain of the matinal skylark—a domain that had now been added, after so many others, to the conquest of the beings with ever-more-insatiable desires known as humans.

One beautiful morning in the early days of Floreal, there was a great excitement in our friends' house. The immense airship was ready, having nothing more to do than raise the anchors that were maintaining it a few meters above the ground in order to rise up with the three travelers and the aerial vessel's crew. Good wishes and farewells were exchanged between the platform and the lawn, where numerous family friends were clustered around Namo's mother and sister.

Although accustomed to sometimes-long absences of the beloved son and brother, the women were more emotional than usual, and had made those departing promise to come back soon. The latter, confident in the already-recognized capabilities of the *Espérance*, promised not to be away longer than a fortnight, for aerial navigation permitted considerable distances to be covered in a short time.

Finally, the airship, liberated from its last attachment, rose majestically in a vertical line, and paused at a few hundred meters in order to describe two or three large circles above the house before setting forth, while hands and handkerchiefs were waved on either side. Then, steering eastwards, without yet leaving the coast, the *Espérance* drew away rapidly and soon disappeared in the distance.

From the platform, the view was presently admirable: on one side, the limitless sea; on the other, beyond the inlets of the coast where navigable streams flowed, was the superb chain of the Atlas mountains, dominated by the snowy summit of the proud Ouarsenis, the Arabs' "eye of the world."[28] And all around, in the valleys and the plains, were cheerful white towns, great and small, which the voyagers recognized and named one after another.

It had been decided, to begin with, that they would continue eastwards as far as the extreme shores of the Mediterranean, but, the pilot having observed that there was a strong north-south current that was impeding the progress of the airship, Alcor had the idea, immediately accepted by his young friends, that they might take advantage of the current without any expenditure of fuel to go further into the interior, in order to give Marius a glimpse of the country, with the probability of picking up a countercurrent thereafter that would bring them back. That was what they did. Aerial navigation did not, in fact, prevent travelers from taking account of favorable atmospheric circumstances when the opportunity arose and economizing on precious supplies of propulsive and ascensional force.

It did not take long for the panorama to change significantly. The sea was soon lost to view; nothing could any long-

---

[28] Ouarsenis—the name of a range of peaks in the Tell Atlas—actually means "nothing higher."

er be seen but tightly-packed mountains rising up to a few principal summits that the airship was almost skimming, and then large valleys—or, rather, veritable plains—and then further chains of mountains that seemed to extend to the horizon. Everywhere there were towns and villages, testifying to the intense life of all those regions.

Although her movement was not sensible on board, the *Espérance* was advancing at that moment at no less than two hundred kilometers an hour.

"A little further," said Marius, "and we'll reach the Sahara Desert."

"Desert?" Namo replied. "What desert? The forest, you mean?"

"You're both right," Alcor put in. "Marius in his time and we in ours. Our immense Saharan forest was once a desert, and the desert of the ancient Bedouins and Tuaregs had previously been the conifer forest of which your contemporary explorers, my dear Marius, found the petrified debris everywhere beneath the burning sand. The desert, the forest and also the sea succeeded one another alternately, it appears, over the centuries in the Sahara. But the day is ending now; the sun is touching the horizon, and if you trust my judgment, my friends, we shouldn't despair from our itinerary any further and ought to land on one of those nearby peaks in order to spend a first peaceful night before retracing our steps tomorrow morning."

At that moment, in any case, the wind that was carrying them weakened as dusk fell, and it was in a relative calm that the airship descended to within range of one of the summits indicated by Alcor and was solidly moored to await the next day's dawn.

The *Espérance*'s platform was, as we have said, very comfortably equipped. The constructors had been able to render that small space, sixty feet long by twenty wide, eminently habitable. The small common room son brought the three friends together in front of a well-served table, to which they did full honor. Then, before going to sleep in the elegant cabins that became the private domicile of each of them for a little while, they took a little stroll back and forth along the platform, imitating the salutary exercise so dear to mariners, who never weary of striding back and forth over the deck of their ship for hours on end.

The darkness was complete by then, a moonless night that allowed the celestial constellations to scintillate in all their glory, while down below, before the eyes of *Espérance*'s passengers, like as many other stars, shone the lights of the habitations that covered the living country.

It was already quite late, and they were talking about separating when several prodigious beams of bright light suddenly rose up from various points of the horizon, which drew an involuntary exclamation from Marius. He did not have to wait long for an explanation of the phenomenon.

"Look! There's the luminous semaphore, about to speak," said Namo. "With whom are we corresponding at present?"

"Doubtless with Jupiter," Alcor replied, pointing to the brilliant planet, which was shining almost at the zenith.

And the spectacle commenced, becoming increasingly astonishing in the strange figures successively designed by the immense streaks of fire that sometimes intersected and sometimes drew apart, or seemed to arch across the heights of the sky—an ever-varying spectacle that lasted for more than an hour.

What series of tentative attempts and fruitless trials had been passed through before it became possible to exchange intelligible signals between two worlds? It had taken a long time, but after having repeated simple designs on one side and the other—a cross, a triangle, a geometric figure, and proving by that alone the existence in each world of intelligent beings with powerful scientific means at their disposal, they had progressed to more complicated attempts, such as designing contours representing the forms of the inhabitants, which had shown the Cybeleans strange figures bearing no resemblance to themselves.

Marius had already heard some mention of that subject, when he had had the opportunity to see what the prodigious telescopes of Cybele were capable of achieving. Thus, on Mars those forms were rather massive; on Saturn, by contrast, they seemed slender and designed for flying, to judge by the wings seemingly indicated by the design. Venus revealed the most curious and most graceful human beings undergoing metamorphoses like our butterflies, and doubtless ending up, like those favored insects, in a final brilliant phase replete with beauty and amour, the inverse of terrestrial human amours. The inhabitants of Jupiter were, however, certainly the most perfect. The Jupiterians, whose image was reminiscent of the one in which all-powerful Buddha is represented in the pagodas of India, possessed numerous arms terminated by different and complicated hands, which gave an impression of a great aptitude for extraordinary manipulations and implied a superior intelligence. They were the ones, in consequence, who had taken the initiative in attempting to communicate with the other planetary humankinds.

After that, allegorical signs had been attempted, and gradually understood; then, finally, that which happens in history to any language and writing transpired, and simple signs conventional had sufficed to express ideas.

In America, ever the country for stunning projects, there had at one time been no hesitation in trying out immense hollow projectiles able to contain an entire written correspondence, which might have inaugurated a routine postal service, and even a certain amount of commercial exchange. By way of projective cannons, veritable artificial volcanoes loaded with nihilite were supposed to launch the new parcels of dispatches as far as the planetary fields of attraction, but in the course of the first trial the planet experienced such a commotion that governments intervened to put a stop to the dangerous game—otherwise, the American gamblers would have increased the force by degrees until the cannon blew up.

But let us return to our friends aboard the *Espérance*, whose conversation was becoming animated.

"Jupiter has known for a long time about the dire fate that is threatening our poor world," the professor continued. "It knows that the signals will soon cease completely, and that will be sufficient to inform it of the disastrous event. In our misfortune, we still have the sad consolation of knowing that our humankind will be sympathetically mourned and regretted by our celestial sisters. Was it not Venus that recently repeated twenty times over the signs signifying: *Hope nevertheless. Trust in God*?"

For the moment, the Jupiterian observers were doubtless recording with religious attention the ideographic signs that Cybele was addressing to them, as one avidly welcomes the words of a friend who has only a short time to live.

"And it's doubtless by similar means that Jupiter will respond?" Marius queried.

"Not at all," the professor told him. "On the contrary, Jupiter, which presents to us a face that is always inundated with light, and which scarcely knows darkness, given its four moons, sends us dark signs—which is to say, projections of black lines. For our part, we employ the same system by day, for—I don't know whether you've been told this already—we've discovered a means of neutralizing light-waves by means of exactly inverted emissions, whose solutions of continuity are as distinctly visible as the sunspots outlined on the sun's dazzling disk."

"Shadows of darkness launched through daylight, just as one launches beams of light through the night? But we imagined that a long time ago in Provence, my friends. In my turn I'm able to talk about something I'll wager you don't know—the old legend of Simon of Carcassonne who had a back so black that whichever way he turned, he projected darkness for three leagues, which gave rise to a popular regional saying: as black as Simon's west."[29]

---

[29] This is a grim joke; Simon de Montfort, the military leader of the so-called "Albigensian crusade" of the early 13th century, ostensibly undertaken to crush the heretic Cathars, but

"Go on, my dear Marius," said Namo, laughing whole-heartedly at the Provençal's wry sally. "With regard to black hearts, I like you better when you have your black ideas."

The luminous signals has ceased completely; darkness was sovereign. It was late, and there was nothing better to do than for each of them to retire to bed, where a reparative sleep would not belong delayed.

Thus, everyone was sprightly and in a good mood when the first gleams of dawn lit up the lower edges of long strips of cloud in the east, from which direction a fresh morning breeze was blowing.

In a matter of minutes everything was ready, the anchors were raised, and the balloon, charged with a full complement of gas, regained the heights, taking advantage of the breeze to gain a little impetus and steering to starboard—a sensibly oblique course that brought the airship back toward the coast while gaining ground. The sea did not take long to appear again, but it was not the same as the day before. The liquid plain glittering in the daylight was only an interior gulf that owed its origin, long before the rise in sea level, to human labor that had once transformed the climate and habitability of that arid region of French Africa. It was the realization of the audacious project, long regarded as chimerical, of a modest pioneer of civilization whose name had survived in the appel-lation given to that extent of salt water, which was still known as the Roudaire Sea.[30]

---

which also had the effect of destroying any hopes that the Languedoc might have had of becoming a separate nation and dividing France in two, remained a significant hate-figure in Provence long afterwards, thus casting an exceedingly black shadow over the history of the region around Carcassonne, where his worst atrocities were committed.

[30] The notion of building a canal to recreate an inland sea in the Sahara, was extensively popularized by François-Élie Roudaire in the 1870s, most notably in an article in the *Revue*

In the afternoon, the *Espérance* flew over a very large city that had been built in the region once occupied by Tunis and Carthage, almost in the same location that the ancient city of Queen Dido had occupied. On a smaller scale, the new Carthage, with its harbor considerable hollowed out be human hands and its grandiose monuments, was reminiscent of Algiers. The explorers did not stop, however. They had resolved to continue following the same course, which ought to permit them to reach Sicily that evening and land for the night—since nothing obliged them for the moment to travel by night—at the station on Mount Etna, one of the largest and busiest in the entire world.

In the meantime, Marius tried to find Malta with his telescope, which ought not to be very far away—but the unfortunate island had already fallen victim to its low altitude in these times of invasion by the sea throughout the hemisphere. Of the ancient domain of the goddess Calypso, and subsequently the pious Christian knights, of the powerful fortress whose flag had finally became and remained Italian, nothing remained but a reef that pilots carefully avoided.

Soon, the airship reached the celebrated volcano. Half way up the mountain there was a veritable port, adapted to the needs of that special navigation, and comfortable hotels striving by means of all possible seductions to retain air tourists for as long as possible—for lovers of aerial travel were numerous. In her journey the *Espérance* had already crossed the paths of a number of other airships flying the flags of many nations, and when she landed, it was in hundreds that the voyagers counted those moored to the enormous solid rings of the port, or even completely deflated.

Here, it was no longer a case of remaining on the platform. The crew were left to guard the ship, and our three

---

des Deux Mondes in 1874. Ferdinand de Lesseps was one of the project's more vocal supporters. Inevitably, it features in numerous French futuristic romances of the period, including Étienne Calvet's *Dans mille ans* (q.v.).

friends used the on-board ladder to descend to the ground, where as many theatrical performances, concerts and engaging taverns as one could wish were on offer, where one might spend a pleasant evening. The professor and his pupil, who were already familiar with the town, took Marius to visit the principal sights: its monuments, its promenades, its capricious lava-flows—which, in times of eruption, had been whimsically molded into mythological colossi—its hanging gardens and, finally, its twin statues of the Montgolfier brothers, who were very much at home in that great port of aerostatic navigation. After that they went into the Hôtel Dupuy de Lôme, where numerous diners were assembled in groups around tables heaped with promise. There were people of every nation there, speaking all languages, mostly unfamiliar to some of their participants but which nevertheless linked together conversations in the casual manner permitted to travelers brought together by the hazards of their journeys.

At the table next to that of our Algerians, half a dozen closely affiliated languages were in full flow. There were Europeans from different countries, who appeared to be engaged in a discussion regarding the comparative merits of Europeans and Americans. One tall bony fellow with a receding forehead and a bold gaze, whose interlocutors were addressing him as "Captain," whose neck, bearded beneath a shaven chin, as well as his strong Yankee accent, denounced a nationality recognizable by the same characteristics as of old.

Jonathan Duck, who commanded a large North American airship, was not, in fact, a man to admit that any other nation was superior to his own in any respect whatsoever. In vain he was reminded of many admirable inventions and all kinds of marvelous progress that had been hatched in the neighboring countries; there were more marvelous and more admirable ones to be cited to the honor of his American homeland.

Was it in Europe that humans had been able to domesticate animal species as rebellious as those of the sea? To train seals, porpoises and even sharks to go fishing in the sea and bring back their catches honestly to their masters, like honest hunting dogs? To have messages carried to the most distant shores? To persuade whales to submit meekly to the yoke of harness and to be drawn along by them on the surface of the sea with the extraordinary rapidity of which those giants of creation were capable, making it possible to travel around the world in less than a fortnight?

It was hardly worth the trouble, in fact, to talk about European inventors! Were there any among them to compare with the engineer from Buffalo who had set out to use the rotation of the globe its self as a motive force, thanks to the invention of a phenomenal suspended pulley that powered a conveyor belt more than ten leagues long—a marvelous pulley that was still, it was true, the secret of that skillful engineer. More than that! He was taking advantage of the same opportunity to straighten the axis of the planet, which was about to tilt under the influence of the imminent catastrophe, thus preventing the disaster.

Ha! He had no fear of comparisons, the brave Captain Duck. It was not in America, the fatherland of immeasurable progress, in the land of "go ahead" that one found arrested populations, fixed, as it were, in physiological state as incurable as that of the degenerate Europeans that he had had occasion to encounter in a few scantly inhabited islands of the old northern and central Europe, fallen so far today from its ancient splendor.

Those unfortunate relics of countries three-quarters swallowed up by the ever-rising waves of the Boreal seas offered, it appeared, in a few places, the curious particularity of having seen the unnatural tendencies of certain Europeans of old continue and further accentuate, fatally, in their descendants. Thus it was that, according to Captain Jonathan, one saw one land of Big-Heads in which the excessive cultivation of brains and the scorning of corporeal vigor had produced a race of human tadpoles whose intellectual faculties were marvelous, since they were born already knowledgeable in all sciences, but never emerged from the domain of pure speculation, and made use of nothing in their existence, which they spent in idleness and poverty.

Elsewhere, the last remains were found of a race of stunted and deformed dwarfs directly descended from ancestors long nourished by the scientific cuisine of the master-chemists of alimentary industries, ingenious inventors of food-stuffs and beverages from which simple nature had been carefully excluded as backward and humdrum. Did they not have the authority of official scientists who estimated that eating a fruit and absorbing the same proportions of nitrogen, carbon and hydrogen that the fruit contained amounted to the same thing?

By contrast, there was to one side of them a heavy race, almost round, with enormous jaws, chops heavy with fat and insatiable guts, which owed that porcine physique and its bestial mores to the gluttony of ancestors who, instead of punishing them severely, had awarded prizes at exhibitions to the breeders of obese animals: impotent pigs; cattle bloated by fat; geese, hens and ducks hypertrophied by means of barbarous treatments. In literature, they remained fervent Zolaists.

Further north, another island contained carnivores to which an appetite even more ferocious, but more exclusively orientated toward the bloody side, had eventually given a savage and sanguinary nature, and had even transformed certain organs, such as the teeth, which had all become canines, and which already distinguished them from other human beings.

Then again, there was also a country of fidgeters, feverish descendants of the neurotics of another era, who lived in a permanent state of nervousness and overexcitement, always in movement and avid for novelties that ceased to be new even before they were born, having been anticipated in advance. Those enervated individuals scarcely took the time to be children and none at all to be young, using up their lives in a matter of a few years, old at twenty, decrepit at twenty-five. They did, however, take their time dying.

"And have you not also visited," replied one of his interlocutors, "a certain country in which dollar fever, by atrophying all uncashable faculties, has also had a retrograde effect on the species, toward an ancestry whose type is still memorable, which retains the hairy collar of the orangutan and the chimpanzee?"

Captain Duck, taking a deep breath, resumed talking, but our three friends were no longer listening. All their attention had been attracted to the News-Screen visible throughout the room—a kind of display in general usage in the epoch. In public places, many establishments like the large hotel, and numerous private houses, a kind of mobile screen could be seen, which registered electrically from moment to moment, almost instantaneously, all the facts and important events that were occurring at all points of the globe.

A central agency that received the communications of its employees distributed all over the world immediately retransmitted the most interesting ones throughout the network of the universal service. Thus, people everywhere, at the same time, had an up-to-date account of the day that was passing hour by hour. It was the ultimate perfection of the newspaper: a perfection that could only be surpassed if a means were to be found of prophesying future events in advance.

At present, the characters that were just appearing at the top of the screen obviously pertained to a subject of great interest, because heads were seen agitating on all sides, and the conversations became louder and more animated in all the groups.

The report commenced thus: *Dore solsilasi domi solsilare*—words comprehensible to speakers of all languages, for a parallel service supplied translations without delay, and a universally-familiar international language was employed, and a mechanism so simple, whose elements were the seven notes of the musical scale, that no other attempt of the same kind, including Volapük, had ever been able to do better. And yet it was, however, a very ancient invention that was attributed to a Frenchman named François Sudre.[31]

This is what the exciting dispatch said:

Ten people from the holy valley of the Patagonians are presently traveling through the city of Magellan, the entire population of which is excited and able to testify irrefutably to the reality of a fact that has been advanced several times by our correspondents—which is to say, the appearance of a new race of extraordinary humans. The same characteristics already identified, which all these individuals present uniformly, exclude without contest the supposition of a unique individual phenomenon, as was thought at first.

The rumor had, in fact, gone around that humans absolutely different from known races, and superior to all of them, had been seen in Patagonia. It was quite natural that such strange news had found echoes on all sides and excited imaginations everywhere. A few rebellious minds refused to believe it, but in those times of fever and apprehension, anything seemed possible to the majority of Cybeleans, even the historically unprecedented creation of a new human race. Why, after all, should the sequence that had caused the commencement of the human species from semi-animal races, and then enabled it improve by degrees, not continue to advance further still, climbing a further step?

The news, positive this time, of the existence of these previously-unknown humans, doubtless more real than Cap-

---

[31] Jean-François Sudre (1787-1862) was a composer and violinst; his musical language, popularized in the posthumous book *Langue musicale universelle* (1866), is known as Solresol. Its brief fashionability was eclipsed by other "universal languages" such as Volapük and Esperanto, which faded away in their turn. In the "words" cited Alhaiza follow Sudre's example in using "si" rather than "ti." I am not able to confirm that the cited phrase really corresponds to the first words of the translation subsequently rendered.

tain Jonathan's Tadpoles and Dwarfs, was, therefore, no longer a surprise for anyone. It had been expected any day—and that was what explains the interest and animation that took possession of the entire audience when the succinct dispatch confirming the event appeared on the screen. Everyone had something to say about it, and remarks and comparisons were being made incessantly on all sides.

For some, it was simply a matter of selection brought about by a long series of marriages between elite individuals, having produced over the generations a physical and mental advancement ever more marked—the realization of what had already seemed possible long ago when, for such a sublime process, the word "megalanthropogenesis" had been invented.[32]

For others, who did not hesitate to devote themselves to more extreme suppositions and who attributed these little-known beings to an absolutely new nature, it was a matter of nothing less than an extra-human species, called to supplant present humankind and relegate its descendants to the rank of animals, with the same separation from the new king of creation as that maintained by the great apes with regard to humans.

Some celebrated the marvelous fecundity of Nature and her treasures of creative power, which eternity could not succeeded in exhausting. Others, more down-to-earth, believers in the "struggle for existence"—with whom our new acquaintance Jonathan Duck energetically joined in chorus—opined that if it were true that a new and superior human race had appeared, it was necessary, without waiting a single day long-

---

[32] The term *megalanthropogénésie* [megalanthropogenesis] was coined by Louis-Joseph-Marie Robert in his *Essai sur la megalanthropogénésie* (1801), which caused something of a stir, exciting comment in Grmanhy and England as well as France. It refers to the art of producing human genius by careful breeding, nurture and education.

er, to make immediate war on it and exterminate it, to the very last representative.

"What about you, my dear Alcor?" asked Marius, stunned by all that he had heard,. "What do you think of all this?"

"One more fact, my friends, before which it is necessary to bow down. Even setting aside what is evidently exaggerated in the stories that have been reaching us from Patagonia for some time, it must nevertheless be admitted that a new step has been taken in the specific advancement of humankind. The strangest thing about it is that in a world as well-known as ours, and as closely linked as all its inhabitants are, one can see the sudden appearance, so to speak, of something as unexpected as a new human species. I don't believe in spontaneous creation, and am inclined to side with those who consider the new development as the work of selection.

"It's necessary to remember that what is known as the Holy Valley in Patagonia has a rather singular history. It was several centuries ago that a religious sect originated in that country of a severe and elevated character, whose role and aim was perfection, in the broadest sense of the word. A few innovators gathered around them a quantity of men and women disillusioned by this discouraging world and predisposed to misanthropy. Offering those sensitive and bruised souls the ideal of an ever-increasing elevation in an existence directed entirely to that sole aim was giving them a new life.

"A monastery was founded in a remote high valley at the southern extremity of the Andes—a valley that subsequently became known in the region as the Holy Valley—and those enthusiasts for perfection gradually isolated themselves further and further from the rest of the living, being self-sufficient by virtue of the cultivation of their domain. They maintained the vigor of their crops by labor while the rest of their time was devoted to the most elevated studies and saintliest practices of the religious ideal, eventually forming a small separate people, whom the populations scattered about the region became accustomed to leaving in their absolute isolation, almost forgetting them until the present epoch, when a few of the transformed offspring of the original zealots of perfection finally decided to come down from their mountains and explore curiously the low country that they had previously been content to contemplate from the heights of their mountains.

"That particular characteristics and new developments should have been fixed over the generations, under the centuries-long influence of a salubrious environment and an intense mental stimulation, is consistent with the ordinary processes of nature. All human races had their beginnings, as did the Aryans of prehistoric times, the future Indo-Europeans whose original nucleus was restricted to the high plateaux of the Altaï in Asia, and for whom the future reserved the domination and conquest of the entire world.

"What has been reported about these mountain folk more than justifies their representation as a race superior to all the others: the superhuman beauty of their features; their tall stature and admirable proportions; the mildness of their mores; and their frugal diet, which proscribes all animal alimentation, are the least of their distinguishing characteristics. What appears to be truly new is the secret and incomprehensible power with which these strangers seem to be endowed of charming and subjugating with a mere gaze anyone who approaches them, when that same gaze does not instantly paralyze a seemingly hostile human or animal.

"Their occult power, it's said, is sufficient to inform them of the sentiments of others and to permit them to suggest their own thoughts without using signs or words, although they are sometimes heard to talk among themselves in soft and harmonious voices. Before the nobility of their attitude, and their air of domination, although the latter is tempered by a supreme expression of kindness, no man can forbid himself an involuntary respect, after the fashion of a legitimately due homage.

"Dare I admit to you, my friends, the thought that has pursued me since the appearance of this new human race was established beyond any doubt? Should I tell you that it is perhaps necessary to see it as the future sovereign of the continents whose deign is about to be completed on our planet for a new period of ten thousand five hundred years? Is it not the ultra-diluvian humankind, already born, which will emerge from its modest cradle in the Holy Valley, gradually spread out and one day reign over the entire globe, where our civilization will be effaced by its own?"

Alcor pressed his forehead with both hands, and murmured: "O Future! Who can ever fathom your mysteries, to reveal to us the ultimate ends of terrestrial destiny?"

X

The *Espérance*, rapidly carried out to sea, had seen the mountainous coasts of Sicily vanish behind her. At present she was heading east-south-east, directly toward Egypt, which she would reach in less than forty-eight hours. From the height at which they were flying, the horizon their eyes embraced was much vaster than that visible to mariners, which scarcely surpasses a radius of four or five leagues. In consequence, the misty coast of Africa was almost always visible, breaking the monotony of the liquid plain that seemed immense, and as smooth as a mirror, dotted here and there by the tiny black hulls of a few vessels.

From time to time they crossed the paths of other airships, which, advancing at great speed, sometimes passed above them and sometimes below. If they had been able to see the submarine boats that were also following their itineraries with similar precision under the water, they would have had before their eyes the three different means of navigation that the voyagers of the ears were able to choose.

Needless to say, the submarine mode, although very amply improved since the attempts of Peral and Goubet,[33] was not the most frequently used, but it had its enthusiasts, and there was no lack of individuals who had directed their atten-

---

[33] The battery-powered submarine developed by Isaac Peral for the Spanish navy was launched in September 1888. It was the first such machine to launch a torpedo under water, but the masters of the Spanish navy could see o future for it and it was abandoned. Claude Goubet's *Goubet I*, launched in 1885, had been the first powered by electricity; the *Goubet II*, launched in 1889, was an improved model, but the French naval general staff proved as short-sighted as their Spanish peers, leaving the field free for the German U-boats that caused so much devastation during the Great War.

tion to that third class of ships to make their preparations for contra-diluvian survival in preference to airships. To take to the same waves that constituted the prospective danger in advance, as a refuge, was a rather ingenious means, which was, after all, not lacking in a certain homeopathic logic.

It must be admitted, however, that the partisans of the latter means of salvation were few in number. As much as the progress of science had improved such machines and provided them with all the means necessary for a long sojourn, and even though perfectly breathable air could be fabricated—even adding water vapor and traces of carbon to the marriage of oxygen and nitrogen in order to contrive a perfect resemblance to atmospheric air, although, like all artificial things, it was inferior to natural air—were there not terrible shocks to be feared that, in a cataclysm such as the one anticipated, might agitate the oceans even in their utmost depths? As we have seen, Namo and his family, like almost everyone else in the world, had adopted the safer and more practical strategy of a rapid flight into the aerial regions.

They came gradually closer to the coast, and were beginning to see distinctly the capricious network of silver ribbons designed, over a vast extent of lowlands, by the numerous branches of the celebrated Egyptian river. White cities along the shore and toward the interior decorated the green background presented by that fertile land, presently adorned in its spring finery. Nothing remained of the cities of old after so many centuries of political vicissitudes and material changes in the delta, which, on the one hand, the new alluvia of the great river tended to increase, while on the other, the rising sea level increasingly submerged. In that contest between the two elements, it was the water that had prevailed over the earth, with the result that it now covered the ancient soil of Damiette, Port Said and the ancient Alexandria, whose famous library the fanatical Omar had once employed to heat the city's public baths for six months.

The *Espérance* was soon flying over the land, and, veering southwards, headed for the capital, which was no longer

187

the Arab city of old, of which nothing remained but the memory. Climatic conditions, reverted to those of the times of the first Pharaohs, had driven the desert back, and rendered all the regions of Egypt fertile—not to mention that the Nile irrigated new expanses of land, thanks to the great barrage that diverted it into several branches and thus considerably enlarged the delta—a simple reiteration of what had been seen in the epoch of the great Sesostris. The latter had appeared in the nudity of a mummy to the scientists contemporary with Marius, who had discovered his sarcophagus and had the signal honor of unwrapping the celebrated monarch from his thirty-six-centuries-old bandages.[34]

Extraordinarily, and without any comparable example in the world, the pyramids were still standing, but were no longer isolated and abandoned in the midst of the sands. The present capital of Egypt was built almost exactly on the ancient site of Memphis, and it enclosed the majestic trio of Cheops, Chephren and Mycerinus, which a local authority respectful of such a venerable past had restored and reestablished in their original state, while still using Cheops as an aerostatic station. It was toward the platform fitted to its summit that the *Espérance* steered, and did not take long to land and moor, in the midst of other airships visiting the great city.

We shall not describe the superb temples, the sumptuous palaces and the immense quarters that extended beyond the pyramids along the left bank of the second branch of the Nile. Our friends were, in any case, only making a brief halt at this point in their journey, attractive as it was. They were only planning to spend a few hours strolling in the most beautiful part of the city. With street-maps in hand they would content

---

[34] Sesostris was a legendary Egyptian king. The reference to a mummy unwrapped by Marus' contemporaries is presumably to the much-publicized unwrapping of the mummy of Thuthmose III, which was carried out by Gaston Maspero in 1886 (although it had earlier been unwrapped by its discoverer, Émile Brugsch, in 1881).

themselves with admiring from the height of their ten-thousand-year-old observatory the monuments and sights that they had within range, rapidly remembering the glorious past and prosperous present of that doyen of civilized lands, which recalled the greatest names in history: the likes of Sesostris, Alexander, Caesar, Napoléon and other ancient heroes.

The movement that had, since the first dynasties, shifted the nucleus of Egyptian civilization further northward, through Ethiopia, Nubia and Egypt proper, had long been reproduced in the opposite direction, without losing any of its conquests to ingrate nature this time. The sands that had advanced to the gates of Cairo had given way to beautiful gardens and rich villas, extending far beyond the places where the ancient capital of the hundred gates had once been resplendent. And if some impossible miracle had resuscitated the pious hermits of the Thebaid, it would not have been the desert, but luxurious fields, that were offered to their astonished gaze. Then, if their ascetic rule had not forbidden it, they would also have been able to appreciate the substantial diet of the news inhabitants, and even wash it down with an Aswan vintage that was easily the equal of the renowned wines of the Egypt of the Pharaohs.

The Egyptian people had paid dearly in times past for their initiation into political life. Curved for an interminable series of centuries under the yoke of different masters, the fellahs, docile and indefatigable serfs, had survived in spite of everything on that ancient land irrigated with their sweat, jealous land that only conserved the descendancy of its own children and drained the blood of foreign races. The present type was thus still that of the Copts and the Arabs, but its new civilization, nurtured primarily under the influence of regenerated Greece, was a direct daughter of Europe, like that of all of north Africa, with social and political mores in conformity with universal progress. It was the same for its morale and beliefs; Muslim fatalism had had its day, as well as Christianity, and the doctrine of Mohammed had gone to join the extinct worship of Osiris and Jupiter-Amon.

Great activity now reigned in the free cities and the terrestrial and fluvial highways, as well as on the ancient Lesseps Canal, considerably broadened since, but scarcely sufficient in spite of that for the maritime traffic that had always increased. The country that our voyagers were now about to leave had realized all the agricultural wealth promised by its great past and its geographical situation, which made it a point of intersection and connection between the Orient and the Occident. The country was, evidently, very different from the one where, on the terrestrial planet, the clever clown John Bull had recently played the comedy of Tel el-Kebir,[35] and was working hard to filch the canal, and the whole of Egypt into the bargain.

The *Espérance* soon resumed her rapid flight toward the other regions she was to visit. On the same day that the travelers left Egyptian territory, they passed over the quadruple liquid highway that linked the two seas and soon saw unfurling before their eyes the plains of Arabia Petraea and then the fortunate land of Canaan that had been the Promised Land of the children of Isaac and Jacob before being the Holy Land of the epic crusades, and which had become a true land of election again by virtue of its new temperate climate and its unequalled fertility. Other great historical memories had come to add to those crowding the thoughts of Marius, whose gaze had searched in vain for the ruins of Jerusalem or Damascus.

Among the memories of that Cybelean past was one rather curious one of which the professor reminded his young friends while all three of them, leading on the balustrade of the platform, were contemplating the uneven ground and the unknown cities that seemed to be gliding beneath them. Toward the end of the twentieth century A.D. an accord had been reached between the various states of Europe, which, after the

---

[35] The battle of Tel el-Kebir, in which British forces defeated those of the rebel army officer Ahmed Urabi, was fought in September 1882. British troops remained garrisoned in Egypt thereafter, considerably increasing British influence over the country and the Suez canal.

experience of all the preceding centuries, had understood the imperious necessity of eliminating the dissolving element of societies known as Judah, still the same in Paris and Berlin as it had been three thousand years earlier in Nineveh and Babylon.

They had agreed to get rid, once and for all, of all of that parasitic race, everywhere inassimilable but so astonishingly able to infiltrate among the constituted peoples, which they would despoil to the point of complete exhaustion if no final reckoning were achieved. Civilized nations as they were, the powers gathered in conference resolved, no longer to expel Jew brutally but to reintegrate all of them in the Judea of old, where they would organize themselves as a family and thus cease to be the leeches of humankind.

To that effect, the rights of the Sultan who then reigned in Asia Minor were repurchased, and the expropriated inhabitants of the territory of Palestine were compensated—a territory vast enough to contain all the children of Israel disseminated throughout the world. Then, allowing them to transport their wealth, a gift was made to them of the land where their ancestors had lived, but with a prohibition against their living elsewhere. It was taken for granted that a people as clever, richer than any other and as generously endowed for its new national debut, would soon be even more prosperous, to its own advantage and that of everyone else.

It appeared, however, that there had been a miscalculation, for two generations had not elapsed before the citizens of the new idea, reduced to exploiting one another without producing anything of their own by hard labor, soon impoverished and feeling lost, began escaping one after another in various disguises, to the extent that the day came when Judea was deserted and all of Judah was spread out once again, as a parasite all the more avid because its suction had been so long deprived of the honey of various human hives. And the annals of Israel counted one exodus more—a voluntary exodus this time, which brought a little gaiety to history for once.

If our friends had had the leisure to head further east-wards and accomplish a more distant voyage, they would have found the rich plains of Mesopotamia—more flourishing than the empires had ever been over which the ancient capitals of Babylon and Nineveh, now vanished without trace, had reigned—and then Persia, India, China and Japan, transformed to the same extent as the rest of the world. That supposedly-immutable Orient had ended up following the general impulsion, and contained an incalculable number of small republics and great confederations, penetrated by the new spirit. But it was necessary to make haste if they wanted to return within the brief span of time that had been granted to them, and the *Espérance*, navigating even by night, continue in a straight line all the way to the mountains of Armenia, a land where an intelligent and strong Aryan race had perpetuated and consti-tuted States of a superior civilization that lost nothing in com-parison with in societies of European origin.

Nocturnal navigation was free of inconvenience, save for the risk of a possible collision with some other airship, but the powerful searchlights with which they were equipped, whose bright beams pierced the thickest clouds, easily warded off that danger. It was at the first light of day that Marius and Namo, awakened by the professor, who had got up to observe the dawn, came to admire the grandiose spectacle of the Ar-menian mountain chains, valleys, rivers and green plains. They did not go on as far as the Black Sea or the Caucasus, but steered westwards before then.

Alcor had thought of suggesting to his companions that they visit Mount Ararat during the day—a place of depressing memory in the present circumstances, to be sure, but which merited a pious pilgrimage on the part of courageous men like themselves who had no fear of looking into the face of any-thing that reminded them of the imminent and inevitable peril. In any case, would not a visit to the celebrated summit where Noah's legendary Ark had stopped more than a hundred centu-ries before, offer them, along with the terrible apprehensions of the present, a consoling hope of deliverance?

An agreement was quickly reached, and the route to follow easily found by traveling up the course of the Euphrates. In the afternoon, rising above the highest Armenian plateaux, two twin peaks appeared on the horizon, of which the higher was the famous mountain that had seen the chain broken by the Biblical Deluge resumed. The same thought that had brought the voyagers of the *Espérance* had been attracting numerous other visitors for some time, so our friends found themselves mingling n arrival with a considerable influx of foreigners from all lands.

Having come incidentally, Alcor and his traveling companions had no intention of staying long. They only took the time to go to the magnificent temple built on the side of the mountain on a vast natural terrace not far from the eternal snows that crowned its summit. The Orient, which loves to devote its moist remarkable sites to religion, had not failed to erect a religious monument on Mount Ararat, which was justly reputed to be one of the marvels of the epoch, and constituted an additional attraction. Festivals and ceremonies of an extraordinary pomp were held there on a daily basis, which further raised the prestige of the location and the great memories that it evoked. As soon as they had satisfied the natural impulse that had brought them, however, the passengers of the *Espérance* re-embarked that same evening and left the extreme point of their voyage to head westwards with all the speed that their excellent aerial vessel permitted them.

In that fashion they rapidly crossed the whole of Asia Minor, whose ancient civilization, interrupted for many centuries by Turkish barbarity, had flourished again under the same Greek influence as before, and had become one of the most prosperous regions in the world.

They were not due to stop until they reached the European territory beyond the Bosphorus, on the fortunate coast that had seen, in times past, the unforgettable Byzantium and the magical Constantinople, and now possessed a new capital seated on a new Golden Horn, rich and still beautiful in its favored situation, but no longer comparable in extent and picturesque quality with the city of the Seraglio, with its mysterious walls, its mosques with high cupolas and vertiginous minarets, and the unique Hagia Sofia, from which the centuries had not effaced the bloody handprint et on its marble by the ferocious Mehmed II.[36] That proud Constantinople with its two existences, so coveted by the Tsars of Russia, so beloved by jealous Sultans, so regretted in advance by the fanatical Ottomans, who, foreseeing its fall, had already wanted their bones to rest in Asiatic soil beneath the gigantic cypresses of Scutari; that marvel of the gate of Europe, had disappeared without leaving any other trace than a few pages of history.

The admirable Bosphorus had retained, very nearly, its ancient appearance, but it was no longer a small inland sea that it linked to the Mediterranean. Its role had grown in becoming the connection between two immense extents of water; the principal sea was now to the north, shallow, it is true, but now continuous with the Polar Ocean. The old Black Sea had been reconnected beyond the Caucasus with the Caspian Sea and, invading the steppes, had gradually swallowed up the vast territory of Russia, in collaboration with the Ocean, which for its part had advanced from the north and the west to meet it, no longer allowing anything to emerge from the waters but a few large marshy islands, several of which were uninhabitable. Cities like St. Petersburg, Kiev and Odessa now lay twenty fathoms deep, and of Moscow the Holy, whose Byzantine bell-towers had once been counted at forty times forty, nothing remained but the site occupied by the superb Kremlin, now a fishing-town that served as the principal port of the islands. Only the great massifs of the Caucasus and the Urals remained intact of what had once been European Russia.

On the other hand, all of the Hellenic peninsula, from the Balkans to the sea, was now at the height of prosperity, and formed a rich and powerful confederation in which the new

---

[36] Mehmed II, also known as Mehmed the Conqueror, put an end to the Byzanine Empire by capturing Constaninople in 1453, after which his new Ottoman Empire expanded vastly.

Byzantium, of which our voyagers were presently the guests, now had no more than a secondary rank among the numerous States of the Hellenic Union.

After having taken the time to let the crew rest and to re-provision the airship, they set out again, heading for the Peloponnese, maintaining a low altitude in order to have the leisure to examine as they passed over the Hellespont that an insane king had had beaten with rods, and the Aegean Sea whose islands and shores where so full of moving memories. Here was the site of Troy, with Mount Ida raising its snowy summit in the distance; there was Lemnos, where Vulcan the son of Jupiter, had fallen from Heaven, rendered permanently lame by the impact; in all directions there were cheerful islands dear to the gods and goddesses of old Homer; further on, the coasts of Continental Greece, which the *Espérance* reached in the evening; and finally, the ancient city of Athens, which, by virtue of an almost unique privilege, had been able to retain through so many centuries its preponderant role and its glorious name. Its Piraeus had been significantly displaced, however, for the sea penetrated much more deeply at that point of the Attic coast.

A part of the Acropolis had been adapted as a garage for aerial vessels. The airship landed there, and the next morning, the three friends got down, promising themselves a pleasant and instructive day. What attracted their attention immediately, would you believe, was the Parthenon, the ancient Parthenon rebuilt and reestablished on the same Pelagic foundations, as it had been in the time of Pericles, with all its marvels of marble animated by the chisel of Phidias, its riches, its dependencies and its grandiose propylea.

The new Greek people, who conserved the religion of their past, had regarded it as a pious duty to their great ancestors to revive a few of their works of genius, especially the unparalleled Parthenon, which human barbarity even more than the scythe of time had once annihilated. If an ancient Greek, shaking off the dust of centuries, had returned to climb the white steps of the holy monument, he would have recognized it in all its aspects, except that other emblems, other priests and other divine hymns would have made him understand that the times were no longer the same and that the new Parthenon was host to another worship than that of Pallas Athene.

The first visit of Alcor and his companion, naturally, was to the marvelous edifice, from which they only came down after having admired the science of its curves and proportions and the harmony of its vivid murals for a long time, and contemplated from the height of the steps of the peristyle the distant celebrated hills of Pentelico, whose precious quarries had not been exhausted by thousands of years of exploitation, and Hymetta, which still yielded the sweet honey of its bees.

Further away, in the gap between the two eminences, were the plains of Marathon where Miltiades was defeated; at their feet was the new Athens, a modern city similar enough to all the others of the epoch, but in which were conserved the richest relics of primitive antiquity, alongside those of more recent epochs, of the Greece that commenced with the Pelagians, and the which recommenced with Constantine Kanaris and his heroic mariners, all the way to the Hellas of peaceful times, devoid of tormented history, that had arrived after those ancient epochs of violence and turbulence.

The flanks of the Acropolis, rendered easily accessible by means of ingenious engines of circulation like those Marius had found in Algiers, now accommodated many places of study or entertainment, restaurants, where our friends savored a Parnes and an Acrocorinth that were still famous, and theaters, especially a splendid edifice that had reoccupied the very stage on which an Athenian public educed to dust for eighty centuries had applauded the tragedies of Sophocles and Euripides. The Greeks were always great lovers of theater, and that virile people had once again become the foremost in the world matters of art, worthily honoring all its interpreters. Each according to his rank, without any risk of ever descending to such a stupid infatuation as that of the Parisians of old, who had glorified poseurs of both sexes as near-equals of demi-gods.

Our strollers loved to mingle with the crowds, which bore them from one meeting-place to another. They observed the serious and taciturn expressions of the Hellenic people, who had conserved the faults as well as the ancient virtues of their people, and who, although they often merited admiration, did not always inspire sympathy. On seeing those cold faces, which did not allow any thought to be divined, the ancient saying returned to memory: "I fear the Greeks, even when they bear gifts." Once more, they observed astonishing permanence of character, mores and ideas conserved by an ancient race through the centuries—which proves that humans are, after all, less changeable and less malleable than certain innovators imagine. One characteristic detail: in the new Greece, as in the one of Marius' century, there were no Jews. The climate did not suit them, it seemed.

Alluring as such a country was, there could be no question of visiting it in detail. That day spent in its principal city sufficed to give a general idea of other Hellenic cities, ancient or recent. From the Acropolis, the *Espérance* traversed the northern part of the Peloponnese toward the Ionia Sea, passing over Corinth, the ancient isthmus of which the human hand had once made a strait. Then, going up the picturesque shore of the western coast of the great Geek Confederation, she soon came within sight of the immense chain of the Tyrolean Alps, without attempting to cross them, which would have been a difficult operation for an airship designed to operate at medium altitude and not to rise up easily to heights of three or four thousand meters. They knew that beyond the mountains they would have found an intact Switzerland and a southern Germany tested by a rigorous climate. They knew too that to the east, there was the Ungaria Sea, and further to the north, the sea covering once again the ancient lands of Prussia and Bavaria, all the way to the great Norwegian island, which was the only considerable land-mass that existed in that direction, already fused over the larger part of its extent with the permanent polar ice.

Having skirted that extremity of the Adriatic and recalled to memory the unfortunate provinces of Venetia and Milan, almost entirely swallowed up, they rose up slightly to pass from the Adriatic into the Mediterranean, thus crossing northern Italy. Poor Venice! It had been, along with the valiant Holland, one of the first victims of the increase in sea level. One day, the horses of San Marco, religiously conserved until then, while the magical cathedral, the Doge's Palace, the Campanile, the Bridge of Sighs and all of the monumental Venice of old had already fallen to the scythe of time, the ancient horses of Corinthian bronze, the only horses of the marine city, had sunk breast-deep in the water, resembling for a while the mythological team of Amphitrite. Then the level of the sea rose further, and continued rising, and finally, the waves of the open sea passed freely, traveling toward other shores, over the eternally-mourned location where so many centuries had contemplated and admired the Queen of the Adriatic.

As for central and southern Italy, which the voyagers left behind, it was only eaten away at a few points along its coast—but what changes there had been since Marius' day! To begin with the ancient capital of the Roman world and the Christian world, who had long seemed to merit the title of the Eternal City, of the Rome of the emperors and the popes, the ever-renewed Rome always worthy of itself and the great Latin people whose splendid capital it had been for so many centuries, nothing had remained for a long time but relics and documents scattered in museums. Naples and Florence had suffered the same fate, and Genoa, the ancient enemy of Venice, was also sleeping the slumber of the dead, like its rival, beneath a liquid shroud.

Understandably, Marius' heart beat more forcefully when he saw that he was skirting the coast of his Provence. It goes without saying that Marseilles, the former capital of the two Frances after Paris, had been included among the principal ports of call of the voyage, and it was, therefore, toward

Marseilles that the *Espérance* now steered, while Marius never took his eyes off the irregular profile of the coast, beyond which rose the rocky chain of the Provençal Alps. He was the first to recognize the extensions of Cap Croisette preceding the spur of Notre-Dame de la Garde, but that was where the signs of recognition ended for him.

As they came closer to the location of the new city, everything became unfamiliar. There was no more colossal statue of the Virgin on the eminence that characterized the topography of the place; no more cathedral with semi-Byzantine domes; no more Palais de Longchamps; nothing any longer of what he remembered so clearly. In their stead there was a great city, still served by a considerable port, with no resemblance to the old one, but considerable depleted since the immense dyke that had once imprisoned the entire bay, to make it the foremost port in the world, had been submerged.

The old city had also retreated before the invasion, and had only been partly saved by moving further into the interior. As in prehistoric times, when the primitive vessels whose debris was once encountered buried in the soil had sunk over the place that the famous Canebière was later to occupy, the sea had retaken possession of all the low-lying quarters, and there were other ships advancing there, other mariners disembarking, careless of all that had once lived and bustled where the calm waters of the new Phocean harbor now stood.

There was no maritime city in the world with a past as distant and constantly prosperous as that of the ancient Masalia of the Ligurians: a past that went back at least nine thousand years; which did not prevent its new citizens from having still present in mind such memories as that of the young Phoceam Euxenes, who had touched the heart of Gyptis, the daughter of the king of Segobriges and established himself with his beautiful wife and his companions in adventure on that fortunate shore, already previously occupied by Tyrians. People there still pronounced with pride names such as those of Pythias and Euthymenes, the audacious navigators who, several centuries before the Christian Era, one of whom had traveled along the entire coast of Hibernia and even to the hyperborean island of Thule, and the other along the African shore all the way to the tropics.

From century to century, without the slightest retreat, Marseilles, which was to have a great era in its history and give its name to the heroic hymn of the French Republic, had always grown. And if, from its beginnings lost in the night of time one leapt to a more recent past, what terms could celebrate the incomparable capital that had merited the honor of replacing and surpassing Paris, and would doubtless have marched to a greater destiny still if Nature herself had not risen against her and finally said "Enough!"

It was, therefore, in a Marseilles in a relatively steep decline that the *Espérance* was about to land at the aerostatic station of the ancient Notre-Dame de la Garde. To believe that Marius took pleasure in scanning the streets and quarters of a city so changed in his eyes would be a great mistake. The poor fellow knew in advance in what epoch he was living, and what a stranger he would be in present-day Marseilles, but that did not prevent his heart swelling at the memory of his schooldays and the distant past that was so recent to him. Rather than stimulate his regrets in the midst of that population of unknowns, he preferred to employ the interval of his sojourn in visiting the surrounding country, which, although also transformed, interested him more by virtue of the products of its new climate, which now made it a land of conifers and renowned hops.

The east, especially the south-east of ancient France, thanks to the mountains of the Alps, the Jura, the Vosges and the Argonne on one side, and the central massif of the Cévennes and the mountains of Auvergne on the other, was the most compact remnant of the great territory of old. Elsewhere, the north and the west no longer offered anything but the sight of large and small islands, increasingly eaten away by the sea. The biggest of those islands was formed by what remained of Brittany and Upper Normandy. As for the southwest, the Gulf of Gascony, which bathed the northern coast of the Pyrenees, had devoured almost all of the unfortunate province that had once borne its name.

It would have been cruel to leave Marseilles without giving Marius the bitter satisfaction of visiting his birthplace, not poor Martigues, long since buried beneath the waves with the entire Rhône delta, but at least its location, in terms of the exact measurement of its latitude and longitude. That was the first thing they did after the airship resumed its aerial journey. Compass in hand, Alcor called a halt at the precise spot, but it was only a momentary affair. He judged that it was unnecessary to put pressure on the still-bloody wound in his young friend's heart.

The latter felt his hands squeezed silently by those of his two companions; then they steered toward the depths of the gulf into which the Rhône poured, thirty leagues further up than its old mouths. The progress of the *Espérance* was hampered slightly at that moment by a fairly strong northerly wind, which, descending the same Rhône valley, reminded Marius of the Mistral that had followed the same route in his own time. It also reminded him of the terrible wind that had denuded the stony hills of Provence of all vegetation, the simultaneously furious and facetious wind whose gusts lifted your hat off your head or tore your newspaper from your hands, to deposit the object in question a few feet away, where it would rest tranquil until you bent down to pick it up, when it would immediately fly away again as swiftly as an arrow.

The *Espérance* took quite a long time to reach the interior of the country, passing over a large number of towns bearing no resemblance to those of old. Only Lyon, always favored by its fluvial situation, had maintained the same location, but only its name, now slightly deformed, perpetuated the memory of the great city that had long retained second rank in the France of long ago.

They passed on. It was agreed that they would not stop now, after having glimpsed the eastern region, until the station marking the place where Paris had been, a place presently uninhabited and uninhabitable, only visited by fervent admirers of history and the glories of the past.

Beyond the former region of Burgundy, the travelers could already see the sea again, a long gulf of which covered a large part of Champagne and had come to recover the large shells of ammonites, the irrefutable debris of a preceding invasion, which the plough had once encountered at the surface of a sandy soil. Then they reached another low-lying coast and a rather extensive and animated land, where they advanced as far as the light wooded eminences surrounding a kind of great marsh, from which emerged a tiny islet covered in brushwood.

The marsh was Paris and the islet was the Butte Montmartre. Even the Seine no longer existed since the change in sea level had disrupted the fluvial regime.

Of that queen of capitals, that nucleus of the genius of ancient European civilization; of that proud Paris which, with her feet in the mud, had nevertheless raised her head above the clouds, summarizing humanity in herself alone, from its lowest depths to its mot radiant summits; of that adored city incensed by the enemies of France, this was all that now remained: the deserted shores and stagnant waters of a marsh, awaiting the imminent arrival of the waters of the ocean—an exact repetition, moreover of something that had already taken place several times in similar anterior periods.

A kind of fortress built on a small elevation that had borne at one time the name of Père-Lachaise, was provided with all the usual accoutrements of aerostatic stations, as well as a hotel. From there one could embrace with the gaze a fairly considerable area, the dismal aspect of which added further to the melancholy of the visitor overwhelmed by the thought of the nullity of human endeavors. From the antique sepulcher of Parisian generations, it was the sepulcher of Paris itself that one had to contemplate in that dormant water, stained in places by glaucous reflections: a lugubrious spectacle depressing beyond all expression for a Frenchman of Marius' epoch, whose mind was still full of his youthful student memories.

On the islet already mentioned stood a bronze obelisk, an authentic funerary monument to which our visitors, before quitting that sad location, went to read the laconic inscription: *Paris was here.*

The date fixed for their return was approaching. There was no time to go on in order to observe that nothing remained of the Belgium of yore but the Ardennes. It was after the annihilation of its rich eastern plains that the old Gallic family had first entered into mourning. The ancient valor of its free and industrious cities, so long prosperous, had been impotent against the implacable liquid element. It had not taken long, however, for what had been the architectural marvel of Europe for centuries, the royal palace that remained a trifle humiliated to have sheltered chicanery at that outset, to cease to extend its last Babylonian entablatures above the waves, marking the place of another unfortunate capital that had disappeared forever.

Further north, although the Celtic population of Great Britain, imprisoned in the ice from a considerable part of the year, still existed in the countries of Wales, Scotland and Ireland, England properly speaking had disappeared—but not the English, who were found scattered and still trading throughout the world, where they had not been assimilated anywhere, like the Jews with whom they were sometimes confused.

Marius, as a man of his time, for whom the exploration of the North Pole had always had the exciting savor of forbidden fruit, would not have been displeased to push on as far as that, but it was necessary not to think of it for the time being. That would be for another occasion. Otherwise, nothing would have prevented our friends from going to plant their feet momentarily in the eternal snows of that mysterious point of the globe that had been the despair of so many intrepid explorers of times past.

This time, the *Espérance* headed directly southwards, with the archipelago of the French islands to her left and the ocean to her right, which extended without limits, not to encounter any other shore on that side until the great continent now tightly extended along the Cordilleras, to which Europe had once owed Americanism, ignoble advertising, phylloxera and other contagions.

Sometime later, they passed over the triple Atlantic wave flowing over the place where ancient Bordeaux lay twenty fathoms deep, and they began to distinguish in the distance the blue-tinted summits of the Pyrenees. Then, little by little, the grandiose chain extending from one extremity of the horizon to the other presented to the gaze the uninterrupted line of its peaks, its gorges and its glaciers, the last-named clearly recognizable by their milky color standing out against the grey or snow-white background of the formidable wall.

In that regard, Alcor reminded his young companions of the ingenious means by which the western Europe of the twenty-fifth century A.D., already sensibly cooler, had been able to bring a new warmth to this region. It was by diverting the major northern branch of the great current of warm water that departed from the gulf of Mexico toward the Old World. The lesser branch of the Gulf Stream, which skirted north-western Europe, had once sufficed to give Brittany, Ireland and even Norway a milder temperature than their latitude implied; it was evident that if the totality of the warm current, more than ten degrees in width, instead of going largely to waste on the coasts of tropical Africa, came to temper the atmosphere of the European north-west, a considerable region would find itself transformed, to the great advantage of its habitability and its agriculture.

To contemplate a project of that magnitude would have seemed absolute madness to the ancient Europeans, always divided in their interests and impoverished of blood and money by their continual wars; even as things were, in spite of all the material and moral progress that had been accomplished, the promoters of the enterprise still required a certain audacity. As the means of the epoch were equal to any endeavor whatsoever, no matter how colossal, they set to work resolutely, and succeeded perfect. An incomparable jetty was extended from the Berlengas, within sight of the coast of Portugal and gradually extended as far as the Azores, barring the way to the southern arm of the current, which was forced to deviate in a northern direction, in such a way as to form a single current with its European branch.

What entered into the materials of such an improbable dyke it is impossible to imagine: not merely all the disposable rocks of south-western Europe, but the entire chain of the Kong Mountains of the Mandigo coast[37] and a part of the Atlas were transported and tipped into the sea. The de Lesseps of the olden days were certainly mere children by comparison with the engineers of the twenty-fifth century. A number of generations profited for a long time from the result of that fine work, but that result could only ever be temporary, and by the time when our friends were heading toward that other rampart nearly a thousand kilometers in length that defends the entirety of northern Spain, even though it was the beginning of summer, at the altitude they were traveling, they would have suffered considerably from the cold had they not been amply furnished with warm furs.

The present climate of France, very cold but very dry under bright sunlight, resembled that which Sweden had once had, whose inhabitants, buoyed up by bright light and good health, had had an open and expansive character, so different from the surly humor usually associated with the people of foggy countries—a character that had sometimes led to them being called the French of the north. It was not astonishing, therefore, that in spite of the climatic transformation, the inhabitants of Old France had not changed, and were still the same amiable and slightly frivolous people.

They needed to reach the Pyrenees, which they were approaching rapidly, not in the heights of their central region but to one side, where they were indented and hollowed out, remaining at a medium altitude and thus accessible to the ascensional force of the *Espérance*. The airship therefore

---

[37] A joke: the Kong Mountains marked on certain old British maps were a product of the imagination.

veered slightly to the west, and was able to find the passage well-known as the Col de Roncevaux, which had once seen the army of a famous paladin lamentably destroyed to the last man by the Basques, those fanatics of independence that even the Romans had not been able to bend to their domination.

In that region there were very few low plains still accessible to the invading sea; and with along the integrity of the territory, national integrity had also been conserved over the centuries: the energetic vitality of a generous and exceptionally proud race that had been one of the first to adopt the principle of the constitution of small States grouped by federal bonds, a system suited in every respect to its traditional tendencies, unifying and particularizing at the same time. It was still the indomitable nation that had once, every time that Europe had bowed down to conquest, had stood up alone and defied the dominators, whether it be the Caesar of Rome, of Aix-la-Chapelle, Paris or Berlin. There too, as in the other ancient peoples, the ancient characteristics of the race had been preserved with the same persistence, still recognizable beneath the accomplished forms of the present civilization.

The slightly degenerate Spain of Marius' century, which scarcely recalled by then the grandeurs of her past, but which, by virtue of a natural attitude, still held her head high and gazed even higher, had got a grip on herself and saved herself from decadence in one of the surges that confounded those who thought they knew her better and which this time, contrary to apparent probability, carried her feverishly toward all the forms of human knowledge. And to general astonishment, a numerous constellation of artists, scientists and writers had surged forth from the torpid nation, animating an extraordinary elevation of spirit, immediately placing her at the head of the intellectual movement in a Europe that stood in great need of being lifted out of the moral abasement and platitude to which it had been reduced by an exclusively mercantile and material positivism.

The Spaniards had not become any more ardent for that in the incessant labors of industry under the yoke of which the men of the north were excessively subjugated and by which they were ground down. Here, the people wanted to have the leisure sometimes to be idle, reaming of chimeras and amour, in return for suffering a few material privations. Perhaps they were not mistaken in that. At any rate, they were no more unhappy for it, even without the civil wars and bullfights that they had repudiated a long time before, at least to judge by the songs that were heard on all sides, and which even repeated once again the old Arab airs of the times of Almanzor and the Abencerrages. And not only did they sing, but they danced, to such an extent that the first Spaniards who perceived the passengers of the *Espérance*, an entire village doubtless engaged in some celebration, formed an immense round, a farandole in which they all joined, young, old and children alike. They were not overly troubled by the prospect of the imminent Deluge!

It was necessary, during that oblique traversal of a part of the peninsula, to maintain the *Espérance*'s balloon at a rather high pressure, even the plains of that region being at a relatively high altitude. In the Spain that they had before their eyes, nothing remained of the cities and towns of old. Needless to say, everything there had been transformed in the same fashion as elsewhere. The marvelous monuments that had once been a part of its glory were no more: no Escorial, no Alhambra, no Alcazars, no Mosque of Cordova. A vestige of the past still remained, however, and even of a fabulous past, in the cyclopean walls of Tarragona, the enormous and unshakable rocks of which had traversed their hundred centuries, still bearing witness to successive generations of the times devoid of history of a primitive humankind, reminding the inheritors of all progress about the people of the Stone Age who also had their grandeur.

They paused briefly on reaching the coast at the station that occupied the location of old Cartagena, just long enough to send a hasty notification to an impatient mother. They were about to cross the Mediterranean again, in the same region where, nearly a year before, Marius had accomplished his miraculous dive. The exact spot had been identified by the professor, who was therefore able to indicate it to his companions with his finger as they passed by.

They were due to be back in Algiers in a matter of hours, about which Namo and Alcor spoke with the visible satisfaction that even the most indifferent individual feels when returning home. As for Marius, however, the thought of seeing the deceptive Junie again was not calculated to make his heart rejoice. He was bringing back to Algiers a soul as somber as at the moment when his friend Namo had come to extract him from his black melancholy once again.

The *Espérance* was flying at that moment with lightning speed. Was it the effect of some favorable aerial current or the zeal of a crew also in a hurry to arrive and stimulating the rotation of the propeller? At any rate, it was sooner than expected that the Algerian coast came into view, and the beloved and splendid capital extended before the eyes of the voyagers, who hastened their preparations for disembarkation.

Namo did not wait for the final maneuvers. Arming himself with his aerovol, he launched himself from the platform and headed straight toward the house and the apartment of his mother and sister, through whose open window he flew, to fall into the arms that the two women were already holding out to him, having been on watch since the morning, and were overjoyed by his return, after an absence too long for their affection.

XI

It goes without saying that an active correspondence had never ceased to be exchanged between the women left behind in Algiers and the travelers, whose first concern, during their numerous stops, had been to run to the improved telephones of the era, which were not limited to transmitting speech, but also reproduced in the communicative dark-room the faithful appearance, the specters of individuals, with an exactitude that created an illusion down to the slightest details, and might have caused uninstructed individuals what they were actually in the presence of their correspondents. Everything—features, gestures and speech—identified the visible but impalpable specter with the individual located a hundred leagues away. They were not only conversations but veritable visits that were made from cabin to cabin.

Thus, our three voyagers had often had the satisfaction of finding themselves, as if they had never left Algiers, in the company of the mother and the daughter—who, for their part, without leaving home, had simultaneously enjoyed the company and conversation of the absentees. If visitors came, they added their presence to the group. Alcor had occasionally conversed with the austere Nea, or exchanged the gazes that were worth more than words, and Marius had also had occasion more than once to shiver on seeing the abhorrent specter of Junie's fiancé surge forth. Even the busy Mirta had occasionally put in brief appearances and said a few words during those pleasant and precious encounters. It was in one of those meetings, in fact, that Marius had learned of the imminent date of the projected marriage, the very idea of which appalled him.

On finding himself once again, this time in the flesh, in the intimate family drawing room, there was, in consequence, nothing much new for him to learn. The conversation was mostly devoted to the preparations that were being made on all sides for the solsticial festival that was going to be held in the Great Temple in a matter of days. It was one of the four principal festivals of the year, one of those that required the collaboration of the entire population, and very serious reasons were required to prevent attendance. All work was suspended, all business put off until later, any absence inexcusable. That was one of the principal reasons for the restricted time that had been granted for the voyage of exploration that had just concluded.

While the *Espérance*, which had stood up to its trials so well, was carefully replaced in its hangar, in a state in which it could be called upon at the shortest notice, daily life was about to resume its accustomed routine. Alcor and Namo went upstairs to reinstall themselves in their adjacent apartments, and prepared to resume their university occupations.

It was now the last days of Prairial, and the heat was making itself very keenly felt while the sun remained high over the horizon, but the nights were cool and clear, pleasant nights propitious to long dreaming, in which Marius liked to indulge while the whole house was asleep, when he went up the little stairway to the terrace, and there forgot himself for hours on end, watching the other Gemma, his own sun, his own world, slowly moving above his head.

He gave no thought to extracting himself from the incessant flow of memories that cradled his thoughts, but the Orient paled at the approach of dawn, eventually warning him that there was not much time to go down and get a little sleep—and, like a silent shadow, he got to his feet and went back to his solitary room without making a sound, where belated sleep often kept him in bed rather late in the morning.

It was thus that the dawn of the first of Messidor 6643 rose in the pure and profound blue of a sky devoid of clouds without Marius waking up. This time, to judge by the agreeable expression that was painted on the sleeper's features, some pleasant dream come from the other world was making him smile and delighting him while awaiting the awakening that would doubtless throw him out of the warm illusion of the dream and into the cold image of reality.

The same happy expression continued to brighten our friend's face even though he had opened his eyes fully to the sparkling golden rays that were coming through his window and illuminating the arabesques of the walls and ceiling with bright colors. That was because, at that moment, a veritably divine harmony coming from he knew not where was filling the air with sweet chords.

Perhaps it seemed to him that the pleasant dream was still continuing under the influence of the magical tones. They were, as you will have guessed, the first preludes to the great solsticial festival, commenced by the divine choir of the re-sounding voices of the sphinxes of the Great Temple—voices softened at that moment in musical modulations that were still sufficiently powerful to be heard throughout the capital.

What completed and elevated the celestial concert of voices was the harmonious and grandiose accompaniment of the giant harps of the same Temple. Nothing so pure and so delightful had yet charmed Marius' terrestrial ears; he felt himself transported, and he listened to that extraordinary mu-sic, that prodigious canticle, in which he distinguished phrases such as "glorious day," "supreme love" and "eternal being."

He would have remained under the spell for a long time, without deciding to obey the invitation of the voices that were already bringing the entire city to celebration, if his neighbor the professor had not come to extract him from the intoxicat-ing torpor in which he entire being seemed to be sunk.

"Come on, get up, my dear idler! We need to go and take our places in the Temple within the hour.

The young man was on his feet in a trice, and while he completed his toilette, he went to throw open the large win-dow that overlooked the surroundings, in order to let the sun-light and the harmony enter more fully. From that height, which was one of the charms of his elegant bachelor apart-ment, and which revealed a considerable part of the city to him, he saw displayed in every direction, and in profusion, immense oriflammes in sky blue and golden yellow, the emblematic colors of the capital, undulating in the fresh morning breeze.

Soon ready, he went in his turn to knock on Alcor's door, and the two of them left together, joined on the patio of the house by Namo, while the women were to make their own way to the place where the female group of which they were to be a part was meeting.

It was the convention of these kinds of festivals that each sex, each age-group and each particular profession should assemble separately, and had its allocated place within the immense temple. An entire people, scattered while it lived and worked at ordinary times, assumed, on occasions such as this, the image of its collective personality and national individuality. It was the whole of living and thinking Algiers that was about to make up a single entity at a sublime rendezvous of religion and patriotism.

The crowd was so big that in spite of all the foresight of the regulations, access to the Great Temple was becoming increasingly difficult from one moment to the next. When the two young men that Alcor had finally left in order to place himself in a row other than theirs, were able in their turn to penetrate the immense enclosure, too narrow for the moment, the view was transformed to the point that Marius could not believe his eyes.

On every side ornament decorations and marvelous decorations could be seen, beneath a firmament of stars that seemed to summarize the universe; gigantic edifices of plants and flowers rose up; crowds were massed in bright festival clothing, and not crowds assembled at hazards but perfect rows of men or women, adolescents of either sex or children, whose sometimes bizarre assemblage appeared to Marius' eyes to be the effect of a capricious art or an incomprehensible plan. He had his own allotted place beside that of his young friend, just as Junie, more ravishing then ever in her white virginal veils, had hers beside her companions of the same age.

In the very center of the innumerable assembly, like a delightful flower-bed, glittering with the thousand colors in which the youngest individuals were adorned, was a host of children, the mere sight of which immediately filled the heart with tenderness. And in the most distant rows, on the heights of the perimeter, the old folk of severe aspect were lined up in their turn, their dark vestments contrasting with the varied colors of the inferior rows that they framed, completing their harmony.

The involuntary impression to which one is always subject in a large assembly can only give a feeble indication of the one that imposed itself in the midst of that immense crowd, which, instead of a confused mass giving only a vague sensation, presented distinct groupings by occupation and by age, from which radiated, like a kind of magnetism and with an extraordinary intensity, the impression appropriate to each of those stations in life.

And those various expressions, to the ensemble of which the effects of the strange strategy of the disposition of groups was added, gradually harmonized, fusing and producing a synthetic whole far surpassing what the best endowed soul was able to conceive of the great and superhuman. It was as if they were in the presence of a more elevated order of life; and that superior vital edification produced an atmosphere of emotion and nobility of thought that transported souls and gripped hearts.

More than anyone, Marius was subject to the influence, so new to him, of that art of arranging the various phases of life, as a composer orchestrates sounds or a painter disposes colors. But he was seized by an indescribable force when, at a signal from the organizer, that entire crowd, activated as if by a single spring and automatically, began to move in unison, describing sinuosities, multiple currents, and figures whose meaning escaped him but in which he sensed a real impression of the vital circulation of a transcendent, supernatural life, while the waves of divine music inundated the space and the air they breathed awoke its own order of indefinable sensations—that of the harmony of perfumes in combination and succession—with an artistry that was a further novelty for Marius.

Yet another novelty to which he was witness, and which would surely have scandalized him if he had not already been somewhat acclimatized to so many strange things, was perceiving, on approaching the extremity of the Temple, a profusion of animals arrange in a scale of vital advancement, summarizing the history of antehuman life. Needless to say, the worthy Hou had an honorable place there.

The idea of allowing to those inferior brethren of humankind to participate in a great religious festival, honoring life even in its most humble manifestations, was entirely natural and dignified for those people, fervent devotees of nature. With the progress of time animals had also raised the general level of their intelligence and sentiment, and it was understood that they could not be completely abstracted from a humankind that was placed at the head of terrestrial life but differed from it only by degree. Henceforth, the time was anticipated of a future fusion of everything endowed with life, a future of synthetic edification, of a perfect organization of the vital element of the entire planet.

Suddenly, at a further command from the organizer, all movement stopped, all sound ceased, and orators appeared at various points on pulpits, whose ardent words, interpreting the elevated thoughts, surges of vision and faith suggested to them by a spontaneous inspiration, were ardently received by the audience. Each orator who finished speaking was swiftly succeeded by another, avid to exhale the enthusiasm overflowing within him, and then by others.

After the speeches, general attention shifted to different stages, on which were represented symbolically the principal fictions of the entirely naturalistic belief of the epoch, including a homage rendered to the star of light, which rose in the sky on that day to the culminating point of its apparent annual course. At the precise moment, the position of the solstice was identified by the brief appearance of a ray of sunlight, which, penetrating from outside by means of a cleverly-designed opening that was only attained once a year, lit with a streak of gold the sacred standard that symbolized the belief, the silken pleats of which surmounted the high altar of the temple.

Afterwards, there were frugal and fraternal ceremonial meals, which brought together in the same admirable order the thousands of assistants, and then hymns and acclamations uttered simultaneously by a hundred thousand voices.

Outside, numerous groups carried deployed banners for long distances through the capital, as if in pilgrimage to religious rendezvous that were situated in entirely rustic locations contrived in the shade of thick woods, which were veritable sylvan temples in which vegetal nature met all the expenses of edification and ornamentation. Those poetic retreats in the middle of the forest seemed, to those distant descendants of Celts, to be a reminiscence of the ancient druidic sanctuaries of their earliest ancestors.

The religious festival was not the whole of the celebration. It was accompanied by games, spectacles and enjoyments of every sort, which animated all the quarters of the great city. Here, theaters open to the sky like the stages of antiquity put on performances to suit all tastes; there dances, decent but full of enthusiasm, brought young people together; elsewhere there were aerovol races, in which innumerable amateurs competed, equipped with apparatus with multicolored wings. There was nothing more striking than the rise, at the moment of departure, of those thousands of human forms obscuring the sky like a swarm of gigantic Lepidoptera.

Another of the principal attractions of the festivals, which lasted for three days, was the aerial battle fought by two formidable squadrons of military airships, in commemoration of a very ancient event that had been epoch-making because it had brought to a permanent end the era of conflicts between the nations of Cybele. The entire planet, since that last act of barbarity, had recognized the supremacy of international courts that were aware of all the different politics and from then on judged people as mere individuals.

That last battle, which had brought American and Europeans into conflict in the region of Santa Maria in the Azores, was universally remembered, and it was its memory that perpetuated the taste for these martial representations, which were also very imposing in themselves. When the rival squadrons racing from the east and the west collided in mid-air, and a thunder of artillery, with its smoke and its flashes, had the effect of ten storms bursting simultaneously, or the long sharp spikes, like enormous lances, with which the airships' prows were equipped ripped enemy airships apart, it was the faithful image of a celestial battle that they had before their eyes.

At intervals, from ships in distress, fully-armed warriors fell like a rain, who, on reaching the ground, went away laughing, with their folded parachutes under their arms, thus reminding everyone that it was no longer anything but an inoffensive and entertaining game. One final exciting episode terminated the action: the single combat of the two aerial flagships, which, in the complete silence of their artillery, attacked one another with the long lances of their anterior projections, clashing like sword-fighters. The two lacerated aerostats, no longer able to sustain themselves in the air, descended side by side, still fencing, and only ceased the combat in the fashion of those knights who were carried away from tournaments as badly wounded as one another.

One could not be everywhere at once; it was necessary to limit oneself—but one thing that Marius did not want to miss was the spectacle of the resurrections that his friends had already mentioned to him, and of which he had been given such curious details. In the crypt of the Temple, where the great men of New France had the most grandiose of Panthéons, a pompous ceremony was to be held on the third day, in honor of the illustrious dead, and there would be an awakening of several of those astonishing volunteers of long lethargic sleep.

Namo and Marius went to the subterranean temple in good time, and when the moment came to summon the testimony of living contemporaries of some of the heroes who were being honored, they lent the closest attention to the arrival and installation on an elevated stage of the sarcophagi, and the awakening of the patients. The latter were surrounded by the most notable citizens of the capital, disputing the honor of being the first to speak to such extraordinary individuals, the youngest of whom was no less than five hundred years old.

The slow and scrupulous preliminary operations required to prepare the bodies to emerge from their long torpor, had been carried out in advance, so that there would not be a long wait to see, one after another, the people whom one would have thought, a few moments earlier, to be corpses, raise their heads and sit up. Then, with the aid of the attendants, they eventually emerged from their seemingly-funereal beds that had been their principal abode for centuries.

A cordial of which they must have been in great need brought them round completely, and on the chairs where they had been placed they were seen to stir, to look around curiously, and then open their mouths, replying to the questions of those who were assisting them, and speaking to one another effusively, like old friends meeting up. They were, in fact, the only people they recognized, mutually, in the midst of the crowd that occupied the stage of the world of their future, in which several generations had gone by.

Soon clad in the costumes of their times, which had been very carefully conserved, they were led to the tomb and placed before the statue of their illustrious contemporary, a poet the equal of Hugo, with whose glory they found themselves briefly associated in the eyes of the multitude surrounding and acclaiming them.

The ceremony was concluded by a speech of welcome addressed to the resuscitated by the principal magistrate of the capital, good wishes addressed to them from various sides for such time as they wished to spend with the present generation, and, finally, by the few words with which the revenants from the past responded, in heartfelt terms, sufficiently distinct for people whose voices must have become a little hoarse over time.

It was dark when the young men set off to return to their dwelling, although the games and concerts were continuing on all sides, and the squares and streets were illuminated by multicolored flames, for that detail of public rejoicing had also made progress.

Instead of the rudimentary illuminations of old, Marius would have been able to admire dazzling phosphorescences that seemed to set all the walls ablaze, where the most various shades and designs were harmoniously extended from one house to the next—but for the moment, Marius was no longer admiring anything. Overwhelmed by the impression that the spectacle he had just witnessed had left, he seemed to be plunged deep in thought, or to be making some somber resolution.

In the midst of so much noise and so much joy, in which all of Algiers was forgetting itself in celebration, who was thinking at that moment about the fatal check of the inevitable catastrophe? With the facility that humans have in setting everything aside, even the expectation of sudden death, were they about to forget that a terrible peril was still present, all the more fearful because its precise moment remained unknown, and might suddenly descended upon the population?

The festivals had not yet concluded when, that same evening, a sinister cracking of the Antarctic ice, like an earthquake, shook the regions neighboring the Austral Pole, and threw panic throughout the entire world, immediately alerted in all its parts. That first tremor of the immense glacial cap would doubtless not long precede the total and final collapse, and the irresistible pressure of an entire ocean that, flowing northwards, was about to break the equilibrium and displace the center of gravity of the globe.

Such a warning immediately changed into public mourning the rejoicing that was still going on. A bleak silence succeeded the joyful cries and resounding orchestral chords. No one any longer had any other thought than that of the frightful event that seemed bound to occur without any further delay.

When Marius went into Alcor's apartment the next morning, the latter was not there. Some urgent concern had doubtless already taken him outside. Then the young man perceived that the professor's bed had not been slept in, and that the work-table was cluttered with books and papers in disorder, in the midst of which an old Bible was visible, open, over which he cast his eyes, distractedly at first, and then more attentively.

The page in view commenced chapter VI of Genesis, where he was able to read: "And the Lord said, I will destroy man whom I have created from the face of the earth; both man, and beast, and the creeping thing, and the fowls of the air; for it repenteth me that I have made them..."

And further on: "And the flood was forty days upon the earth...

"And the waters prevailed exceedingly upon the earth; and all the high hills, that were under the whole heaven were covered...

"And all flesh died that moved upon the earth, both of fowl, and of cattle, and of beast, and of every creeping thing that creepeth upon the earth, and every man...

"And the waters prevailed upon the earth an hundred and fifty days..."

Then came the moving episode of Noah saved, with his family, and a pair of all the animals, by the Ark that carried them, and which, on the twenty-seventh day of the seventh month, the waters having receded, ran aground on a mountain in Armenia; the release of the crow that flew off and did not come back, not because the deluge was over but because it had found its pasture in the cadavers floating on the surface of the waters; then, a little later, the flight of the dove, which came back with an olive branch in its beak, covered with new foliage, which showed that the earth was becoming habitable again, and that the time had finally come to leave the Ark.

It was evident that Alcor had spent part of the night reading every detail of Moses' great story. A bookmark placed in the final pages of the venerable book showed that he had also paused briefly over the terrible words of St. John relating to the end of the world, in Chapter VI of the Apocalypse:

"And the sun became black as sackcloth of hair, and the moon became as blood.

"And the stars of heaven fell unto the earth, even as a fig tree casteth her untimely figs, when she is shaken of a mighty wind.

"And the heaven departed as a scroll when it is rolled together; and every mountain and island were moved out of their places."

The professor was, therefore, no more exempt from somber preoccupations than anyone else. Many others must have suffered mortal dread that night. Many families were not even waiting any longer to commit their airships to the wind and prudently remove themselves out of range of the catastrophe, although, at the latitude of Algeria, there was bound to be several hours of respite between the signal of the unleashing of the frightful tide and the arrival of the fatal wave.

The days went by, however, and the signal did not come.

Gradually, people resumed living, and even hoping. Perhaps it was simply one more false alarm. Might not the cataclysm foreseen by old Adhémar be postponed after all, by another human lifetime?

In the meantime, all the preparations for Junie's marriage were completed. The prospect of the redoubted upheaval would not prevent a union whose future would doubtless continue beyond the present state of affairs. Was not the *Espérance* another Ark of salvation for the lovers, which held all the promise containing in the good omen of her name?

The hour was about to chime. The wedding was finally to be held no later than the following day. The friends of the family had been invited and the temple awaited the coming of the future spouses. In the house, everything assumed an appearance of rejuvenation under the vigilant direction of the valiant Mirta, who did not allow herself a moment's rest.

Cam, Junie's fortunate fiancé, had just arrived, radiant with happiness. It was his final visit as a suitor of the woman that he would call his wife on the morrow. And poor Marius, a neglected witness of that family celebration, saw himself in his imagination beside his Jeanne, in the midst of vey similar preparations in his house in Martigues. Oh, no, he certainly could not bear the bitter sight of such derision of his own vanished happiness.

This time, his decision had been made, irrevocably. He would go to occupy a place among those discouraged by contemporary life, who had requested a centuries-long slumber, the forgetfulness of the present and the hope of a better future.

If, a long time hence, he resumed the course of his existence, the unwitting torturers of his lost love would no longer be there to torment his still ulcerated heart. And if he did not wake up again, if the Deluge claimed him, well, so much the better. Tonight would be the last that he would spend under the roof that had been so hospitable to him, but where he had found such an inconceivable deceptive echo of all his affections and everything that his life on Earth had been.

In the fever of his thoughts, afflicted simultaneously by a thousand disordered memories, he did not think about sleeping. What point was there, for a man who was perhaps about to descend forever into an absolute repose?

He did not intend to see his friends Alcor and Namo again, to voice difficult farewells, although he owed them such warm impulses of affection and so many instructive lessons, which had helped him to support an entire year of exile in a world so different from his own. Above all, he would not see Junie, that perfect and despairing image of his beloved Jeanne. His only adieux would be for the woman who was still present in his heart, even though she was far away in the sidereal heavens; for his true and still living fiancée, whose existence was confused for him in the soft radiance of a star.

At that late hour he emerges from his retreat, and goes down into the garden, which reminds him of the one he knew before, and in the great silence of midnight, along with his gaze, he raises his entire soul toward the celestial immensity, where, among so many resplendent constellations, he seems only to see one: the fateful Crown in which Gemma is enthroned, the pearl, the queen, the sun of his homeland and his ineradicable love.

But what's that?

What sounds, what melodious sighs are reaching his ears?

Oh, he knows those hardly-distinguishable notes well, which are falling discreetly from half-closed windows where, it appears, someone else is awake:

My heart cannot change;
Remember that I love you!

Jeanne! Jeanne! Adieu! Adieu!

He wants to go away, to flee those chords, which, at that moment, at such an extremity, are breaking his heart—but emotion chokes him and annihilates him.

His head reels, his eyes cloud over, his legs buckle, and he loses consciousness...

Was he dreaming, or were his now-reanimated senses really perceiving those terrible noises?

What, then, was that frightful bellowing that was tearing the air and importing a new terror into the recovered consciousness of his soul?

There was no possibility of error. It was the chorus of the formidable voices of the Great Temple, the unparalleled roar of the twenty-four sphinxes, which, with all the might of their brazen lungs, were hurling to the four winds of the capital, in a harrowing crescendo, that terrible word: "Deluge! Deluge! Deluge!"

And while that terrible tocsin fell from the clouds and filled the air, the ground trembled, and, seemingly coming from afar, increasing from moment to moment, the confused rumble of a storm was punctuated by piercing clamors.

Great God! What was happening now?

Marius understood. He tried to flee, launching himself forwards, but it was impossible. An insurmountable weight was crushing his breast and nailing him to the spot.

Now the distant rumbling had drawn closer, and the sound of a hundred thunderclaps drowned out the panicked cries of an entire people, and the very voices of the sphinxes, which had spoken for the last time.

Finally, rising all the way to the clouds, a chain of liquid mountains raced from the horizon, sweeping cities and monuments before it in an inconceivable surge—cities and monuments that were seen being lifted up and rolled together, like the pebbles of a beach.

Not long thereafter, there was peace, solitude, and the universal silence of death in the tranquil desert of the new Great Boreal Pacific Ocean.

XII

The shock had been such that Marius had definitely woken up this time, for good and all, and that which summoned him woke him up to the true reality of his positive earthly existence.

It really was in a garden that he found himself, but his own, in his house in Martigues, and if he had not realized it at first, it was because the deep hypnotic trance to which he had fallen prey for the entire night still held him in torpor, and the extraordinary dream from which he had scarcely emerged had obsessed his brain too forcefully to be able to dissipate instantaneously. So he did not understand his true situation immediately, or the words full of solicitude that a well-known voice, a true voice with the accent of the Bouches-du-Rhône, was repeated beside him, punctuating them with anxious interjections

"What! God, is it possible? Monsieur Marius! Monsieur Marius! Oh, sinner, it's here that you're sleeping!"

Thus was groaning the worthy Martine, who, having not found her young master in his bed, still intact, when she had brought him his morning coffee as usual, had been running around in search of him for some time, rendered distraught by his inexplicable disappearance.

"Deluge! Deluge! Every man for himself!" Marius repeated to himself unconsciously, whose closed eyes were as yet only able to see inwardly, and were taking their time to open to external reality, while his respiration was halting and nervous tics shook him.

"What bad dream has gripped him as hard as that? Wake up, Monsieur Marius!"

"Where am I?" the young man finally murmured, as his haggard eyes encountered the face of excellent woman who was leaning over him. "Is that you, Mirta? Why am I not dead?"

"What's he saying now? It's not natural. He's been taken ill, poor fellow. And on a day like today! Good God, what a misfortune! Come and put yourself to bed, Monsieur Marius, you're not well." The worthy Martine, greatly troubled, already had tears in her eyes.

Meanwhile, our friend gradually pulled himself together, turning his head curiously to the right and the left, his gaze sometimes pausing on the flowers and the shrubs that surrounded him, all moist with the nocturnal dew, sometimes on the walls of the silent house, and then on the sky, were a little light vapor gilded by the rising sun promised a warm and splendid summer day.

"It's true, though, that all of that wasn't just a dream, and the dream of a single night! Junie, Alcor, Namo…Gemma, Cybele, New France, the Deluge…how could so many things, so many strange adventures, which are still so present in my mind, have taken only a few hours?" Then, as if inundated by a sudden felicity, he said: "Jeanne! Where's Jeanne? I have to see her, to speak to her, right away."

"What are you thinking, Monsieur Marius? At five o'clock in the morning! Mademoiselle isn't up yet."

He remained momentarily as if in ecstasy, contemplating for afar the little shuttered window of the house next door, where his beloved Jeanne was asleep at that very moment. Then, abruptly, he stood up.

"My dear Martine," he exclaimed, embracing the housekeeper furiously, "I'm too happy! If you knew! Oh, Monsieur Cam, you've given me such a hard time!" Then, perceiving the worthy Houzard, who had woken up in his turn and was clamoring for his attention, he added: "And you're here too, good dog? You have no suspicion of the voyage we've just undertaken together."

The worthy woman, who had began to feel reassured, was gripped once again by a serious anxiety. No, it wasn't natural. And on such a day!

And this time, poor Martine began weeping copiously.

"Come on, come on, my dear—are you mad? What's got into you now? Yes, I can see that you don't understand me very well, that you take me for a lunatic—but don't worry; it's only the effect of the immense and real joy that I've found instead of an imaginary misfortune. God! This greenery that surrounds me, that blue sky resplendent up above, that sea scintillating on the horizon—how beautiful it all is! And today is the great day! Come on, quickly, let's hurry up and get ready."

In the Honorat household too, it was not long before there was an animation greater than usual, and earlier. The mother and daughter, after embracing one another as soon as they awoke with a tender effusion, set about their toilette, which was no small affair on such a day.

In such important circumstances, no matter how well everything has been anticipated, there is always some unexpected snag at the last moment, which it is necessary to overcome, and the time goes by, and one trembles in case one is not ready when the solemn moment arrives. Fortunately, active friends had come to the aid of the ladies in question, commencing with Mademoiselle Renée, Jeanne's former governess and ever-faithful companion.

As for Numa, who sensed that he was excess to requirements amid all that feminine coming-and-going, he went out to smoke a cigarette, taking a long walk through the streets of the dear little town of his birth, before eventually ending up at the house of his friend Marius—where he was awaited with great impatience by Martine, who had not yet recovered from the derangement of her young master's habits and his incoherent speech. Still very emotional, she told Marius' friend about what had just happened, and the vague dread that she could not help feeling.

"For sure, something's wrong with Monsieur Marius," the excellent woman repeated continually—but she fell silent as soon as she heard a door open and the person about whom she was talking run downstairs.

The young man was already fully dressed in his ceremonial costume, completely ready although he was much too early.

"Oh, my dear friend, it's really you this time!" he exclaimed, throwing himself recklessly into the young officer's arms. "Here you are, really!" Then, as the old notary, the grave Monsieur Foulane, appeared on the threshold of his apartment, Marius collected himself, in order to go to his father and lavish further effusions upon him, as if he were suddenly seeing him again after years of separation.

There is, indeed, something about Marius that isn't natural, Jeanne's brother said to himself, anxiously. *Is it just joy that's turning his head momentarily? Might it be some disturbance? I'm uneasy!*

And while Martine exchanged an anxious glance with him, he went to link arms with Marius. He drew him gently toward the main pathway of the garden.

"Come on, my dear fellow, let's chat for a while—we have time, since it's only seven o'clock and we don't have to be there until noon. Damn! You're up very early, you know! Already under arms, cravated and gloved. Why so much unnecessary haste?"

"Impossible! Is it still as early as that?" the young man replied, in surprised. He had not thought to look at his watch, and time seemed to have lost its habitual measure.

"Come on, Marius, look at me, face to face, your eyes looking straight into mine."

And as that mute examination was prolonged, and a keen anxiety was painted on Numa's features, Marius quickly came to understand, and suddenly burst out into frank and sane laughter.

"Ha! You too! I really must seem slightly unhinged this morning. But don't worry, my friend; I'm only crazed with happiness, and if I seem to you to be a trifle eccentric, as I do to the worthy Martine, it's because, you see, I've just had an extraordinary adventure, which, I admit has turned my mind

227

upside-down. And yet it was only a dream…but a kind of dream that one doesn't have every day."

As the officer's face still gave evidence of some uncertainty, he continued: "Come on, my dear Numa, I don't have to explain to you what a profound hypnotic action can do to a man. All night, I haven't belonged to myself, and on that bench you see there I've lived an entire other life. I've suffered, I've learned, I've traveled—oh, traveled, especially! It's as if I changed my existence, and with such an appearance of reality that the slightest details of my imaginary tribulations are still present in my mind, as if they couldn't have been a simple illusion.

"Anyway, I'll tell you all about it soon. In my turn, I've known and visited curious peoples and distant countries, and from now on, I can compete with you in telling interesting and extraordinary stories, I promise you. So much happened in such a short time—which is no less marvelous than all the rest!

"Do you remember that story in the Thousand-and-One Nights, about a sultan to whom a magician gave a magic bowl and asked him to plunge his gaze into it momentarily? Scarcely had the sultan done what the magician asked than a new life commenced for him. Having been the sultan, he became the most unfortunate man in his State, had a hundred adventures, each more tragic than the one before, which were about to conclude with his execution, when having raised his eyes from the enchanted bowl, he found himself exactly as he was before. The long and miserable existence he had just lived had only lasted a minute.

"Well, something comparable to that has happened to me. In a single night I've lived the entirety of a most extraordinary existence, which had nothing in common with my real life except that my personality remained almost intact, and that the faces of the strange people I encountered out there, by a bizarre singularity, were those I knew the best: yours, for example, my dear Numa, for you were also my best friend in that other world. And another face too, but that one…"

Marius stopped, because a tremulous sigh, seemingly coming from far away, had just cut off his speech.

The young man soon continued, however: "Oh, I haven't been happy in that second existence, I can assure you! So my return to the sweet reality of a happy day like this one has delighted me with a frantic joy, whose effects probably seem slightly odd to you. Isn't happiness made, above all, of sufferings and chagrins avoided, even if they're chimerical? Come on, are you reassured now?"

All that was said in a tone so true and so natural that Numa was entirely reassured, and laughing in his turn, wholeheartedly, at the suspicion that had brushed him momentarily, he shook hands effusively with the man that he would shortly and forever be able to call his brother.

Time passed, however, and the rumble of carriages was heard in the street. Guests arrived; compliments were exchanged. Before the appointed time, the pretty Mairie of Martigues was invaded by a numerous gathering of high society in formal dress.

At noon precisely, the bride's carriage arrived, from which the divine white-clad Jeanne got down, immediately surrounded, admired and accompanied to the hall of honor—in which Marius, who had already arrived, had to contain himself in order not to commit some new folly at the radiant appearance of the most ravishing of brides.

Before the Maire, an old family friend, smiling profusely without ceasing to be as solemn as the occasion required, two "I dos" were finally pronounced that were veritably overflowing with conviction and ineffable promises.

In the church, there was the same affluence and even more solemnity. Before the flamboyant altar, in the fumes of incense expanding from the choir in all directions, beneath the old arched vaults in which the chords of the great organ reverberated, a wedding mass was celebrated that filled the souls of all those present with the purest and most tender emotion.

And that evening, in the notary's house, those who saw Marius, as if transfigured, traverse the old drawing-room, re-decorated and adapted as a ballroom, with his Jeanne on his arm, certainly saw the most complete image of human felicity.

In a corner of the room, a late-arriving guest who appeared to have been absorbed for some time in a conversation, doubtless very engaging, with Mademoiselle Renée, only perceived the presence of the newlyweds when they arrived very close to him. He got up swiftly and put out his hand to shake that of the happy Marius.

"So you're here at last, my dear Al…Monsieur Coral?" exclaimed our friend, impetuously, shaking hands with the worthy professor, who was slightly disconcerted by such an excessive demonstration. "You'd never believe how much I missed you."

Then, all of a sudden, Marius' features contracted, and he squeezed Jeanne's arm forcefully.

She was astonished by the swift change in his attitude. It was because he had just seen, looking out through an open window, his unwitting Cybelean torturer, Monsieur Camoin, the justice of the peace, who was passing by and had yielded to the bitter curiosity of glimpsing the radiant Jeanne on the arm of his fortunate rival.

"What's the matter, my love?" she asked.

"Oh, my Jeanne, my Junie, if you only knew…"

"Junie? Who's that?"

"It's stifling in here—let's go out for a moment to breathe the night air. Oh, come along dear heart, so that I can tell you how mad I have been, and how much I love you."

The orchestra had just resumed its joyous chords, which were fading now as the lovers advanced further into the shady pathways of the garden.

"Look up there. In that starry sky, almost exactly above our heads, there's a scintillating diadem in which the beautiful Gemma is shining with a particular brightness. Gemma is a sun like ours, which lights and warms a world exactly similar to this one, where that Junie lives, who is the deceptive image of my adored Jeanne. But Gemma possesses a terrible and mysterious power. She draws toward her imprudent individuals who abandon their gazes to her for too long, Look away from her, my love!"

And, fearful that Jeanne might not comprehend the danger quickly enough, Marius, frantic with love, drew that dear head toward him and deposited long thirsty kisses, on the already-moist eyelids of the emotional child, which were only the first steps of a new celestial voyage, as distant as and far happier than the one from which he had just returned.

SF & FANTASY

Adolphe Alhaiza. *Cybele*
Alphonse Allais. *The Adventures of Captain Cap*
Henri Allorge. *The Great Cataclysm*
Guy d'Armen. *Doc Ardan: The City of Gold and Lepers*
G.-J. Arnaud. *The Ice Company*
Charles Asselineau. *The Double Life*
Cyprien Bérard. *The Vampire Lord Ruthwen*
S. Henry Berthoud. *Martyrs of Science*
Aloysius Bertrand. *Gaspard de la Nuit*
Richard Bessière. *The Gardens of the Apocalypse*
Albert Bleunard. *Ever Smaller*
Félix Bodin. *The Novel of the Future*
Louis Boussenard. *Monsieur Synthesis*
Alphonse Brown. *City of Glass; The Conquest of the Air*
Emile Calvet. *In a Thousand Years*
André Caroff. *The Terror of Madame Atomos; Miss Atomos; The Return of Madame Atomos; The Mistake of Madame Atomos; The Monsters of Madame Atomos; The Revenge of Madame Atomos; The Resurrection of Madame Atomos; The Mark of Madame Atomos*
Félicien Champsaur. *The Human Arrow; Ouha, King of the Apes; Pharaoh's Wife*
Didier de Chousy. *Ignis*
Jules Clarétie. *Obsession*
Michel Corday. *The Eternal Flame*
Captain Danrit. *Undersea Odyssey*
C. I. Defontenay. *Star (Psi Cassiopeia)*
Charles Derennes. *The People of the Pole*
Georges Dodds (anthologist). *The Missing Link*
Harry Dickson. *The Heir of Dracula*
Jules Dornay. *Lord Ruthven Begins*
Alfred Driou. *The Adventures of a Parisian Aeronaut*
Sâr Dubnotal *vs. Jack the Ripper*
Alexandre Dumas. *The Return of Lord Ruthven*
Renée Dunan. *Baal*
J.-C. Dunyach. *The Night Orchid; The Thieves of Silence*
Henri Duvernois. *The Man Who Found Himself*
Achille Eyraud. *Voyage to Venus*
Henri Falk. *The Age of Lead*

Paul Féval. *Anne of the Isles; Knightshade; Revenants; Vampire City; The Vampire Countess; The Wandering Jew's Daughter*
Paul Féval, *fils. Felifax, the Tiger-Man*
Charles de Fieux. *Lamékis*
Arnould Galopin. *Doctor Omega; Doctor Omega and the Shadowmen* (anthology)
Judith Gautier. *Isoline and the Serpent-Flower*
Léon Gozlan. *The Vampire of the Val-de-Grâce*
G.L. Gick. *Harry Dickson and the Werewolf of Rutherford Grange*
Edmond Haraucourt. *Illusions of Immortality*
Nathalie Henneberg. *The Green Gods*
V. Hugo, P. Foucher & P. Meurice. *The Hunchback of Notre-Dame*
Romain d'Huissier. *Hexagon: Dark Matter*
Michel Jeury. *Chronolysis*
Gustave Kahn. *The Tale of Gold and Silence*
Gérard Klein. *The Mote in Time's Eye*
Fernand Kolney. *Love in 5000 Years*
Paul Lacroix. *Danse Macabre*
Louis-Guillaume de La Follie. *The Unpretentious Philosopher*
Jean de La Hire. *Enter the Nyctalope; The Nyctalope on Mars; The Nyctalope vs. Lucifer; The Nyctalope Steps In; Night of the Nyctalope; Return of the Nyctalope; The Fiery Wheel*
Etienne-Léon de Lamothe-Langon. *The Virgin Vampire*
André Laurie. *Spiridon*
Gabriel de Lautrec. *The Vengeance of the Oval Portrait*
Alain le Drimeur. *The Future City*
Georges Le Faure & Henri de Graffigny. *The Extraordinary Adventures of a Russian Scientist Across the Solar System* (2 vols.)
Gustave Le Rouge. *The Vampires of Mars; The Dominion of the World* (w/Gustave Guitton) (4 vols.)
Jules Lermina. *Mysteryville; Panic in Paris; To-Ho and the Gold Destroyers; The Secret of Zippelius*
André Lichtenberger. *The Centaurs; The Children of the Crab*
Jean-Marc & Randy Lofficier. *Edgar Allan Poe on Mars; The Katrina Protocol; Pacifica; Robonocchio; Return of the Nyctalope;* (anthologists) *Tales of the Shadowmen 1-10*
Xavier Mauméjean. *The League of Heroes*
Joseph Méry. *The Tower of Destiny*
Hippolyte Mettais. *The Year 5865*
Louise Michel. *The Human Microbes; The New World*
Tony Moilin. *Paris in the Year 2000*

José Moselli. *Illa's End*
John-Antoine Nau. *Enemy Force*
Marie Nizet. *Captain Vampire*
C. Nodier, A. Beraud & Toussaint-Merle. *Frankenstein*
Henri de Parville. *An Inhabitant of the Planet Mars*
Gaston de Pawlowski. *Journey to the Land of the 4th Dimension*
Georges Pellerin. *The World in 2000 Years*
Ernest Pérochon. *The Frenetic People*
Pierre Pelot. *The Child Who Walked on the Sky*
J. Polidori, C. Nodier, E. Scribe. *Lord Ruthven the Vampire*
P.-A. Ponson du Terrail. *The Vampire and the Devil's Son; The Immortal Woman*
Edgar Quinet. *Ahasuerus*
Henri de Régnier. *A Surfeit of Mirrors*
Maurice Renard. *The Blue Peril; Doctor Lerne; The Doctored Man; A Man Among the Microbes; The Master of Light*
Jean Richepin. *The Wing; The Crazy Corner*
Albert Robida. *The Adventures of Saturnin Farandoul; The Clock of the Centuries; Chalet in the Sky; The Electric Life*
J.-H. Rosny Aîné. *Helgvor of the Blue River; The Givreuse Enigma; The Mysterious Force; The Navigators of Space; Vamireh; The World of the Variants; The Young Vampire*
Marcel Rouff. *Journey to the Inverted World*
Han Ryner. *The Superhumans*
Brian Stableford. *The New Faust at the Tragicomique;The Empire of the Necromancers (The Shadow of Frankenstein; Frankenstein and the Vampire Countess; Frankenstein in London); Sherlock Holmes & The Vampires of Eternity; The Stones of Camelot; The Wayward Muse.* (anthologist) *News from the Moon; The Germans on Venus; The Supreme Progress; The World Above the World; Nemoville; Investigations of the Future; The Conqueror of Death*
Jacques Spitz. *The Eye of Purgatory*
Kurt Steiner. *Ortog*
Eugène Thébault. *Radio-Terror*
C.-F. Tiphaigne de La Roche. *Amilec*
Louis Ulbach. *Prince Bonifacio*
Théo Varlet. *The Golden Rock. The Xenobiotic Invasion; The Castaways of Eros; Timeslip Troopers* (w/André Blandin); *The Martian Epic* (w/Octave Joncquel)
Paul Vibert. *The Mysterious Fluid*
Villiers de l'Isle-Adam. *The Scaffold; The Vampire Soul*

Philippe Ward. *Artahe*
Philippe Ward & Sylvie Miller. *The Song of Montségur*

MYSTERIES & THRILLERS

M. Allain & P. Souvestre. *The Daughter of Fantômas*
A. Anicet-Bourgeois, Lucien Dabril. *Rocambole*
A. Bernède. *Belphegor*; *Judex* (w/Louis Feuillade); *The Return of Judex* (w/Louis Feuillade); *The Shadow of Judex*
A. Bisson & G. Livet. *Nick Carter vs. Fantômas*
V. Darlay & H. de Gorsse. *Arsène Lupin vs. Sherlock Holmes: The Stage Play*
Séamas Duffy. *Sherlock Holmes in Paris*
Paul Féval. *Gentlemen of the Night; John Devil; The Black Coats ('Salem Street; The Invisible Weapon; The Parisian Jungle; The Companions of the Treasure; Heart of Steel; The Cadet Gang; The Sword-Swallower)*
Emile Gaboriau. *Monsieur Lecoq*
Goron & Emile Gautier. *Spawn of the Penitentiary*
Rick Lai. *Shadows of the Opera: Retribution in Blood; Sisters of the Shadows: The Curse of Cagliostro*
Steve Leadley. *Sherlock Holmes: The Circle of Blood*
Maurice Leblanc. *Arsène Lupin vs. Countess Cagliostro; Arsène Lupin vs. Sherlock Holmes (The Blonde Phantom; The Hollow Needle); The Many Faces of Arsène Lupin*
Gaston Leroux. *Chéri-Bibi; The Phantom of the Opera; Rouletabille & the Mystery of the Yellow Room; Rouletabille at Krupp's*
Richard Marsh. *The Complete Adventures of Judith Lee*
William Patrick Maynard. *The Terror of Fu Manchu; The Destiny of Fu Manchu*
Frank J. Morlock. *Sherlock Holmes: The Grand Horizontals; Sherlock Holmes vs Jack the Ripper*
Antonin Reschal. *The Adventures of Miss Boston*
P. de Wattyne & Y. Walter. *Sherlock Holmes vs. Fantômas*
David White. *Fantômas in America*
Pierre Yrondy. *The Adventures of Thérèse Arnaud*

SCREENPLAYS

Mike Baron. *The Iron Triangle*
Emma Bull & Will Shetterly. *Nightspeeder; War for the Oaks*

Gerry Conway & Roy Thomas. *Doc Dynamo*
Steve Englehart. *Majorca*
James Hudnall. *The Devastator*
Jean-Marc & Randy Lofficier. *Royal Flush*
J.-M. & R. Lofficier & Marc Agapit. *Despair*
J.-M. & R. Lofficier & Joël Houssin. *City*
Andrew Paquette. *Peripheral Vision*
Robert L. Robinson, Jr. *Judex*
R. Thomas, J. Hendler & L. Sprague de Camp. *Rivers of Time*

NON-FICTION

Stephen R. Bissette. *Blur 1-5. Green Mountain Cinema 1; Teen Angels*
Win Scott Eckert. *Crossovers* (2 vols.)
Jean-Marc & Randy Lofficier. *Shadowmen* (2 vols.)
Randy Lofficier. *Over Here*

ART BOOKS

J.-M. Lofficier & D. Taylor. *Tongue*Lash*
Jean-Pierre Normand. *Science Fiction Illustrations*
Raven Okeefe. *Raven's L'il Critters; Rave's Faves*
Randy Lofficier & Raven Okeefe. *If Your Possum Go Daylight...*
Daniele Serra. *Illusions*

HEXAGON COMICS

Franco Frescura & Luciano Bernasconi. *Wampus*
Franco Frescura & Giorgio Trevisan. *CLASH*
L. Bernasconi, J.-M. Lofficier & Juan Roncagliolo Berger. *Phenix*
Claude Legrand, J.-M. Lofficier & L. Bernasconi. *Kabur*
Franco Oneta. *Zembla*
L. Buffolente, Lofficier & J.-J. Dzialowski. *Strangers: Homicron*
Danilo Grossi. *Strangers: Jaydee*
Claude Legrand & Luciano Bernasconi. *Strangers: Starlock*